THE
TIME~LAPSED
MAN

and other stories

THE TIME~LAPSED MAN

and other stories

ERIC BROWN

DRUNKEN DRAGON PRESS
Birmingham England
1990

This edition published 1990
by Drunken Dragon Press Limited
84 Suffolk Street, Birmingham, B1 1TA

Published by arrangement with Pan Books Ltd.

First Hardcover Edition
October 1990

Standard Edition
ISBN: 0-947578-03-X

De luxe edition, limited to 100
specially-bound,
signed and numbered copies
ISBN: 0-947578-53-6

04553122

Printed and bound by
The Longdunn Press Ltd, Bristol

For my Parents
for Liz & Graham, Bob, Gin & Frank

ACKNOWLEDGEMENTS

"The Time-Lapsed Man" first published in *Interzone* 24, 1988.
"The Karma Kid Transcends" first published in *Opus*, 1988.
"Big Trouble Upstairs" first published in *Interzone* 26, 1988.
"Star-Crystals and Karmel" first published in *Interzone* 30, 1989.
"Krash-Bangg Joe and the Pineal-Zen Equation" first published in *Interzone* 21, 1987.
"The Girl Who Died for Art and Lived" first published in *Interzone* 22, 1987.
"Pithecanthropus Blues" and "The Inheritors of Earth" appear for the first time.

The Time-Lapsed Man

Thorn was not immediately aware of the silence.

As he lay in the tank and watched the crystal cover lift above him, he was still trying to regain some measure of the unification he had attained during the three months in flux. For that long – though it had seemed a timeless period to Thorn – he had mind-pushed his boat between the stars: for that long he had been one with the vastness of the *nada*-continuum.

As always when emerging from flux, Thorn sensed the elusive residuum of the union somewhere within him. As always, he tried to regain it and failed; it diminished like a haunting echo in his mind. Only in three months, on his next shift, would he be able to renew his familiarity with the infinite. Until then his conscious life would comprise a series of unfulfilled events; a succession of set-pieces featuring an actor whose thoughts were forever elsewhere. Occasionally he would be allowed intimations of rapture in his dreams, only to have them snatched away upon awakening.

Some Enginemen he knew, in fact the majority of those from the East, subscribed to the belief that in flux they were granted a foretaste of Nirvana. Thorn's Western pragmatism denied him this explanation. He favoured a more psychological rationale – though in the immediate period following flux he found it difficult to define exactly a materialistic basis for the ecstasy he had experienced.

He eased himself up and crossed the chamber. It was then that he noticed the absence of sound. He should have

1

been able to hear the dull drone of the auxiliary burners; likewise his footsteps, and his laboured breathing after so long without exercise. He rapped on the bulkhead. He stepped into the shower and turned on the water-jet. He made a sound of pleasure as the hot water needled his tired skin. Yet he heard nothing. The silence was more absolute than any he had experienced before.

He told himself that it was no doubt some side-effect of the flux. After more than fifty shifts, a lifetime among the stars, this was his first rehabilitation problem, and he was not unduly worried. He would go for a medical if his hearing did not return.

He stepped under the blo-drier, donned his uniform and left the chamber. Through the lounge viewscreen he could see the lights of the spaceport. He felt a jarring shudder as the stasis-grid grabbed the ship and brought it down. He missed the familiar diminuendo of the afterburn, the squeal of a hundred tyres on tarmac. The terminal ziggurat hove into sight. The ship eased to a halt. Above the viewscreen a strip-light pulsed red, sanctioning disembarkation. It should have been accompanied by a voice welcoming ship personnel back to Earth, but Thorn heard nothing.

As always he was the first to leave the ship. He passed through check-out, offering his card to a succession of bored port officials. Normally he might have waited for the others and gone for a drink; he preferred to spend his free time with other Enginemen, and pilots and mechanics, as if the company of his colleagues might bring him closer to that which he missed most. This time, though, he left the port and caught a flyer to the city. He would seek the medical aid he needed in his own time, not at the behest of solicitous colleagues.

He told the driver his destination; unable to hear his own voice, he moved his lips again. The driver nodded, accelerated. The flyer banked between towerpiles, lights flickering by in a mesmerizing rush.

They came down in the forecourt of his stack. Thorn

2

climbed out and took the upchute to his penthouse suite. This was the first time he had arrived home sober in years. Alcohol helped to ease the pain of loss; sober, he was horribly aware of his material possessions, mocking his mortality and his dependence upon them. His suite might have been described as luxurious, but the blatant utility of the furnishings filled him with nausea.

He poured himself a Scotch and paused by the piano. He fingered the opening notes of Beethoven's *Pathétique*, then sat down in his recliner by the wall-window and stared out. In the comforting darkness of the room, with the lights of the city arrayed below him, he could make-believe he was back aboard his ship, coming in for landing.

Of course, if his hearing never returned . . .

He realized he was sweating at the thought of never being able to flux again. He wondered if he would be able to bluff his way through the next shift.

He was on his second drink, twenty minutes later, when a sound startled him. He smiled to himself, raised his glass in a toast to his reflection in the window. He spoke . . . but he could not hear his words.

He heard another sound and his stomach lurched with sickening confusion. He called out . . . in silence. Yet he could hear *something*.

He heard footsteps, and breathing, and then a resounding *clang*. Then he heard the high-pressure hiss of the hot water and an exclamation of pleasure. His own exclamation . . . He heard the roar of the blo-drier, then the rasp of material against his skin; the quick whirr of the sliding door and the diminishing note of the afterburners, cutting out.

Thorn forced himself to say something; to comment and somehow bring an end to this madness. But his voice made no sound. He threw his glass against the wall and it shattered in silence.

Then he was listening to footsteps again; his own footsteps. They passed down the connecting tube from the ship

3

to the terminal building; he heard tired acknowledgements from the port officials, then the hubbub of the crowded foyer.

He sat rigid with fright, listening to that which by rights he should have heard one hour ago.

He heard the driver's question, then his own voice; he stated his destination in a drunken slur, then repeated himself. He heard the whine of turbos, and later the hatch opening, then more footsteps, the grind of the upchute . . .

There was a silence then. He thought back one hour and realized he had paused for a time on the threshold, looking into the room he called home and feeling sickened. He could just make out the sound of his own breathing, the distant hum of the city.

Then the gentle notes of Beethoven's *Pathétique*.

The rattle of glass on glass.

He remained in the recliner, unable to move, listening to the sound of his time-lapsed breathing, his drinking when he wasn't drinking.

Later he heard his delayed exclamation, the explosion of his glass against the wall.

He pushed himself from the recliner and staggered over to the vidscreen. He hesitated, his hand poised above the keyboard. He intended to contact the company medic, but, almost against his will, he found himself tapping out the code he had used so often in the past.

She was a long time answering. He looked at his watch. It was still early, not yet seven. He was about to give up when the screen flared into life. Then he was looking at Caroline Da Silva, older by five years but just as attractive as he remembered. She stared at him in disbelief, pulling a gown to her throat.

Then her lips moved in obvious anger, but Thorn heard nothing – or, rather, he heard the sound of himself chugging Scotch one hour ago.

He feared she might cut the connection. He leaned forward and mouthed what he hoped were the words: *I need you, Carrie. I'm ill. I can't hear. That is —*

He broke off, unsure how to continue.

Her expression of hostility altered; she still looked guarded, but there was an air of concern about her now as well. Her lips moved, then she remembered herself and used the deaf facility. She typed: Is your hearing delayed, Max?

He nodded.

She typed: Be at my surgery in one hour.

They stared at each other for a long moment, as if to see who might prove the stronger and switch off first.

Thorn shouted: *What the hell's wrong with me, Carrie? Is it something serious?*

She replied, forgetting to type. Her lips moved, answering his question with silent words.

In panic Thorn yelled: *What the hell do you mean?*

But Caroline had cut the connection.

Thorn returned to his recliner. He reflected that there was a certain justice in the way she had cut him off. Five years ago, their final communication had been by vidscreen. Then it had been Thorn who had severed the connection, effectively cutting her out of his life, implying without exactly saying so that she was no match for what he had found in flux.

Caroline's question about the time-lapse suggested that she knew something about his condition. He wondered – presuming his illness was a side-effect of the flux – if she was aware of the irony of his appeal for help.

One hour later Thorn boarded a flyer. Drunk and unable to hear his own words, he had taken the precaution of writing the address of the hospital on a card. He passed this to the driver, and as the flyer took off Thorn sank back in his seat.

He closed his eyes.

Aurally, he was in the past now, experiencing the sounds of his life that were already one hour old. He heard himself leave the recliner, cross the room and type the code on

5

the keyboard. After a while he heard the crackle of the screen and Caroline's, 'Doctor Da Silva . . .' followed by an indrawn breath of surprise.

'I need you, Carrie. I'm ill. I can't hear. That is —' Thorn felt ashamed at how pathetic he had sounded.

Then he heard Caroline's spoken reply, more to herself, before she bethought herself to use the keyboard and ask him if his hearing was delayed. 'Black's Syndrome,' she had said.

Now, in the flyer, Thorn's stomach lurched. He had no idea what Black's Syndrome was, but the sound of it scared him.

Then he heard his one-hour-past-self say, 'What the hell's wrong with me, Carrie? Is it something serious?' The words came out slurred, but Caroline had understood.

She had answered: 'I'm afraid it is serious, Max. Get yourself here in one hour, okay?'

And she had cut the connection.

Caroline Da Silva's surgery was part of a large hospital complex overlooking the bay. Thorn left the flyer in the landing lot and made his way unsteadily to the west wing. The sound of the city, as heard from his apartment, played in his ears.

He moved carefully down interminable corridors. Had he been less apprehensive about what might be wrong with him, and about meeting Caroline again after so long, he might have enjoyed the strange sensation of seeing one thing and hearing another. It was like watching a film with the wrong sound-track.

He found the door marked Dr Da Silva, knocked and stepped inside. Caroline was the first person he saw in the room. For a second he wondered how the flux had managed to lure him away from her, but only for a second. She was very attractive, with the calm elliptical face of a ballerina, the same graceful poise. She was caring and intelligent, too, but the very fact of her physicality spoke to Thorn of the manifest impermanence of all things physical. The flux promised, and delivered, periods of blissful disembodiment.

Only then did Thorn notice the other occupants of the room. He recognized the two men behind the desk. One was his medic at the Line, the other his commanding officer. Their very presence suggested that all was not well. The way they regarded him, with direct stares devoid of emotion, confirmed this.

The realization rocked Thorn with the impact of a physical blow, and a combination of drink and shock pitched him into unconsciousness.

He awoke in bed in a white room. To his right a glass door gave on to a balcony, and all he could see beyond was the bright blue sky. On the opposite wall was a rectangular screen, opaque to him but transparent to observers in the next room.

Electrodes covered his head and chest.

He could hear the drone of the flyer's turbos as it carried him towards the hospital. He sat up and called out what he hoped was: *Caroline!* . . . *Carrie!*

He sank back, frustrated. He watched an hour tick by on his wall-clock, listening to the flyer descend and his own footsteps as the Thorn-of-one-hour-ago approached the hospital. He wondered if he was being watched through the one-way window. He felt caged.

He looked through the door into the sky. In the distance he could see a big starship climb on a steep gradient. He heard himself open the surgery door, and Caroline's voice. 'Ah . . . Max.'

Then – unexpectedly, though he should have been aware of its coming – silence. This was the period during which he was unconscious.

He glanced back at the sky, but the starship had phased out and was no longer visible.

Thorn tried not to think about his future.

★

7

Caroline arrived thirty minutes later. She carried a sketch pad and a stylus. She sat on a plastic chair beside the bed, the pad on her lap. She tried to cover her concern with smiles, but Thorn was aware of tears recently shed, the evidence of smudged make-up. He had seen it many times before.

How long will I be in here? he asked.

Caroline chewed her lower lip, avoiding his eyes. She began to speak, then stopped herself. Instead, she wrote on the sketch pad and held up the finished product.

A week or two, Max. We want to run a few tests.

Thorn smiled to himself. *What exactly is this Black's Syndrome?* he asked, with what he hoped was the right degree of malicious sarcasm.

He was pleased with Caroline's shocked expression.

How do you know that? she scribbled.

You mentioned it over the vidscreen, Thorn told her. *I didn't hear it until I was coming here . . . What is it, Carrie?*

She paused, then began writing. Thorn read the words upside down: Black – an Engineman on the Taurus Line out of Varanasi. After fifty shifts he developed acute sensory time-lapse. It's a one-in-a-thousand malady, Max. We don't know exactly what causes it, but we suspect it's a malfunction in the tank leads that retards interneuron activity.

She paused, then held up the message.

Thorn nodded. *I've read it. So . . .?*

She turned to a blank page, stylus poised.

How long did he last? Thorn asked, bitterly. *When did the poor bastard die?*

Quickly she wrote: He's still alive, Max.

Thorn was surprised, relieved. If the present condition was the extent of Black's Syndrome, then what was to prevent him fluxing again?

He wondered at Caroline's tears. If his disease was only this minor, then why all the emotion?

Then he thought he understood.

When can I leave, Carrie? When can I get back to the flux?

8

He was watching the pad, waiting for a reply. When he looked up he saw that she was crying, openly this time.

He laughed. *You thought you had me, didn't you? Discharged from the Line, your own little invalid to look after and pamper. You can't stand the thought that I'll recover and flux again, can you?*

Despite her tears she was scribbling, covering page after page with rapid, oversized scrawl.

When she came to the end she stabbed a vicious period, ripped the pages out and flung them at him. She ran from the room, skittling a chair on the way. Thorn watched her, a sudden sense of guilt excavating a hollow in his chest.

His gaze dropped to the crumpled pages. He picked them up and read:

Acute *sensory* time-lapse. Not just hearing. Everything. In a few days your taste and smell will go the same way. Then your vision. You'll be left only with the sensation of touch in the 'present'. Everything else will be lapsed . . .

It went like this for a few more pages, the handwriting becoming more and more erratic. Most of it reiterated the few known facts and Caroline's observations of Black's decline. On the last page she had simply written: I loved you, Max.

Thorn smoothed the pages across his lap. He called for Caroline again and again, but if she heard she ignored him. He wanted to apologise, ask what might happen to him. He tried to envisage the sensation of having all his senses time-lapsed save for that of touch, but the task was beyond his powers of perception.

He lay back and closed his eyes. Later he was startled by the sound of his voice, his cruel questions. He heard Caroline's breathless sobs, the squeak of the stylus, a murmured, 'I loved you . . .' to accompany the written assurance. He heard her run crying from the room, the chair tumble, the door slam shut.

Then all he could hear was the sound of his breathing, the muffled, routine noises of the hospital. For the first time in hours the sounds he heard were synchronized with what he could see.

He slept.

On the morning of his third day in hospital, Thorn's senses of taste and smell went the way of his hearing. This further time-lapse dashed any hope he might have had that Caroline's diagnosis had been mistaken.

He had not seen Caroline since her hurried departure on the first day. He had been examined and tested by medical staff who went about their business in silence, as if they were aware of his outburst at Caroline and were censoring him for it. On the third morning in hospital, a black nurse brought him his breakfast.

He began eating, and soon realised that he could neither taste nor smell the bacon and eggs, or the coffee, black and no doubt strong.

He finished his meal. He watched the nurse return and remove the tray, sank back and waited.

Two hours later he heard the sound of the trolley being rolled in, the rattle of knife and fork. Seconds later the taste of bacon, then egg yolk, filled his mouth. He inhaled the aroma of the coffee, tasted it on his tongue. He closed his eyes and savoured the sensation. It was the only pleasurable effect of this strange malaise so far.

Then he sat up as something struck him. *Two hours*! . . . The delay between eating the food and tasting it had been two hours! Likewise the sound of the nurse's arrival.

If his hearing, taste and smell became delayed at the rate of two hours every three days – then what would it be like in a week, say, or a month or a year?

And what of his eyesight? How would he cope with seeing something that had occurred hours, days, even weeks ago? He resolved to find out what had happened to Black, how he was coping. He sat up and called for Caroline.

She did not show herself for another three days.

10

Thorn was attended by an efficient platoon of medics. They seemed to rush through their duties around him with a casual indifference as if he had ceased to exist, or as if they assumed that his senses had retarded to such an extent that he existed alone in a bubble of isolation. On more than one occasion he had asked whether he could be cured, how much worse it might become, what had happened to Black? But they used the fact that he could not immediately hear them as an excuse to ignore him, avoiding not only his words but his eyes.

On the morning of his sixth day in hospital, he awoke to silence and ate his tasteless breakfast. The sound of his waking, of the hospital coming to life around him, the taste of his breakfast – all these things would come to him later. He wondered if he could time it so that he tasted his breakfast at the same time as he ate his lunch?

He waited, and it was four hours later when he tasted toast and marmalade, heard the sounds of his breathing as he awoke.

Later, a nurse removed the electrodes from his head and chest. She opened the door to the balcony and held up a card which read:

Would you like to go out for some air?

Thorn waited until the nurse had left, shrugged into a dressing gown and stepped onto the balcony. He sat down on a chair in the sunlight and stared across the bay, then up into the sky. There was no sign of starship activity today.

He realised that, despite the seriousness of his condition, he still hoped to flux again. Surely the state of his senses would have no detrimental effect on his ability to mind-push? He had already decided that when his condition deteriorated to such an extent that he could no longer function without help, which must surely happen when his sight became affected, he would volunteer for a long-shift. He could push a boat to one of the Rim Worlds, spend a year of ecstasy in flux. It would probably kill him, but the

11

prospect of such rapture and a painless end was preferable to the life he could expect here on Earth.

Caroline appeared on the edge of his vision. She placed a chair next to his and sat down beside him, the sketch pad on her lap. She seemed fresh and composed, the episode of the other day forgotten.

I've been wanting to apologize for what I said, Carrie. I had hoped you'd visit me before now. And he cursed himself for making even his apology sound like an accusation.

Caroline wrote: I've been with Black.

Thorn was suddenly aware of his own heartbeat. *How is he?*

She wrote: Only his sense of touch is now in the 'present'. All his other senses are time-lapsed by nearly a day.

How's he coping?

She paused, then wrote: Not very well. He was never very stable. He's showing signs of psychosis. But you're much stronger, Max —

He interrupted: *What happens when his sense of touch retards?*

Caroline shrugged. Thorn read: It hasn't happened yet. It's difficult to say. In a way, if it does occur, it will be easier for him as all his senses will be synchronized in the 'past'. But he'll be unable to mix with people, socialize. How could he? Their presence would be delayed subjectively by hours, days. There would be no way for him to relate . . .

He could still flux, Thorn said.

Caroline looked away. Tears appeared in her eyes. Then she scribbled something on the pad:

Is the flux all you think about?

It's my life, Carrie. The only reason I exist.

She shook her head, frustrated by this clumsy means of communication. She wrote out two pages of neat script and passed them to him.

I could understand your infatuation with the flux if you thought the experience had religious significance; that you were in touch with the Afterlife. But you don't even believe that! To you it's just a drug, a mental fix. You're a flux-junky, Max. When you left me you were running away from something you couldn't handle emotionally because you'd never had to in the past. For most of your life, Max, the flux has provided you with a substitute for human emotion, both the giving of it and the taking. And look where it's got you!

Thorn sat without speaking. Some part of him – some distant, buried, human part – was stunned by the truth of her insight.

You just feel sorry for yourself because you didn't get me, he said weakly, trying to defend himself.

Caroline just stared at him. She shook her head. With deliberation she wrote one line. She stood up and tore off the top sheet, handed it to him and left the balcony.

I'm not sorry for myself, Max. I'm sorry for you.

Thorn pushed the meeting with Caroline to the back of his mind. In the days that followed he dwelled on the hope that he might one day be able to flux again. If his sense of touch did retard, then, as Caroline had suggested, all his senses would be synchronized and his condition made considerably easier. He might not be able to socialize, but that would be no great loss. His only desire was to rejoin the Line.

On his ninth morning in hospital, Thorn opened his eyes and saw nothing but darkness. He called for the lights to be switched on, but instead someone spoon-fed him breakfast. He was unable to tell if it was Caroline; he could neither see, hear, or even smell the person. He asked who it was, but the only response – the only one possible in the circumstances – was a gentle hand on his arm. After his first breakfast in darkness he lay back and waited.

His sensory delay had expanded to six hours now, and it was that long before the darkness lifted and he was able to see the sunlight slanting into the room. He had the disconcerting experience of lying flat on his back while his gaze of six hours ago lifted as the Thorn-of-this-morning sat up and prepared for breakfast. In his vision the black nurse positioned his tray

13

and fed him bacon and eggs. Thorn felt that he could reach out and touch the woman. He tried, and of course his hand encountered nothing.

He had no control over the direction of his gaze; his unseeing eyes of that morning had wandered, and he found himself trying to bring his errant vision back to the nurse, when all he saw was the far wall. His vision was interrupted by frequent, fraction-of-a-second blanks, when he had blinked, and longer stretches of total blackness when he had closed his eyes. The only benefit of this visual delay was that now his sight and hearing, taste and smell were synchronized. He saw the nurse lift a forkful of egg to his mouth, heard the sound of his chewing and tasted the food. The only thing missing was the egg itself; his mouth was empty.

'There we are,' the nurse said, proffering Thorn a last corner of toast. He wanted to tell her to stop treating him like a child, but that was the big disadvantage of his present condition: what he experienced now had happened six hours ago. The Jamaican nurse would be elsewhere in the hospital, the bacon and egg digested, the sounds and aromas dissolved into the ether.

Over the next few days he remained awake into the early hours, watching the happenings of the previous day. At four in the morning, then six, darkness would descend, and Thorn would settle down to sleep. Around noon he would wake, spend several hours in darkness, then watch the sun rise eight hours late. If the delay between occurrence and perception continued to increase by two hours every three days, as it was doing, then Thorn foresaw a time when he would be spending more time in darkness than in light.

He would be able to cope. There had been many a long period in the past, between shifts, when he had locked himself in his darkened apartment, with drink and fleeting memories of flux.

★

14

After almost two weeks in hospital Thorn began to weaken. He passed through periods of physical nausea and mental confusion. He hallucinated once that he was fluxing again, this time without the usual euphoria of the union.

The day following this hallucination he awoke early and felt the warmth of sunlight on his skin. Eight hours later he was aware of the sun coming up over the sea. He would have liked to watch it, but his eyes of eight hours ago were fixed on the foot of his bed. The frequency of his 'waking' blinks gave the scene the aspect of an ancient, flickering movie. At least it wasn't silent: he could hear the hospital waking around him, the distant crescendo of a starship's burners.

Later, after someone spoon-fed him a tasteless lunch, he felt a soft hand on his arm. He moved his head, as if by doing so he might see who it was. But all he saw was the same old far wall of eight hours ago; all he heard was his own breathing. He recalled the touch of the black nurse, but that had been light, platonic, reassuring him like a child that everything was all right. There was nothing platonic about this touch. As he lay there, helpless, whoever it was pulled back the sheets and divested him of hospital garb. He shouted out in silence, tried to fend her off – 'her' because his flailing arm caught the softness of a breast. But he could not see the woman and he was unable to prevent the ludicrous rape. He felt a warm, soft weight straddle him, her breasts loose against his chest, and the sensation was what he imagined it might be like to be taken by a succubus.

Caroline? he said. He moved his arms in the clumsy description of an embrace, touched her familiar warm and slender body. He was aroused now despite himself. She found him and he moaned without a sound, ran his fingers through her black invisible hair. He recognized Caroline's brand of love-making from the past, went along with it as though they had never parted, and when climax came it was as he remembered it from many years ago – a brief ecstasy soon gone, like a second in flux but not as satisfying. Even

15

the unusual circumstances of the union, the fact that he could not see Caroline, that the source of his pleasure was as it were disembodied, could only intimate a greater rapture and not fulfil in itself.

The invisible weight of her lay against him now, heavy and sated after orgasm, which Thorn had experienced through the silent contractions of her body. She kissed him, and he felt salt tears fall on his face.

Caroline . . . Why . . .?

Her lips moved against his cheek, her breath hot as she formed words. It was like being kissed by a ghost, bestowed silent prophecy.

In the calm aftermath of the act, Thorn began to feel revulsion. The bizarre nature of their love-making sickened him. He felt a return of the old guilt which he thought he had long since banished. It was as if the union was a symbol of their relationship to date; for years Thorn had played at loving someone whose essence was invisible to him, while Caroline for her part had wasted her life chasing someone who was emotionally forever elsewhere.

He cried out now and pushed her from the bed. He felt her fall and almost heard her cry of pain. *Get out, Caroline! Go away!* He faced where he thought she might be, but could not be sure. *I don't want you, for God's sake! All I want —*

She attacked him then. She came at him with painful blows and slaps, and no doubt cries and accusations. Thorn was aware only of the physical violence, the punches that struck from nowhere without warning. And he was aware, too, that he deserved everything he was getting.

He lay on the bed, battered and exhausted. Caroline had ceased her attack. He had no way of knowing whether she was still in the room, but he sensed her continued presence. *I don't know why you came here*, he said. *I don't know what you want from me . . .*

He half-expected another hail of blows, and flinched in anticipation. But none came.

16

When he thought he was alone he dragged the bedsheets around him protectively, lay back and recalled Caroline's tears on his cheeks.

There could only be one explanation for her visit.

Thorn felt himself weaken further during the hours that followed.

He waited with mounting apprehension, his body covered in chill sweat. Visually it was four o'clock in the afternoon, but the real time was around midnight. It seemed a lot longer than the delayed eight hours before Caroline entered his line of sight.

She moved out of it quickly as she came to the side of his bed. She reached out and touched his arm, and Thorn expected to feel her now, but of course her touch had startled him eight hours ago. Then, Thorn had turned his head abruptly, and now he saw Caroline full on. She wore only a white gown and nothing beneath, and she was crying.

He watched as she undressed him, and the sight of her doing this now brought a hot flush of shame and resentment to his cheeks. The sensation of her touch had passed, but as he watched her slip from her gown and climb on to him he experienced a resurgence of the desire that had overwhelmed him eight hours earlier.

The Thorn-of-now lay still in his bed. He was making love to Caroline, but, with his memories of the physical act already eight hours old, he felt like a voyeur in the head of his former self. He could see her, frenzied blurs of flesh and hair and tongue; he could smell her, the perfume she used and the sweat of sex that overcame it; and he could hear her small moans of pleasure, her repeated cry of his name as she approached climax.

He heard his slurred question: 'Caroline . . . Why . . .?'

They had finished their love-making and she lay in his arms. 'Because I loved you, Max,' she had said. 'Because I *still* love you.'

17

He knew what happened next. Again he experienced that overwhelming sense of revulsion, brought about by guilt. He watched helplessly as he pushed her from the bed. 'Get out, Caroline!' he heard himself cry. 'Get away!' He saw her expression of pain, the acceptance of rejection in her eyes, and had it been possible he would have stopped himself saying what he said next. 'I don't want you, for God's sake! All I want —'

She came at him and hit him again and again.

The Thorn-of-now flinched, as if the blows he could see coming might indeed inflict pain upon him; he raised his arms as if to protect himself.

Caroline backed off and yelled at him.

He heard himself say: 'I don't know why you came here . . . I don't know what you want from me . . ,'

Caroline was crying. 'I came because I loved you, Max. I came to say goodbye.'

She lowered her gaze and murmured, more to herself than to Thorn: 'Black died two days ago . . .'

Eight hours later Thorn lay quite still.

He deteriorated rapidly over the next few days.

The knowledge of Black's death robbed him of any will he might have had to fight. In his final hours he experienced a gradual diminution of his senses. His hearing left him first – then his taste and sense of smell.

Later, his vision dimmed and went out, and a familiar euphoria flooded through him as he became aware of himself as a small, blind intelligence afloat in an infinite ocean.

The Karma Kid
Transcends

I had my twelfth birthday on the way back from star Capella. I didn't celebrate. I stuck to my berth, drank acid shorts and poked tongue at my reflection. I didn't tell Jacques, either. He wouldn't give a damn how old I was. To him, I was just another telepathic-navigator, and the only thing that distinguished me from most of the others in the fleet was the fact that I was a girl. Even so, I was nothing special. I'd blooded a month before my birthday, but I was still unattractive – as if I'd expected, at the onset of womanhood, to be transformed butterfly-like into something beautiful. I was still short and plain, padded with puppy-fat in all the wrong places. Even my Asiatic origins did nothing for him. But what did I expect from a starship Captain who'd seen a hundred aliens more exotic than myself?

In the two years I'd worked for Jacques I'd often tried to get to know him better, establish a rapport that might in time have led to something more. But that proved impossible. Jacques wore a mind-shield. I had probed him on our very first meeting but came up with nothing. Since then I'd slipped probes towards him at regular intervals, but his mind was as elusive as a Lyran silver eel – and the fact that he constantly wore a shield frightened me. What was he hiding? Only criminals and psychopaths wore those things all the time, people who had something real bad to hide, who didn't want telepaths probing by accident. The longer I knew Jacques, the more worried I became.

Then, at the beginning of this trip, as we lighted out of Sol System bound for star Capella, he let his defences drop.

I knew from his manner that something was bothering him. We were carrying a representative of the Telemann-Vonhoff corporation to the seventh world of Capella – an uninhabited, Earthnorm planet out of bounds to all but approved star traffic. Jacques' attitude towards the official was, at best, brusque; he made it obvious that for some reason he resented the woman. He avoided her when he could and tried to ignore her when he couldn't. He was preoccupied and nervous and he spent most of his time in the flight-pod.

We were four days from star Capella; it was a routine haul and we were cruising. Jacques was flying and I was navigating. I'd mind-vectored ahead to the planet-bound telepath who charted our position and future flight-path, and then I fed the information through to Jacques.

I was about to close down when I picked up stray thoughts from our passenger. Nothing special – just superficial mindmush like how she couldn't wait to bed her girlfriend when she got back to Earth.

Then I got something else. Jacques' angst overcame his shield, and I was blitzed into unconsciousness by a two-second burst of brainhowl. I awoke disoriented, and only after minutes realised what had happened. I tried to recall the content of the contact, but it was like snatching at fragments of a forgotten dream. I came up with ill-defined images and fleeting sensations. I saw dead bodies and experienced quick cerebral stabs of ecstasy, followed by plummeting depression. I saw enough to realise that Jacques needed help, and who knows maybe even love. I decided to confront him when I was next off-duty. I'd had enough of his keeping away from me, avoiding contact. I'd give him no choice now; he'd either reject me or take me, and either way I might learn something.

We were a day away from Capella when I made my way to the flight-pod and sneaked in. Jacques was strapped into the traction-nexus like a fly in a spider's web. He'd just finished a stint in flux, and he was on his way down. Sweat saturated his uniform a shade darker than the usual sky blue. The sight of him made my stomach flip.

When I met Jacques two years back it was love at first sight. I was fresh out of navigator-training school and he was my first Captain. What I felt for him then, and still felt, wasn't just the neophyte's infatuation with the romantic mystique of a lone starship Captain. Okay, maybe that had something to do with it, at first. He cut a wild, wayward figure in his tight-fitting pilot's garb – but my love for him was more than just an attraction to his physical aspect and rank. There was something about him that cried out for help and protection. He was scared and he needed *someone*. I was a telepath, wasn't I? If only he'd open up and share his tortured psyche with me, allow us to become one . . . I might not be a stunning beauty, but love is more than just good looks. I knew I could give him what he'd never had before.

I touched his foot. He opened his eyes immediately and I caught my breath, managed a timid smile. He lifted his head and stared at me. I perched myself on the rim of the nexus. 'Jacques . . .'

'What do you want?'

He said it sharply, as if what I wanted wasn't obvious. I'd changed from my silversuit into a short slip. Telepathic therapy was always enhanced during sex. My face burned. I ran my hand along his leg.

'Jacques . . . Please let me help.'

'I need no help, least of all from you . . .'

His words hurt. 'The other day I . . . I read you briefly. I don't understand what I saw, but I know you need help. Let me —'

He sat up. 'How much did you read?' He leaned forward and stared at me with anger in his eyes.

'Hardly anything . . . I felt you needed help, that's all. Please, Jacques – let me in.'

I tried a probe, got nothing.

He felt warmth in his head and hit out. His fist caught my cheek. I jumped up and backed away.

Jacques pushed himself from the nexus and stood shakily. He was weak after the flux and he leaned against the wall for support. He pointed at me, and the deliberation of the gesture scared me more than the punch. 'You stupid little fool! How could you ever hope to understand? I need no one!' He came for me then, lurching forward. 'Get out!' he yelled, and the emotion he generated overcame the restraint of his mind-shield. I was rocked by a wave of raw feeling that hit me with the force of a physical blow. Jacques hated himself. He hated me, too – but in the brief second that he was open I saw that he hated not me personally, not Dhondup Ysomo, tele-navigator, but what I represented. He hated the temptation that I and all living beings held for him. I was shocked and bewildered then, and only much later did I learn why he hated – and the reason he hated himself with such corrosive, almost suicidal energy. Sobbing, I fled the pod.

For the rest of the journey I kept my distance. I thought it best not to antagonize him. He needed time to cool off, and I needed time to plan my next move.

Only later, when the trip was over and we were coming in to land on Earth, did it occur to me that perhaps Jacques' depression, his *weltschmerz*, had something to do with the presence aboard the ship of the Telemann-Vonhoff official, Hallelujah Birmingham.

We screamed out of hyper-light drive.

Jacques dropped the ship through the plane of the ecliptic and up again, heading for home. We were on automatic now, but he chose to remain in the flight-pod. My tour of duty officially finished here. Now we were out of hy-c, all communications could be handled conventionally. I slipped the ferronniere from my shaven head and left the navigation follicle. I dropped two decks to the lounge and sat, yogi-fashion, in the dome that obtruded through the skin of the ship. I stared out at the planets and wondered what I was going to do with Captain Jacques Latrouche.

In whichever port we docked, Jacques always used his ship as base. He spent his nights in the city and his days sleeping it off in his berth. I was barred from the ship while it was in port, given my pay and papers and the time of the next burn-out. A couple of times I'd tried to stay with Jacques, even suggested that I show him Lhasa or Kathmandu. But he was always at his most irritable at the end of a run, strung-out and impatient to be rid of me. He made it clear that he wanted to hit the city alone and I always felt abandoned when we said goodbye. This time, I decided to remain in the city where we landed and stick close to him.

I was so absorbed in my own thoughts that I failed to register those of our passenger until she laid a hand on my shoulder. Then I was aware of the warm glow high above my head. In the concave surface of the dome I could see the tall reflection of Hallelujah Birmingham.

'We're almost home, Dhondup,' she smiled.

Folding herself neatly, she sat down beside me. She was outfitted in a smart red company uniform and she carried her case, ready to disembark when we docked.

The moment she boarded the ship three months ago, I was jealous. I was convinced that Jacques would make a move for her. She was a tall, beautiful Nigerian, with all the poise and grace of her race. I guessed she was around eighteen, and consoled myself with the thought that maybe in five or six years I might look as good.

As things turned out, for some reason Jacques ignored her, and I got to know her well. Between shifts in the tele-communications nacelle, I played her at chess and beat her, and we'd rap for ages about our families and friends and things.

'What you doing this furlough, Dhondup?' she asked now.

23

I hesitated. 'Oh . . . I'll visit my mother in Lhasa, I think. I haven't seen her for a while. She'll be wondering where I've got to. You know what mothers are like . . .' I lapsed into silence, staring out. We were cruising above the asteroid belt; the silvery nodes arced away in a perfect parabola towards the far side of the sun.

She rested a warm hand on my thigh. 'Hey, believe me – he isn't worth it.'

I probed her. 'Who isn't?' I said, shocked that I was so readable. As a telepath I was accustomed to reading the thoughts and emotions of others and keeping my own well under wraps.

'You can't kid me, kid. I know you're crazy about him.'

Hallelujah Birmingham was one of the most genuine people I'd ever met. She was honest; her words corresponded with what she thought, always, and this was rare. Now I read a warm compassion for me – and lust as well – but more than that, a sympathy for my unhappiness. At times I came up against areas of her mind that were guarded, that my probes glanced off and could not penetrate. This was usual with company representatives and people in big business. There were some things that had to be kept secret, and rather than employ shields, which were not always effective, corporations had ways of hynotizing employees so that certain subjects in their heads were never readable. I'd probed Hallelujah many times and discovered that one of the things concealed behind her mindblock was this mission. It was top secret and priority A, and the Telemann-Vonhoff people wanted no one, not even lowly young tele-navs, to know what was going on.

'Dhondup, why not forget Jacques and come with me this furlough? You can visit your family some other time. Have you ever been to New York?'

'Of course I have,' I said, probing her. 'I *know* it's a dangerous place and I'm not scared, so don't get that idea.'

Hallelujah smiled and raised her palms in mock capitulation. She leaned back against the wall of the dome and appeared to be suspended in space, with Mars on her right, Venus on her left and Earth eclipsed by her afro. 'Well . . . how about it, Dhondy? Why not come with me when we land?'

'I prefer Jacques,' I said in a whisper.

Hallelujah just shrugged, smiling.

We'd made a rough touchdown on Capella Seven, and Jacques hadn't even shown himself to apologize. Seven was a virgin world, the temporary base of a small team of Telemann–Vonhoff scientists. Hallelujah Birmingham had spent three days with her colleagues in the spacious living domes at the head of a beautiful valley, and we were requested to remain aboard the ship. While Miss Birmingham was away, I took the opportunity to go through her berth. I found she was a xenobiologist specialising in alien pharmaceuticals, which was an area of information blocked off in her mind. On the third day, Miss Birmingham returned with a freezer carricase and we lighted out for Earth.

'What were you doing on Seven?' I asked now.

She gave me a cool, appraising look. 'If I tell you . . . will you accompany me to New York?'

I decided to lie. 'Hokay.' I shrugged. 'Why not?'

I probed her and found doubt, hesitation; but desire overcame any qualms she might have had at breaching company guidelines.

'You've heard of the drug DLa, or Spice as it's called on the street?'

'Do I look like a dummy?' I asked. The drug was used by non-telepaths to gain states of brief telepathic awareness. The user could read minds, but not as clearly as true telepaths, nor for any sustained periods. The usual trip lasted about ten minutes and left the user blasted. Spice was not addictive, but one trip could kill. The drug had become the focus of a sick cult in the Western world.

The Freaks, as the cultists were called, used Spice to ride 'dead' minds to the white light.

The fact of Afterlife was established at the end of the last century. It was ironical that life after death, the state of being that mystics had foretold for thousands of years, was eventually proven by the unforeseen result of a scientific breakthrough.

The first person to undergo neuro-surgery to bring about telepathy was a four-year-old Peruvian girl. On waking from the operation, she reported that an old man in another part of the hospital, who, according to the minds of the doctors and nurses was dead, was in fact still alive. She claimed that she had travelled with the old man into the sky towards a bright light that emanated peace and tranquillity. There the girl had been repulsed, and the old man left her and became one with the light . . . More children were made surgically telepathic, and they all affirmed the experience of the first child: after the 'death' of the body, the mind, or perhaps even the soul, lived on.

I had experienced close contact with a departing mind only twice. The first time was after a loading accident at Varanasi spaceport; I had travelled with the 'dead' loader as far as a brilliant white light in a transport of incredible ecstasy. Even though, as a Buddhist, I believed in transcendence after bodily death, nothing could have prepared me for the actual wonder of the experience. The second time, when I had a hotel room next to that of an old woman who died in her sleep, there was no diminution of effect. The supernal delight of rising with her to the next stage of existence was such that the return to life on Earth came as a crushing disappointment.

I could understand how the Freaks became hooked on the thrill of riding . . .

We landed.

We sailed into a stasis grid and magnetic grabs lowered

26

us to the shunting lanes. A hovertug hauled us at walking pace towards the terminal ziggurat. It was dark outside, and the dazzling illumination of photon tubes prevented identification of the city beyond the perimeter crash barrier. We might have been in any one of a dozen major spaceports on Earth.

I said, 'What was your mission on Seven?'

Hallelujah smiled at me. 'You know what? I reckon our relationship should be more than just platonic . . .'

I didn't flinch. She was being honest, after all. Which I wasn't when I said, 'I might like that, maybe.' And I smiled, too.

'Very well, then . . .'

And she proceeded to tell me that the scientists on Seven had been working on a new version of the drug DLa. The old drug was extracted from flora on the colony world of Emerald – illegally. A Telemann–Vonhoff exploration team had discovered a similar strain of vegetation on Capella Seven, and tests to date had shown it to be even stronger than the regular DLa.

'So?' I shrugged. 'Why is your company interested in a drug stronger than Spice? I thought the authorities were trying to clamp down on the import of the stuff?'

'On the *illegal* import of DLa,' she said. 'We intend to bring the new drug to Earth, *legally*, and test it for certain properties . . .'

I shrugged again.

Hallelujah smiled. 'We have reason to believe that the drug will take the user not only to the white light, but beyond. Let's just say that my company has a certain interest in discovering Heaven . . . or even Nirvana.'

The ship trundled to a halt. External clunkings and pneumatic sighs indicated that we had docked with the entry chute of the terminal ziggurat. Behind the rectangular viewscreens of the building I could see the small figures of spaceport personnel at work.

'Where are we?' I asked.

'New Seattle. Independent Pacific Northwest. I recognise the zigg.' She smiled at me. 'I have to deliver this case to New York in four hours, but I've a few calls to make first. How about I meet you back here in say two hours?'

'I . . . There's a bit of work I have to clear. I might be late.'

'Hey, don't back out now, kid. Remember your promise . . .'

'I'll be through in two hours,' I said.

She kissed my forehead. 'I'll see you then, my little Tibby-tan,' she said, mimicking the way I pronounced the word. She picked up her case and stood on the down-disc, wiping a circular wave in the air as she descended.

The voice of an Android official sounded through the ship, enumerating disembarkation procedure. I jumped from the dome and found my tricorne and moccasins in the sunken lounger where I'd thrown them earlier. I had no intention of keeping the rendezvous with Miss Birmingham, and I planned to be out of the ship when she returned. I'd hang around and follow Jacques when he left.

I was adjusting my tricorne at a cool angle when Jacques appeared at the far end of the lounge. 'Where is she?' he yelled. He braced himself in the entrance, panting.

I felt an irrational pang of jealousy. 'Who?'

'Who the hell do you think? Birmingham!'

'She just left. I didn't know you —'

He cursed again and jumped on the down-disc, stabbing the sensor impatiently. He dropped. 'Jacques – wait!'

I rushed to the chute, then remembered my exit card and dashed to my berth. When I returned, Jacques had been processed and the chute was free. I hopped aboard and closed my eyes. I was voided in a peristaltic rush and landed dizzy at the terminal check-out. Jacques had already been cleared. I saw him pushing through the crowd beyond the barrier. I passed my card to the Andy officer and waited, trying to conceal my impatience. His nod signalled my release and I took off. The unshielded mindmush of the crowd came at me in a wave of mixed emotions. I damped my receptivity and the noise modulated to a background hiss like static on a bad vid-soundtrack. I scooted through the foyer and attracted a posse of bodyguards who surrounded me like beggars with offers of security for the next twenty-four hours. They took my age and the fact I was Asiatic to mean I'd be needing their protection in the big bad Western world outside. I cursed them, then scoured their heads with a blowback of the loathing I felt towards parasites. They fell away. I slipped through the exit gate, feeling great.

After the solitude of deep space, New Seattle jumped me like a familiar nightmare. It was three in the morning, but the early hour did nothing to slow the pulse of life. Slideways carried crowds between serried citystacks. Fliers swept fast and silent overhead, and photon displays strobed ads into the dark night sky. Superimposed over all this was the incessant brainhowl of urban citizens. Dizzy, I paused for breath, clamped in a crowd surging towards a flier platform. Invisible hands frisked me expertly, found nothing worth picking and moved on. Dubious voices hissed for my attention. The usual hassle. It took some getting used to after space, but I'd survive.

I squirmed through the crowd and probed the take-off ramp. If Jacques had taken a slideway, then he was lost. My only hope was that Miss Birmingham might have boarded an air-cab, and Jacques had followed her. Most of the drivers were Andys, and my probes got nothing. Then I scanned a human driver and picked up the quick recognition of a spacer, and the merest mentalized suggestion of the stench. I was familiar with Jacques's flux-spiced body odour from the nexus, and my heart began a laboured pounding. His cab was moving up the take-off ramp, jets glowing. I jumped the queue and dived aboard the next cab in line, flashing the order to follow without saying a word. Take-off was immediate, pushing me into the padded seat. Jacques's cab was speeding ahead, weaving through the 'stacks. His driver had Miss Birmingham's cab in sight and was moving in. I ordered my driver to accelerate, leaned forward and watched the chase. I was desperate to find out why Jacques wanted to catch Birmingham. I *had* to know. I intended to be in there, probing, when they met.

As we raced over the city I was briefly aware of vibrant minds going out as suicides made it and left. The distance between us was too great to allow me to ride them, and for that I was thankful. The two occasions I had ridden departing minds to the white light had been enough for me to appreciate the experience; any more and I faced the danger of becoming hooked. I knew a few tele-navs who couldn't get enough of death, and worked the terminal wards during furlough. To these people everyday life, mundane reality, was an anti-climax. One guy I'd schooled with had jumped to his death from the cargo hatch of a landing lightship, just to have the final thrill. It was one way out, but not an exit I cared to contemplate. The white light was there at the end of it all like a promise, but I planned to make the most of my life before then.

Jacques' cab was gaining steadily on the one in front of it, and I prepared myself for the imminent confrontation – but I should have known. Without warning, a stasis grid came down on our lane and held us immobile. Overhead a freighter from Callisto trundled in, its passage churning a wake of turbulence which would have capsized our cab. Jacques' cab had been halted too – but Miss Birmingham's had slipped through. The stasis grid lifted and Jacques' cab moved off, slowly now, the chase abandoned. I probed Jacques' driver and read his new instructions: a dive in the Android quarter. I told my driver the same place and sat back, rehearsing the questions I'd ask when I finally caught up with him.

I stood across the slideway from the *White Ride* and watched Jacques dodge peds and run down the stairs to the underground club. I followed. He'd already entered when I reached the door, and a tall Andy barred my way.

When I tried to push past, a powerful arm stopped me. His transistorized thumb toyed with the option of clamping my carotid. His optics registered the connected-minds symbol tattooed on my cheek. 'Tele-snoops and kids,' the Andy purred, '*persona non grata*. Fly.' His thumb became more familiar. I'd heard of malfunctioning Andys before. A slip of his cogs and I'd be Angelled. I flew.

I took a drink in a bar above the slideway. I'd wait until Jacques came out and pick him up then. As I drank I watched the entrance, and the one next to it. From time to time a gang of girls descended the stairs to the second entrance. They were gash – I could tell that from their clothes, or rather the lack of them. They were ugly, too. I found myself thinking that I was more attractive at twelve than any of them. And to think that men paid . . . I was jolted by a sudden fit of bourgeois jealousy. Jacques! The dirty slumming bastard!

I ran across the slideway and tagged on to three gash as they went down the stairs. At the bottom we passed through a door, under the gaze of an uninterested Andy. Once inside, the gash went one way and I ran the other – in the direction, I hoped, of the bar and Jacques. I strode down a dark corridor and came to a swing door, opened it and peered in. Through a haze of euphor-fumes I made out a crowd of quiet drinkers. I painted a rouge nova over my tele-symbol, pushed through the door and played it cool. Jacques slouched alone in a private booth, staring into a crimson drink. I joined him, climbing aboard the opposite stool.

'Jullay, handsome,' I wisecracked brightly.

His reaction was tardy. He blinked twice, focusing on me. 'Dhondy . . . What you doing here?'

'I might ask you the same thing,' I said. I was suddenly aware that I was the youngest person in the bar. My moccasins dangled inches above the floor.

He regarded me blankly. 'How'd you get in?'

'I snuck,' I told him. 'Aren't you going to buy me a drink?'

I glanced around. All the drinkers wore guarded expressions, and their minds were guarded too, shielded. The only open minds in the place belonged to the girls I'd followed in, three points of warmth somewhere beyond the bar-room. I recalled the Andy-doorman's injunction against telepaths. It was the first time I'd ever been in a crowd and deprived of my tele-sense. I was frightened. What had they to hide? I glanced timidly at Jacques, but my probe ricocheted.

His attitude towards me, as he languidly sipped his drink, was that of an adult plagued by a bothersome kid: ignore it and it might *vamoose*. Well, this was one kid who wasn't going to be got rid of that easy.

'Why did you follow Birmingham?' I asked, ordering my own short from the press-select panel on the table.

He sighed. 'Let's just say we have some unfinished business to clear up.' He was watching the timer on the wall of the booth.

'What business?' I demanded. I reached across the table, but he pulled his hand away. He looked at me. In his old, wise eyes I saw the weight of weariness, as if he'd seen everything and everything was too much.

'Let me help you, Jacques,' I said. 'I'm a telepath, remember? If you open up and let me in . . . We all have secrets we like to keep hidden —'

'Even you?' He was mocking. 'Even little Dhondup?'

My gaze fell to my stubby fingers, spread on the table. 'Of course even me. We all have things to hide, things that are better shared. Open up, Jacques. Let me see what's in your head and I'll show you what's in mine. Then you'll realise . . .'

'I'm old enough to be your father, Dhondy. You can't help me.'

I hated him then, briefly. He was mocking me, trying to belittle the genuine affection I felt for him.

I tried something else. 'How desperately do you want to find Miss Birmingham?' I asked.

He affected disinterest, but his unshaven cheek twitched.

'I know where she'll be not long from now,' I went on.

'How do you know?'

I shrugged. 'I arranged to meet her.'

Jacques was in a dilemma: he wanted to ask me where she would be, but at the same time he didn't want to involve me.

The silence stretched. I considered asking him the question I'd dreaded all along. In a whisper I said, 'Is it something to do with the drug, Jacques?'

'What drug?' He sipped his drink, casual – and I knew I'd scored a hit.

'You know what damned drug! DLa. Spice.'

'What the hell are you getting at?' he laughed. And his question seemed so genuine that for a second he almost had me conned. But only for a second. I was unable to probe him, but my talent enabled me to match facial expressions to the psychology behind them. I'd read many a lie when the expression appeared truthful, and I had come to recognize the face of dishonesty.

Jacques knew very well what I was getting at.

'You want the drug, Jacques,' I said in a small voice. 'The new stuff discovered on Seven.'

He smiled to himself. 'I heard a rumour that a new strain had been developed . . .'

I felt tears swell in my eyes. 'You're hooked on riding, aren't you?' I could hardly bring myself to look at him. 'You're one of those Freaks who bum around outside hospitals and retiring homes . . .'

He reached across the table and took my cheek in the palm of his hand. He thumbed tears from my eyes. 'Honest, Dhondy, I do none of those things.'

'Then why?' I bit my lip, unable to go on. Then I managed, 'Jacques, let me help you. We could find a hotel room and merge and I promise you that everything will be better by morning. If you're hooked on the stuff, on the need to ride, I'll show you . . .' I whispered what I'd show him: 'Love . . . I know it might not compensate for the ecstasy of the white light, but it's the only thing I have to offer.'

'You don't understand, Dhondy. You're still a kid —'

'Not in here I'm not.' I pointed to my shaven skull. 'You can't say what I am until you've experienced a merging. At least give it a try.'

He sighed. His hands were shaking and he looked wrecked, as if he needed another trip with a departing Angel, or something only I could give him.

He said, 'This . . . *merging*. What exactly happens?' He forced himself to look away from me, as if afraid he might relent and accept my therapy.

'We merge, Jacques. Become one. We pool our strengths to overcome our weaknesses. It's an accepted psychiatric practice now. If the telepath is strong enough to take the subject's psychosis —'

He smiled. 'Are you strong enough?'

'I wouldn't make the offer if I didn't think I was . . .'

Jacques hesitated. Then: 'Very well,' he said.

I choked on a sob. 'You will? You'll try it?' I began to cry with relief. 'Really honestly? Now?' I clutched his arm as if afraid he was about to leave.

'I'll let you do whatever it is you do,' he said. 'On one condition . . .'

I slumped in my seat and stared at him.

'Where did you arrange to meet Birmingham?' he asked.

'You bastard,' I said in a whisper.

'Dhondy . . . Look, I swear – once I've seen her I'll come back to you.' He touched my hand. 'Honest, kid. Believe me.'

I stared at my bitten finger-nails. I felt the weight of a great depression bearing down on me. What was there to lose? If I refused to tell him, he would hardly agree to our

34

merging. If I told him . . . then maybe there was a chance that he'd keep his word, allow me to help.

'She'll be back at the ship in,' I looked at my watch, 'in about fifteen minutes. She wanted to take me to New York.'

'Will she have the carricase with her?'

'Jacques . . .' I began to cry again.

'Will she?' He shook me, and my head jogged a grudging assent. He stepped from the booth and pushed his way through the crowd. I watched him go, unable to do anything to stop him, a hard knot of anguish in my chest.

The timer on the wall pulsed red, and an impersonal Android voice said, 'Table eleven, your room is ready. Table eleven . . .' I bit back another fit of sobbing and slipped from the stool, stumbled to the bar and ordered a drink. I found a niche by a speaker blaring an assault of electro-horn and pipes. The euphor-fumes got to me and I giggled stupidly.

I was wondering what to do next when I felt a sudden warmth in my head. One of the gash had moved closer to me, and in lieu of any other open mind in the vicinity my tele-sense seized on it. Idly, to take my mind off myself, I probed. The woman entered a room behind the bar and stood facing a tall man. I probed the guy, too, but his mind was shielded. The woman undressed and walked across the room. She unzipped her customer's suit, then dropped to her knees and took him in her mouth.

She died without fully understanding why. She saw the silver glint of the knife and felt it grate through her ribcage and into her lungs. Unable to scream, she choked – and I felt a dull pain within my chest in psychosomatic sympathy. She was still alive when the guy laid her on the bed and injected himself with Spice; he tensed as the drug took him. Then he entered the dying woman and thrust repeatedly, brutally. I collapsed against the wall, the woman's dwindling consciousness bequeathing me the vicarious terror of rape. She died, then, and I was rising with her, taken in a breathless rush beyond the confines of my physical form

35

and into a wondrous realm transcending all Earthly reality. I was one with the 'dead' gash and riding her towards eternity . . . There was another consciousness there, too. Hard and cruel and masculine – a mind closed but nevertheless evident to me as the killer's rapture overcame the mechanics of his shield.

We flew into the white light.

Then it was over.

The trip was through and I was squatting down against the wall, my legs sticky where I'd pissed myself in delight. Beyond the after-effects of the ecstasy, and the disappointment of withdrawal and comedown, I felt the first vague stirrings of dread.

I recalled the events of the last hour, the fact that Jacques had booked a room. Across the haze-filled bar, in the booth we had occupied, the red light flashed on and off.

I opened my mouth, but the scream was drowned by electro-horn. I thought of Jacques and Hallelujah Birmingham and I screamed again. I ran in blind panic from the *White Ride*, past the Andy-doorman and up the stairs.

There was a cab-ramp a block along the slideway. I jumped aboard the moving strip and ran, passing tired night-shifters. It was the beginning of a new day, and the sun was rising behind the citystacks. As I ran, it began to rain; a fine drizzle that soaked me in seconds.

I jumped from the slideway and ran to the ramp, barging through the crowd on the platform. Ignoring protests, I reached the first cab. I was almost aboard when some jerk grabbed the hood of my silversuit and yanked me back. I spun, half strangled, lashed out and missed. I slipped and fell to the ground, gashing my knee. The crowd affected not to notice. I staggered to my feet and charged them again. I made it this time and ducked aboard the flier, my anger replaced by a brief sense of achievement.

'Spaceport. Crew check-in.' I turned towards the side-screen, hiding my tears.

We climbed and banked. The driver accelerated and the stacks flickered by in a dizzying rush. I sent out a probe, but the port was too far away for me to reach without the amplification of my ferronniere. All I got was the chaos of a thousand intervening minds. This morning, the collective consciousness of mankind seemed a shade darker.

We slipped into the port stasis grid and I was sprinting again, into the zigg and through the departure lounge. I was brought up short by the check-in. The Andy official took my card and observed my distress, allowing me through only after scrupulously checking my credentials.

At the tube-booths I took the chute to the hangar where the ship was racked. As I was flushed through the chute, I shut my eyes and probed. Distinct among the minds of mechanics and servicing engineers, I found Miss Birmingham's familiar mental warmth. She was running through the ship, her metabolism adrenalized with terror.

And Jacques was chasing her.

Then I read him. He'd removed his mind-shield to experience the full force of the new drug and his *angst* came at me like a bad attack of migraine. Over all else – over his fear and self-loathing – I experienced his ferocious craving, his need of ecstasy after so long in space.

I cried that I was coming, that I could help. In his mania to get at Birmingham he was hardly aware of my mental presence. The only image of myself that I managed to dredge from his mind was that of someone who mattered very little, a minor annoyance he could ignore.

The chute ejected me and I stumbled along the corridor, off balance. I fell again and my knee blazed in pain. I limped to the upchute and threw myself in, crying at the delay as I was carried to the highest shelf. One part of me repeated over and over that I was not to blame, but another voice reminded me that if only I'd realized Jacques's motives while we were in the club . . .

This time I landed square and sprinted limping along the catwalk. A variety of lightships were racked in individual berths. Our cruiser was the sixth along. I palmed the entry-sensor and rode the lift. I probed again, dreading what I might find.

I was rocked by a chaotic discord of two minds so close that they came to me as one – a schizophrenic blast of terror and desire. They were in the lounge, near the dome, and Jacques had Birmingham in the sights of his laser.

My sudden appearance on the disc startled him. He looked around, crazed with need and attempting to judge the threat I represented. I ran at him, was almost on him when he turned and fired. For one frozen second I was incredulous at the fact of my death. The bolt threw me off my feet and into the dome. I lay, immobilized but still alive, sick with the realization that Jacques had had no idea whether the laser had been on stun, or kill. I tried to move, but the shot had paralysed me, and all I could do was stare into the lounge with mounting horror.

Jacques caught Birmingham and thrust her to the floor, then he opened her carricase and fumbled a cartridge. He loaded it into a hypo-ject gun and banged it into his arm. His eyes closed and his body swayed as the new drug took him. He stood over Birmingham and adjusted his laser to kill. He took aim and fired, opening a bloody hole in her chest. Then he dropped to the floor and embraced her in a grotesque parody of affection.

I wanted nothing to do with the euphoria that rushed me then. I tried to withdraw my probe, close myself off, but the combined power of two open minds, one of them resonant with the new drug and the other already transcending, overcame my resistance and carried me away.

I soared, freed from paralysis and admitted into a realm of tranquillity and sublime peace. The joy of this trip was accentuated beyond anything I had ever experienced before. I was one with Birmingham and Jacques, and through him the new drug gave me a heightened perception of Afterlife. My last thought was that soon I would be experiencing the revelation of what lay *beyond* the white light.

Then the brightness came from everywhere, surrounding us and rushing in for the ultimate act of consummation. I was charged with wonder, with anticipation of what incredible sensation awaited us.

The white light exploded.

An instant blackness replaced the light – a cold, inimical void redolent of vague despair, just as the realm before it suggested hope. I found myself in a hostile element, like a non-swimmer thrown into the sea, and my mind reached frantically for some point of contact. I located Jacques, and beyond him, rushing away from us, bright shards and slivers of light, like the fragments of a smashed mirror reflecting the shattered image of something that was once complete. I probed towards one, and found a memory, the dwindling recollection of an African childhood; then another, Hallelujah Birmingham's first lover; then later scenes from adult life, along with love and joy and pain and regret . . . Then the images became weak, tenuous, and the cold reality of nothingness annihilated their former warmth.

The darkness faded then, became ever more remote like the haunting memory of a nightmare, and I found myself back in the lounge. Hallelujah Birmingham lay in the corner. Some residual effect of the drug in Jacques allowed me to probe deeper into her mind than my normal tele-ability would permit. I saw the last fragments of her subconscious, her last thoughts and memories, close down and die.

Before the full horror of the revelation came to me, Jacques screamed. He crawled away from the body and vomited, then collapsed. Tentatively, I probed him, found his guilt and despair. I opened up and thought love at him. I found I could move and, with pain and difficulty, dragged myself across the floor. I pulled Jacques to me and held him like a child, moving into him and letting him move into me. We merged.

How can you . . .? he thought.

Love you? I asked. *It's the only way, Jacques. I know you like I know myself. The only way I can help you is to love you, and you need my help. We have no secrets from each other, now.*

But you're not . . . his thoughts exclaimed.

Of course I wasn't Tibetan, or even Buddhist, really. I was the bastard of some lousy Chinese-American gash, who dumped me at birth on a slideway for a patrolling cop-flier to pick up. At four I was diagnosed a latent telepath, and I had the cut. At six I sprang myself from state creche; I couldn't take the regimented routine imposed on me, so I quit. A girl has to look after herself in the big bad world, and what I needed most back then was an identity. I met a Buddhist nun on a sub-orbital bound for Leh, and we hit it off. I dug her belief system and took it as my own, along with the exotic notion of Tibetan nationality, and the tag. It was a hard life, but then whose isn't? I had little love when I was young, and even less when I was on the run. For a year I bummed from job to job, living on my wits between times. Then suddenly things began to go right. At eight I was selected for tele-nav training school, and two years later I teamed up with a weak wreck of a bastard called Jacques Latrouche, barely twenty-five and in need of help . . . After all the shit, I got lucky.

Irony is, I'd always kidded myself that I must have been real bad in a previous incarnation, and the misfortune had carried over into this life.

So much for the Karma Kid.

I was just plain *me*, now.

I held him and he screamed again, screamed with grief for all the women he'd consigned to oblivion, horror at the new order of reality revealed by the drug.

We knew the truth. There was nothing beyond the white light.

Jacques reached out as he descended into a mental hell, and I held him. Of course, there was no guarantee that he'd ever get back.

But I'd be with him all the way.

Big Trouble Upstairs

I'm on the Barrier Reef pleasure plex, looking for a year-wife. Someone small and dark this time – Oriental maybe. The jacuzzi lagoon is foaming around me and my lover, a cute Kampuchean fluxer, when my handset goes *ber-leep*. I wade into the shallows, the kid big-eyed on my hip, and take the call.

'Sorry to come between you and your fun, Isabella.' Massingberd stares up from the back of my hand, playing the chaperone. 'But you're on.'

The spacer senses the goodbye and lays a soft cheek against my breast. I enter her head, tone down the love I've been promoting thus far, damp her synaptic fires.

'Give it me, Mass,' I sigh.

'You're gonna love this one,' he begins, and gives me a big wink.

There's a laser-slayer loose on the Carnival Sat, wasting innocents like mad-crazy. The bastard zeroed the security team first, along with the mechanical defences – and he has a dozen workers imprisoned on the satellite, to pick off at his leisure.

'It's your kind of Job, Is. You're going in there alone.'

'Say, thanks . . .'

'A shuttle's on its way,' he says, and signs off.

Soo-Lee clutches me. 'Isabella . . .'

'There'll be other times,' I soothe. But not with me . . . Why do I do it – *why*? It was love at first sight. I felt that yearning, gut pang the second I set eyes on Soo-Lee a week

41

back. She was picking scabs from her new hand-jack on the beach outside my villa. Of course, she wouldn't have given me a second glance, but I have *ability*.

Ten years ago I tested psi-positive and had the cut; but the operation went wrong. It was *too* successful. Instead of coming out plain telepathic, I emerged *mega*-telepathic. Which meant that, as well as being able to read minds, I had the power to control a subject's thoughts, make them do just whatever the hell I wanted. Pretty neat, okay.

I was the first of a new line.

We're a dozen now, closely supervised.

And I have this thing about kids. Whenever I see one I like I get in there and tamper, fix, and soon they're all gooey-eyed, eager.

This past week on the plex we made a striking couple: an anorexic, slit-eyed Enginegirl and a six-six eighteen-year-old Rwandan Watusi with scarified cheeks and dreads. That's me.

The love I promote is doomed, of course. I can't sustain that degree of adoration in a subject for long. The past few years I've instilled ersatz-love for the period of a six-month or one-year marriage contract – then withdrawn. It's kinder that way, to both parties. A year is long enough to live a lie, even when you're in love.

I dump Soo-Lee on the golden sand and sluice apathy around her frontal lobe, and by the time I step into my villa she's beginning to wonder what she ever saw in me. Soon Isabella Manchester will be nothing more than a pleasant event in the memory of her childhood, and then not even that.

Massingberd knows. He was the only person I could bring myself to tell. He once asked me why I didn't turn my ability on myself. 'Why don't you cure yourself, Is? Fix your head so you don't lust after these kids . . .'

It's no longer illegal, but oldsters like Mass have throw-back morality.

"Cos if it wasn't kids it'd be women or men. I'd be no

better off, just the same. I need love, okay? I guess I'm insecure. I can't change what I am because of *why* I am —' and stopped there.

I didn't even know Massingberd well enough to tell him why I am.

'I need love and it's so easy for me to get it,' I'd often say. 'But how can that be love?'

Skip two hours and I'm aboard the shutt on autopilot, heading away from the plane of the ecliptic towards the Carnival Sat. And mine's the only vessel going thisaway: all the other traffic is streaming Earthwards, sunlit specks corkscrewing down the gravity-well like gene-data on a DNA helix.

From this far out the satellite is an oblate spheroid, a yuletide bauble set against the Pleiades. The lower hemisphere is in darkness – the maintenance section that keeps the whole show ticking. Above, the working end of the Sat is a fuzzy golden blur. Closer proximity provides resolution: I see avenues and arcades, rides and sideshows. One big fun city down there.

Massingberd's saying: '. . . carved up two hundred Japanese and American tourists before the emergency shuttles could get the rest out. There's around a dozen workers still in there, plus the killer —'

'You sure he didn't sneak out on a shuttle?'

'I had a head screening every ship that left, Is.' He looks up at me solicitously. 'Hey, you be careful, okay?'

The sentimental old bastard. 'I'll be fine, Mass.'

'I'm putting you through to the Director who's still in there —'

But he's cut off by a screenful of static. I shake my hand impatiently and the screen clears. Now another mugshot regards me – the big cartoon head, all ribbons and grin, of Minnie Mouse.

'I'm fouled up with an entertainment channel, Mass!' I yell. I'm approaching the Satellite fast and I need the

Director's talk-down. I can't hit destination cold. I'd be easy meat for the laser-slayer.

'Massingberd!' I cry again.

'Manchester?' Minnie Mouse asks.

'Huh?' I goggle.

'Are you reading, Manchester?' Minnie's fatuous grin belies the impatient tone.

'Reading,' I say. 'Who the hell . . .?'

'Director Maria Da Souza,' Minnie says, a girl's voice muffled by latex.

'Why the fancy dress, Director?'

'You'll find out when you get here. Frankly, your surprise cannot equal mine. I was expecting a combat squad, at least. We have a maniac rampant up here, and they send me a . . .' she subvocalizes the rest, not for my ears, but I make out what might be, '. . . a witch-doctor.'

I smile. 'What's the score, Minnie?'

'I'll meet you at rim-lock twelve. The killer's somewhere on the far side of the complex. Could be anywhere within an area of twenty square kilometres. My workers are in the central plaza, in the dorms. They fled there when the shooting began.' I have the weird sensation of watching a kids' video crossed with the soundtrack of a cop show. 'They're pinned down and can't get out.'

'Have they tried?'

'You're joking, of course. The fire came from the far rim, and the dorms open on to the central concourse. It'd be an automatic death sentence for the first person who shows their face. You've got to get these people out —'

'My job is to get the killer,' I tell her. 'Then they're safe.'

'In that case I hope you're well armed,' Minnie says condescendingly.

I have the last laugh. 'As a matter of fact I don't believe in the things,' I say.

The Minnie head deprives me the satisfaction of seeing her face drop. She grins idiotically until I cut the link.

The shutt makes one hi-altitude orbit of the satellite and

glides towards the docking rig in the underbelly, blindside of the killer. We contact with the delicacy of balloons kissing.

Seconds later I float out, cycle myself through the airlock and peer cautiously into the long, curving corridor. I scan for the killer's manic brainvibes, but the coast is clear. I move inside.

Minnie stands arms akimbo, awaiting me.

Maria Da Souza is tense and afraid, of course: but beneath this on a deeper level I access her identity. She's an intelligent, lonely kid, and in any other circumstances I'd like to get to know her better.

As it is . . .

'So here you are at last!' She kicks something towards me, a black rubber puddle sprouting ears.

'What the hell?'

'Get into it. Don't argue.' She looks me up and down, appraising. 'You're tall, but you'll fit at a stretch.'

I pick it up. A Mickey suit. I step into the booties and pull up the clinging rubber leggings over those of my onepiece. 'Now, if you don't mind telling me what all this is about?' I could take time off scanning for the killer and read her, but I'm jumpy at the thought of being fried alive.

'This allows us greater freedom,' Da Souza says. 'The killer isn't potting cartoon characters – they're all robots. I was in the storeroom when the killing began. I saw what was going on and dug these out. They're the last we have in stock, from the days before actors were superseded by 'bots.'

I stretch the torso over each shoulder and let go with a snap. Then I pull on the zippered head; my own bulges between the ears like a big egg. Mickey's never been so tall.

'You weren't kidding, were you?'

'Eh?' I'm having difficulty with the zipper.

'You aren't armed.'

'Told you so.'

'Then how the hell do you hope to kill the killer?'

I give her a big smile before fastening the zipper. 'An old African custom,' I say. 'I'll *think* him dead.' Which isn't that far off the mark, minus the ethnic bit.

'Okay, just one more thing,' she says. 'You gotta walk like the real Mickey. Like this.'

I stare at her through the gauze where Mickey's tonsils should be. She's strutting up and down the corridor, waving her arms, twitching her ass. If only Massingberd could see us now.

'Your turn, Manchester.'

So I strut my stuff before her, elbows working invisible bellows. 'Point your boots! Swing your tail! This has to be perfect, Manchester. If this bastard so much as suspects . . .'

She doesn't have to finish that line.

'Fine. You got it. Now where you want to go first?'

The thought of parading myself out there like a sitting duck – or rather mouse – gives me the heebies.

I quit wriggling and squat on my heels. The suit is tight and uncomfortable, squashing me short. 'First, before I start risking my life – 'cos I don't want to be seen dead in this fucking thing – first I want to know more about the killer. Like how he managed to waste an entire security team *and* blow the defence system?'

I keep a probe out for the killer. I have a range of just over a kilometre, though it's getting weak by then. We're quite alone at present.

'The security unit? The killer sprayed them with Procyon animalcules. They reduced the unit to slush one hour before the fireworks began.'

'*Yech*! And the mechanical defences? The 'bots?'

'Deactivated beforehand. That should have set off an alarm in computer control, but that'd been fixed too.'

'Whoever the killer is, he sure knows his stuff. Could it be someone who works here?'

She shrugs. 'Why not? We employ nearly twenty thousand permanent staff.'

'Most of them evacuated with the trippers? So that leaves only the dozen workers holed up in the dorms —'

'Plus the killer.'

I think about it. 'Has there been any shooting since the dozen staff made it to safety?'

'No . . .' Da Souza is getting my drift.

'So perhaps, just *perhaps*, the killer is a worker. He or she hides with the others after the firing's through – providing an alibi.'

'You think that likely?'

'At the moment anything's possible,' I say.

Da Souza pushes herself from the wall with a practised rubber bounce. 'Any more questions?'

'Yeah . . . how come a girl as young as you gets to be the Director of an outfit as big as this?'

That stops her in her tracks.

'How do you know how old I am?'

'I'm well informed,' I tell her. 'Well?'

She shrugs. 'I work hard.'

'You must be very talented.'

She's suddenly uncomfortable, under the Minnie suit. I read that she was a solitary kid, bullied at school, whose only way of showing *them* was to succeed. But there's still something lacking, I read. Success isn't all.

I have the almost irresistible urge to go in there and help her out, ever so gently. But I restrain myself. This is neither the time or the place – and there's work to be done. Besides, I'm getting to the stage where I need *real* love, love that isn't forced.

'Lead the way,' I say.

'Where to?'

'The workers' dorm, or thereabouts. I can do my stuff at long range.'

She regards me. 'Okay. You ready?'

We cake-walk into the open, beneath the arching crystal dome, along with hundreds of other cartoon characters. They're operating with an attention to duty that could be mistaken for macabre celebration of the surrounding carnage.

The fear I feel at our vulnerability is soon replaced by horror. Gobbets of human flesh occupy parks and gardens, tree-lined boulevards and exhibitions and fun-rides. Families lie in messily quartered sections, each chunk still grotesquely parcelled in the appropriate portion of clothing. Lower halves of once human beings sit in the seats of whirlers and spinners, still whirling and spinning in mechanical ignorance of their dead cargo.

And – this somehow makes the slaughter all the more tragic – robotic Mickeys and Minnies, Donalds and Plutos move from body to lasered body, patting dismembered heads, shaking lifeless hands, posing for pictures never to be taken beside the lacerated remains of Junior and Sis . . .

Da Souza continues galumphing along. She's seen it all before. I slow and stare aghast until I hear a 'Psst!' and see a tiny gesture from Minnie up ahead. I quicken up and join her, strutting like a fool.

We leave the boulevard, cross a facsimile Wonderland and come to the croquet lawn. The Queen of Hearts strides around and calls imperiously, 'Off with their heads!' And by some ghastly coincidence the Alice 'bot stands, hands on hips, her head removed by a freak sweep of this killer's laser.

Da Souza ducks behind a hillock and points. 'There,' she says, indicating the entrance of a large rabbit burrow.

I close my eyes and concentrate on the workers' dorm beneath this make-believe world.

'What are you doing?' Da Souza asks in a whisper.

'Just casting dem ol' black spells,' I jape.

I make out eleven minds down there. I go through them one by one, discarding each in turn as innocent. The killer isn't among them, of that I'm sure. All I read is fear and apprehension and, in a couple of cases, even hysteria. I'm looking for the bright brainvibes of a maniac. This bunch is clean.

'You a telepath?' Da Souza asks in a small voice as I open my eyes and clear my head with a shake.

'Something like that,' I tell her. 'I thought you said there were a dozen workers? I scan only eleven.'

'Over there.' She points a white-gloved hand beyond the burrow to a hulking structure moored in a white, simulacrum river, part of another facsimile. I recognize it. The steamboat from Huck Finn. 'He didn't make it to the dorm,' she says.

I concentrate, get nothing. There's a blank where the person should be. The boat's within range, and there's nothing wrong with my ability as I can still sense the eleven down the rabbit hole.

'There's no one there,' I say. 'You sure . . .?'

Then I glimpse movement.

Between balustrades I see a guy sitting on the steps of the upper deck. He's garbed in ancient costume: cloak, frilled shirt, tight breeches and big-buckled shoes. He's there, okay.

Fact remains – I scan nothing.

'I don't get this one bit,' I murmur. 'You see a guy over there? Or am I hallucinating ghosties?'

'Sure. That's him. He's an Andy, an A-grader. He plays the part of Dr Frankenstein in our latest spectacular.'

'Thanks for telling me,' I say. 'You think I can scan cyber-junkboxes just like living minds?'

She gets the message and stays mute.

So our Dr Frankenstein's an Android? A tank-nurtured artificial human, playing the lead in the Gothic classic. I reckon Mary would just love that.

As for me, I'm suspicious. I have this aversion to Andys. Okay, so this guy's a citizen-grade Android from a reputable clinic, a fellow sentient with all the civil rights of you and me. But he still doesn't scan. I can't read Androids.

Prejudice, I know. And me of all people . . .

Nevertheless, I avoid them at parties.

'What do you know about this guy?' I ask. And I read her to ensure she's telling me all she knows.

'Well, he's an exceptionally talented actor. He applied for the role of the Doctor in the Frankenstein show. He auditioned well and got the part.'

'You think he might be the killer?'

'Him?' She's surprised. 'No . . . I don't think so. When we met he seemed very —'

'Okay, okay. I don't want a character reference. They say the Boston Strangler was a charmer.'

'But what makes you think . . .?'

I shrug. 'A hunch, that's all. The eleven workers are clean, and here we have an unscannable Andy.'

'The laser fire did come from the other direction.'

'Has it occurred to you that he might have got where he is now after he quit firing?' I say in a tone that suggests she shut up.

But why would an Andy go berserk like this, I ask myself.

I'm about to suggest we get the hell out in case the Andy is our man, when he sees us. He stands and stares across the river at the two cartoon mice no longer in role.

I take Da Souza by the hand and put the Duchess's cottage between us and the Android. 'The best way to prove your Andy innocent is if I grill him,' I say, pulling off my left glove.

Most Androids are equipped with handsets, and Dr Frankenstein is no exception. His face, heavily made-up with age-lines and dark smudges beneath the eyes to suggest overwork, frowns out at me.

'Worry not, good Doctor. Your circuits have not fused.' I unzip the Mickey head and tip it back. 'Isabella Manchester. Tactical Telescan Unit. I'm here to save you people like a regular superhero.'

The Android inclines his head, not taken with my humour. 'I wondered when help might arrive.' His tone is measured, cultivated. I almost understand why citizen-graders are so sought after at all the big social events.

'A few questions, if you please.'

He inclines his noble head again.

So I ask him where he was when the firing began, what he saw of the slaughter, where does he suspect the killer is now? I try every trick in the book to make him incriminate himself, but he's not that dumb. He answers the questions with a slight Germanic accent, and I get the impression he's mocking me, as if he knows what I'm doing and wants me to know that he knows. He's pointedly civil in his acceptance of suspicion.

I thank him, assure him that I'll get the killer and quick, and cut the link. 'Well?' Da Souza asks.

'What do you expect?' I say, frustrated. 'That he admits he's the bad guy?'

'What did he say?'

'He was rehearsing when the killing began and made it as far as the showboat. He saw nothing of the massacre after that. He kept his tin-pot head down.'

'You still think he did it?'

'I never said I did . . . But anything's possible.'

'And now?' she asks. She's far from impressed by my uncertainty.

'Where did you say the last fire came from? Across the complex? Okay, so I'll make my way around the perimeter until I come within range. If I were you I'd remain here. I don't want your death on my conscience.'

'I feel it my duty to accompany you,' she says.

I nod. 'Very well, then. Okay.' I grab her hand and look for a route out of the Andy's possible line of fire.

She restrains me. 'Remember the walk!'

So we be-bop into the open again, heading towards the multiple amphitheatres that scallop the perimeter of the complex. Our only comfort is the knowledge that we're indistinguishable from hundreds of other strutting cartoon characters.

At least, I *thought* we were.

The killer knows better.

The first bolt amputates Minnie's tail at the rump with a quick hiss and a coil of oily smoke. The second bolt misses

51

me by a whisker and roasts a passing Donald Duck at short order.

Da Souza drags me into the cover of a stage set and we crouch behind a chunk of lichened stone. I trace the bolts back to their source: across the complex beneath the far arch of the dome. I concentrate, but the distance defeats me.

'So the Android *can't* be the killer,' Da Souza claims.

I laugh. 'No? You sure about that? Think again, girl. In our disguises we were safe among all the other characters – then we're seen by the Andy. He's the only person who knows we're in this get-up.'

'But the fire came from the opposite direction,' she complains, reasonably.

'So the Andy has an accomplice, yes?'

That silences her.

Belatedly I realize that we're on the set of Frankenstein. The scientist's lab is caught in flickers of electric blue, revealing eerie contraptions, improbable machines. The monster is on the slab, awaiting reanimation.

'And I don't know why we're wearing these stupid things,' I say, unzipping the head and flinging it back. Out there, the killer is busy frying every Mickey and Minnie in sight.

Da Souza says: 'But why should he want to . . .?'

'Slipped cog?' I suggest facetiously. I kick my suit away and it shivers against the wall like an animated jelly. 'Take yours off,' I tell her. 'You're a marked mouse if you don't ditch that suit.'

I waste no time and get through to Massingberd.

'Is! You okay?'

'I'm fine, Mass. Look, I need some info. You ready?'

I look at Da Souza. She gives me the Andy's tag and classification, and I relay this to Mass with the rider: 'Not that he's filed under that. Check wide. You know where to find me.' I cut the link.

'You not out of that thing yet?' I stare at her. 'Hey, you got something to hide?' Which, considering I have access to her head, is cruel.

I peep over masonry. I can't see the Andy or his boat from here, but his accomplice is still junking robot rodents. Bolts hail continuously from the far side of the complex.

'Come on!' I say.

She's out of the suit and staring defiantly at me.

The right side of her face is disfigured by a long scar more suited to Frankenstein's monster. Even in the flickering light I can see that it was once far worse, before plastic surgery. And it's still ugly. She's a nice kid, too – a small, dark Peruvian with skin like Aztec gold.

The scar's much deeper, of course. The surface damage is superficial; it's the scar inside her head that causes all the pain.

I give her my hand. 'There must be a service hatch somewhere,' I say. 'We can approach the killer from below without being seen.'

She leads me to a concealed swing door and we hit the underside. Less attention has been paid to illumination and glitz down here. Glo-tubes rationed to every ten metres stitch the gloom. The thunder of machinery is deafening. We jog along a vast, curving gallery, mirror image of the corridor top-side where I met Da Souza.

And I'm scanning all the time for the killer.

My hand bleeps and we stop to take the call.

'You're right, Is,' Massingberd raps. 'The droid isn't on our files – under that tag. I came up with a likely candidate, though. A B-grade Andy manufactured in the Carnival clinic twenty-five years ago. It was employed for the first ten years as an extra in kids' films. It applied for up-grading several times but got nowhere. It was transferred to Disneyworld Shanghai, where it worked for another decade. Then – get this, Is – five years ago this droid was reported rogue. It dropped out and disappeared. We have a few reports on file as to its alleged activities during the next five years. Apparently it joined the outlawed Supremacy League, that crackpot band of droids who demand the rule over humanity. It was involved in the bombings of '65, but

53

was never apprehended. We have a number of reports that it underwent a programme of training as a cyber-surgeon so that the League could expand its up-grading of all the droids who joined them. We lost trace of it earlier this year, Is – around the time that your droid joined the Carnival outfit. It's quite feasible that it gave itself new retina-, finger- and voice-prints, doctored certificates and became the actor who played Dr Frankenstein. The droid returned home, Is —'

'To do a little counter publicity for the largest manufacturers of B-grade Androids,' I finish.

'You got it.'

'I'll keep you posted, Mass.'

We set off again.

Da Souza is murmuring to herself. 'And he seemed so genuine at the audition . . .'

I ignore her and concentrate on the sudden flare of sentience that's just appeared a kilometre up-front. I've never before scanned anything like it. As we draw closer I realize that I'm not dealing with a normal human being. The thing up there overwhelms me with fear and pain and regret and guilt.

I go for the killer's identity, but I'm either too far away or the signal is weakening. I get the impression, then, that the killer is losing his strength, dying . . .

We're almost underneath the place where the maniac made his stand. To our right is a viewscreen, showing space and the quiet Earth. On our left we pass a pair of green swing doors, marked with hieroglyphs: the representation of a man and what might be an icicle.

It doesn't hit me for another five paces.

There's something in the head of the killer above us that has no right to be there . . . something that's keeping him alive.

I retrace my steps and regard the swing doors.

'Isabella?' Da Souza says.

'Christ,' I murmur. 'Jesus Christ . . .'

I push through the doors at a run.

54

'Isabella!' Da Souza rushes in after me.

We're in an operating theatre, and the only way it differs from the one in Dr Frankenstein's castle is in the modern fittings; the overhead halogens and the angle-poise operating table. They've both seen the same deed accomplished, one in fiction and one in fact.

I move towards a green, vertical tank as if in a trance.

'Isabella?' Da Souza is staring at me. 'Didn't you know? We brought him up here years ago, equipped this place for when the time is right to bring him back to —'

I open the tank and it's empty.

'Where is he?' she screams at me as I run from the theatre and through the nearest hatch to the upper hemisphere.

I've never really credited Androids with any of the more complex human emotions, like love or hate . . .

Or even irony.

By playing his role of Dr Frankenstein to the full, this Andy has proved me wrong.

Back in the sixties of the last century, the king of the greatest entertainment industry on Earth was corpsicled. Put on ice and stacked away until such time as his cancer could be fixed. And now . . .

Now Walt stands on the balcony of a fairytale castle. Ten metres separate him from where I crouch on the gallery that circles the complex. He rests his weight on a laser-rifle, crutchlike, and sways. His shaven head bulges at the left temple with a dark mass like some morbid extra-cranial tumour: it's a cyber-auxiliary, wired in there by the Android. It's this that is powering him, that motivated him to commit the slaying of the innocents. He's so feeble now, so near death a second time, that it has little control over his body or his mind. For the first time since his resurrection, he is himself.

He sees me and smiles sadly.

His skin, blanched with a hundred years of death, is puckered and loose, maggotlike. He is barely conscious, yet a flicker of tragic awareness moves within him. The chemical that is keeping him alive is almost spent.

'Is this a nightmare?' he asks in a voice so frail it barely reaches me.

'A dream,' I say.

'Where am I?' I read his lips. 'In Hell?'

I almost reply: 'In your Heaven, Walt,' but stop myself.

I follow his gaze to the deck, as he surveys the carnage of his own doing.

'Watch out!' Da Souza appears beside me and drags me to the ground. Walt is making one last feeble attempt to lift and aim the laser; it wavers in our direction. I can read in his eyes that he has no desire to kill us, but the choice is not his. The Frankenstein Android controls the cyber-auxiliary.

I close my eyes.

In the nightmare of Walt's failing brain I open the floodgates of anger. I motivate him into action, give him the will to revenge himself.

And while I'm doing this I realise something. How can I ever again use my ability to induce love after using it to promote so much hate?

Da Souza clutches my arm. 'What —?'

I concentrate. 'Just call it black magic, Maria.' And as I speak, Walt swings his laser-rifle, the desire for revenge overcoming the Android's final command.

He cries out and fires.

The showboat disintegrates in a million shards of synthi-timber, and Dr Frankenstein explodes like a grenade in a brilliant white starburst.

Walt lets the laser fall and slips quietly into his second death, smiling with induced euphoria all the way.

Three hours later and we're surfing down the helix of the gravity-well. Back on the Sat, Walt is being returned to ice, the slaughter mopped up. Maria is taking time off, dirtside.

I break the silence. 'Were you orphaned, Maria?' Gently.

She looks at me, suspicious. 'How do you know?'

I reach out and touch her head. 'Big trouble upstairs,' I say. Then: 'We're very much alike, you and me.'

She gives me the story that I know already, but it helps for her to talk about it. Her mother died when she was ten, and she was taken from her father following the attack that left her scarred. 'And you?' she asks. 'Were you orphaned?'

'Something like that . . .' and stop.

My parents' tribe was hungry and poor. I was their third and youngest daughter, and I checked out psi-positive. A hundred thousand credits bought a lot of cattle, back then.

So the Telescan Unit wasn't exactly slave labour . . .

But try telling that to a lonely nine-year-old.

'Perhaps you'd like to tell me about it?' Maria asks, with affection.

Get that —

Genuine Affection.

I smile. 'I think perhaps I might,' I say.

Star-Crystals and Karmel

I was on Addenbrooke for three months before I met Lorraine Lomax – which, I later learnt, was something of a record. Lomax kept herself to herself, for obvious reasons, and not many of the settlers in Magenta Bay had made her acquaintance.

The meeting – I feel like calling it my audience – came about unexpectedly one warm evening towards the end of Spring. I was savouring an imported whisky on the verandah and watching Torr and Shama walking hand in hand along the beach, for all the world like human lovers. My reverie was interrupted when a ground effect vehicle pulled up beside the A-frame. I tried to decide if I felt bitter that my privacy was about to be invaded, or glad of the company. I think I secretly welcomed the opportunity to talk to someone other than myself – then the wing-hatch of the vehicle hinged up and the invalid carriage glided out.

I'd heard a lot about Lorraine Lomax. She was the talk of the township, which was to be expected as the only other topics of interest were the tourist trade and the weather. The regulars down at the Magenta Bay Club were lucky to have such a focus of interest in the vicinity; and fortunate also in that Lomax's arrival on the colony planet pre-dated their own, so that there was no way their gossip might be verified, or dismissed.

Lomax was the first settler on this northerly continent, ten years ago, and the events surrounding her injuries had never been disclosed. Rumour had it that they were the result of a mechanical accident; another that she had fallen prey to a jungle predator. Her determination to continue running the plantation and her reclusive existence in the mansion over at Barnett's Landfall served only to add to the mystery.

As I watched the carriage hover from the vehicle, my apprehension had nothing to do with the fact that her visit would soon be common knowledge. I could put up with any amount of gossip, and had done so since the day of my arrival. The reason for my unease was that I felt uncomfortable in the presence of beautiful women and those physically less fortunate than myself – and Lomax just happened to be both.

She settled her carriage beside me with a barely perceptible whirr of a-grav turbos, smiled and held out a hand in such a way as to leave me in doubt whether she wanted it kissed or shaken. 'Henderson – *so* pleased to meet you at last. I've heard a lot about you.'

I murmured that this was surely an exaggeration and took her hand in a loose shake. I busied myself fixing her a drink and stole glances while she sighed and smiled at the view of the bay.

Just as the beauty of the *Venus de Milo* is emphasized by the absence of arms, so Lorraine Lomax's poised elegance seemed to be accentuated by the fact that her torso terminated abruptly just below the ribcage. Her carriage was bulky and ugly, but she had managed to transform the life-support mechanism into a throne; there was something almost regal in her demeanour.

We drank and exchanged idle chatter. I found myself talking about my past and the reason I came to Addenbrooke, something which I usually keep to myself. A couple of whiskies later I was aware that I'd run off at the mouth like a damned fool, and also that I knew next to nothing about Lorraine Lomax.

She was staring at the Ring of Tharssos, the arc of silver moonlets that embraced the hemisphere from horizon to horizon. I took this opportunity to mention the alien festivities due to take place in less than a week. Lomax made some off-hand comment about the '*natives*', pronouncing the word with a certain venom I was to notice later in her dealings with all things alien.

She changed the subject. 'You're probably wondering why I called on you?'

I shrugged. 'A social visit?' My humour was lost on her.

'I've seen some of your stones, Henderson – those *star-crystals*, I think you call them. I'm quite impressed. And my daughter likes them, too —'

'Your daughter?' I must have sounded surprised – certainly I could never recall hearing that Lorraine Lomax had a daughter.

'Karmel is at that difficult age when children are satisfied with nothing. I need something to keep her out of my way while I work.'

I felt a sudden resentment of Lomax, then; it often comes over me when I encounter parents who do not fully appreciate how fortunate they are to have children.

'Do you think you might run over with a consignment of star-crystals tomorrow? Payment on delivery?'

I wanted to ask her why she could not take a 'consignment' back with her this evening, but her manner intimidated. She was obviously accustomed to having her every word obeyed, her purchases hand-delivered, and would brook no dissent.

I began to pity poor Karmel.

She finished her drink and thanked me for a pleasant evening. I watched the carriage glide from the verandah and slot itself into the ground effect vehicle. 'Are you sure you're okay in that thing?' I called from the top of the steps. 'You've had a bit to drink.'

She smiled up at me. 'That's quite all right, Henderson. Alcohol has no effect on me. I have an artificial liver implant that purifies all harmful fluids . . .'

I watched her reverse down the drive and accelerate along the coast road, resentment burning in my chest. I did not like

Lorraine Lomax – and it had nothing to do with the fact that she had consumed my whisky without due appreciation. I disliked her attitude, her assumed superiority. At the same time I could not deny that I was strangely attracted to her physical aspect, the little of it that had survived the accident unscathed.

I finished the bottle, by which stage I hated myself thoroughly, staggered into the lounge and fell asleep on the chesterfield while the vidscreen repeated an old romantic movie from Earth.

The following evening I shut the showroom and drove along the coast road for a kilometre, then turned inland through the rain-forest. I passed files of small, semi-naked Ashentay walking along the roadside; these were tribes from outlying areas, making their way to the local clan dwelling-places around the bay. When human colonists first settled in Magenta, many Ashentay moved out rather than have their way of life changed by what they saw as human materialism; a few remained and worked in the shops and boatyards around the settlement. In general, the aliens and humans kept themselves to themselves, though I'd heard that in the capital, a thousand miles down the coast, and in some of the larger cities of the south, alien-human relations were such that inter-marriage was not uncommon. In some areas, a first generation of Ashentay-humans were growing up.

Now the *emigrés* were returning for the festivities, the *Say-nath'an-dar*. I had to admit that I knew very little about the aliens, even though I'd been on the planet almost three months. I'd heard talk of the *Say-nath'an-dar* down at the club, but all I could recall was that there was a special, or privileged, clan of nomadic Ashentay who spent their lives following the Ring of Tharssos around the planet, and that the ceremonies would begin with their arrival in Magenta Bay.

The Lomax plantation was a small concern, just ten square kilometres of lush interior land. The base of the operations, an old-style colonial mansion, was situated a kilometre beyond the perimeter fence, along a straight track hemmed in by files of alien fruit trees.

I drew up before the steps of the mansion and climbed out, case in hand. The house was old, certainly pre-dating the time when the planet was settled. I guessed that the building, foursquare and brooding in the twilight, had been telemassed directly to Addenbrooke from the continent of Africa, Earth.

'Henderson!'

I turned. Lorraine Lomax was approaching the house in her carriage, gliding along at a height of one metre. From a distance, the contraption reminded me of nothing so much as an old boot. Coupled to its heel was a long train of wheeled containers, brimful with shiny purple fruit the size of melons. A tall, six-legged spider-bot clanked alongside. As they approached, the robot uncoupled the containers and continued with them around the house.

Lomax gestured. 'Henderson, you must forgive me. I've been working since six this morning, and as you can see . . .'

She indicated her face, masked with perspiration and greasy fingermarks. She wore a loose khaki shirt, and the last stud was unfastened so that I could see where the tanned skin of her slim stomach fitted into the collar of her life-support system.

She escorted me through the mansion to a long verandah overlooking a valley patterned with rows of fruit trees. She indicated a small table laden with a variety of bottles. 'Please make yourself at home. Excuse me while I change and find Karmel.' She smiled, turned and hovered back into the house.

I poured myself a Scotch and stared into the valley. Whereas yesterday Lorraine Lomax had seemed distant, even cold, this evening she was just the opposite. I wondered if she was one of those nervous people who are never very good at initial encounters, but who take only one meeting to form an opinion of one's character.

I operate quite differently. In my line of work it helps if I get along with everyone I meet; but I take a long time before I can say whether or not I like someone. I was still very unsure about Lorraine Lomax.

I was on my second drink when she returned.

She pushed through the French windows with the toe of her carriage. 'Henderson, meet my daughter, Karmel. Karmel, this is Mr Henderson. He's brought you something.'

Karmel was perhaps ten years old; she was tall and sun-browned – a big girl for her age. Her face was triangular, disconcertingly equilateral, and her eyes were large and green.

She beamed at me. 'You've brought the crystals?'

She sat cross-legged on the floor while I lay the carricase before her and opened the lid. The dozen gems scintillated against the black velvet. The girl stared at them with the eyes of a cat suddenly transfixed. 'May I?'

'Go ahead.' I smiled up at Lomax.

Her expression was aloof; she was watching her daughter with barely concealed impatience. I remembered her attitude towards Karmel last night, and that she regarded her as a minor nuisance who could be kept quiet with gifts.

Karmel reached into the case and pulled out a star-crystal. She held it tightly in her fist, then pressed it against her cheek.

She dropped the crystal, a slight frown marring her features, and picked up another. She went through the same performance with this one, and again discarded it. Then another, and another. Soon the case was empty and the discard pile was a small mountain, winking rainbow colours. Karmel looked up at me with tears in her lustrous eyes.

'But they aren't *right*,' she cried in a piping voice. 'They're . . . *spoiled*!' She looked up at her mother and brought her hands down on her knees in a frustrated palms-up gesture. Then she switched her exasperated attention to me. 'I'm sorry, Mr Henderson. But don't you see? They're too full of *you*!'

I laughed. 'Full of me?'

'I thought you were bringing crystals like the other one, only . . . *warmer*.'

'Do you still have that crystal?' I asked.

'I'll go and find it,' Lomax said.

While her mother moved back into the house, Karmel poked a finger into the pile of star-crystals and stirred.

'What do you mean, Karmel – they're too full of me?'

She shrugged. 'I don't know. They're . . . You cut them, didn't you? You put yourself into them.' She gestured again, frustrated at the hopelessness of trying to explain to an adult what was obvious.

Lomax returned with the crystal and passed it to me.

It was one of my earliest efforts, crude and amateurish. I'd cut and polished to the best of my ability, but I'd been unable to unlock the promise of the star-crystal burning beneath the surface.

'This isn't half so pretty as those,' I pointed out.

Karmel took it from my hand and smiled. 'But it feels so much better!' she cried.

I looked at Lomax. 'It's strange, but have you noticed that the Ashentay often carry them around? They finger them like worry beads . . . If you like,' I said to Karmel, 'you can pop round to my showroom after school sometime. I'll show you some that I haven't got round to cutting yet. You might like those.'

She was staring into the original crystal. 'I don't go to school, Mr Henderson.'

Her mother explained: 'We have a terminal in the study. She has all the latest lessons telemassed from Earth.'

'In that case why not bring her over tomorrow?' I think I said this because I felt sorry for the girl, imprisoned in the mansion with a mother whose idea of affection was an expensive present.

Karmel looked from me to her mother. 'Will you?'

Lomax sighed. 'You can go, but one of the automatons will have to drive you. I'm much too busy with the harvest.'

Karmel smiled at me and went running off into the house, tossing the gem into the air and catching it like a ball.

I packed away the star-crystals.

Later we sat on the verandah, sipping mint tea from china cups and admiring the sunset. Down in the valley, mechanical harvesters moved along the rows of fruit trees. The green plantation was networked with a silver web of tracks; spider-bots supervised the picking and drove container trains to packing stations.

I mentioned something that I had noticed earlier. 'Don't you employ Ashentay?' I asked.

I'd heard a rumour that, ten years ago, Lorraine Lomax had been in dispute with a group of native workers, and the upshot was that she had fired them on the spot and vowed never to employ them again.

She sipped her tea, considering my question. 'The Ashentay are poor workers, Henderson. They're hunter-gatherers in their natural environment, and they don't adapt well to farm work. Automation is much more cost-effective.'

A little later it occurred to me that the plantation must hold bad memories for her, and I wondered why she stayed on. 'Haven't you ever thought of selling up and leaving Addenbrooke?' I asked her.

She hesitated, then said, 'With a little luck I'll be leaving quite soon, Henderson.' She gazed out over her plantation. 'Did you know that the latest resurrection techniques can equip me with an extended spine, a new pelvis, hips and legs? They have clinics on Earth that clone the requisite parts.'

I whistled. 'That must be expensive.'

She looked at me. 'Why do you think I've remained here for so long, Henderson?'

We finished our tea. Lomax excused herself and I drove back to Magenta Bay.

In the morning I set off along the beach in search of 'unspoilt' crystals for Karmel. In their natural state, the stones were unspectacular, even ugly; they could be found only in coastal areas, lying where the Ashentay had picked them up, caressed them and put them back down again. Only my training as a geologist had drawn my attention to them three months ago – I had known that within the unsightly, calcined gobbets there were things of lapidary beauty.

As I walked, I kept a look out for a certain type of crystal that I had only ever seen once before; these were twice the size of the regular crystals, and dull, but with a stone inside that would make the *Koh-i-noor* look like a pebble. Soon after my arrival on Addenbrooke I had come across an old Ashentay sitting on a rock on the headland, gazing out to sea and turning just such a stone in his fingers. I had made him an offer for it, but in his halting English he conveyed that no amount of my money could pay for the *thole*, as he called it. He was right, of course, for the crystal was priceless – though I rather think that it was worth more to the old alien than it would be to any human being. Now, I selected the largest crystals I could find and made my way back home.

I was in the workshop an hour later when the Lomax ground effect vehicle pulled up. I stepped outside just as Karmel jumped down from the passenger seat. She was wearing an old pair of dungarees, with the legs rolled up to just below the knees, and a frilly white blouse.

'Hi, Mr Henderson. I'm here.' In the vehicle, a gleaming silver spider-bot sat in the driver's seat, jacked into the steering column.

'Have you got the good crystals, Mr Henderson?'

'Let's go and have a look, shall we?'

As we walked to the house, Karmel slipped her hand into mine and jumped up the steps one by one. It came to me suddenly that no daughter should be without a father, and I remembered the rumours that Lorraine Lomax's husband had moved to Earth soon after her accident.

I fixed Karmel a tumbler of orange juice, and when I came in from the kitchen I saw that she was tapping the holo-cube that stood on top of the vid-set. The figure of the young girl, locked inside the plastic, began smiling and talking.

Karmel gulped down the juice. 'Who's that?' she asked.

I began to tell her, and then she saw the carricase on the chesterfield. 'The crystals!' she cried.

I opened the case on the floor and she fell to her knees and stared with wide eyes at the treasure. She reached out; hesitantly, it seemed, as if she did not want to be disappointed for a second time. When her fingers came into contact with the first stone she shrieked as if electrocuted.

She scooped up the stones and pressed them against her cheek as if they were baby chicks. She giggled with delight and seemed totally oblivious of my presence. For the next twenty minutes I watched her inspect each stone in turn, talking to herself in an excited whisper. I asked if I could hold one, but when I failed to feel anything she shook her head in exasperation, before losing herself again in rapturous communion with the crystals.

It occurred to me that perhaps the mystery was not in the crystals themselves, but in the mind of the recipient, and maybe human adults had outgrown that vital spark of imagination needed to believe . . . Watching Karmel as she played among the stones, I saw that as a cold and cynical rationalization. We try to explain away what we don't understand, and I certainly didn't understand how something as inorganic and stable as the crystals could be *warm*.

'Can I have one?' she asked at last. 'Can I take one home with me?'

'You can have them all,' I said.

I packed the uncut crystals into the carricase, except one which Karmel carried back to the ground effect vehicle. As she was about to climb inside, Shama and Torr appeared in the driveway. Karmel stopped and stared at them, her eyes widening. I realised that, due to her isolation up at the plantation, this was perhaps one of the few times Karmel had actually seen an alien at close quarters. They returned her stare, just as curious. As the vehicle reversed down the drive, all I could see of Karmel was the top of her head as she peered timorously out at the Ashentay.

I waved down at Shama and Torr. 'I'm about to eat,' I called. 'You're welcome to join me.'

They came to tend the grounds of my A-frame every week, and I always invited them in for lunch. They never accepted, however, often saying that they had eaten already, or were fasting.

I was therefore surprised when Torr said, 'Thank you, Ben. We will.'

They entered the lounge, and while Torr assisted his pregnant wife to the floor – she was hugely swollen and ungainly – I fetched food from the kitchen and joined them.

We ate in silence. I wanted to ask what had brought them here today – it was obvious that they needed to see me about something, I reasoned, or they would have refused my offer of food. But questions were unknown in Ashentay conversation, and in consequence there were no such things as answers. A dialogue with the aliens proceeded in a series of personal statements, to which an individual might append a subjective observation if sufficiently interested.

This peculiar form of stilted dialogue was one of the reasons why the human settlers on Addenbrooke looked upon the Ashentay as alien and therefore 'unknowable'. To a straight question, an alien would merely blink at the effrontery. There was little else dividing the two races, other than the difference of life-styles. The Ashentay were a small, slight people – I often thought of them as Nordic Japanese; individually, they would not be out of place in a crowd of *Homo sapiens*. They could even speak English in a quiet, whispery fashion.

As we finished the meal of bread, cheese and a local sap-derived beverage, I opened the exchange. I wanted to know what importance the aliens attached to the crystals – if they too found them warm.

'I am ignorant of the crystals that your people use,' I said.

They exchanged a glance, remained silent.

'Karmel tells me that they are *warm*.'

I waited. Often, if they did not wish to speak of a certain subject, they remained obdurately silent until I happened upon a topic of mutual interest.

Torr spoke at last. 'We are not empowered to speak about the *kantha-dan* – the crystals,' he said.

I nodded. The silence stretched. My guests showed no inclination to break the ice and tell me why they were here. At last I said. 'I am surprised to find you here today . . .' In other words, what the hell do you want to see me about?

Shama sat with her distended belly resting in the bowl of her crossed-legs. She regarded her folded hands with downcast eyes and said quietly, 'I learnt one week ago that I am with *Say-na* – and therefore privileged.'

My immediate impulse was to ask what was *Say-na*? I remembered myself and said, 'I am ignorant of the phrase *Say-na*.'

Torr said, on behalf of his partner, 'It means, translated literally, "chosen one or wanderer".'

Shama, regarding her jutting pregnancy, flushed with pride.

'I'm pleased for you both,' I said, somewhat puzzled.

'Therefore,' Torr continued, 'Shama can no longer work for you, and I soon must migrate to the western coast, as is our custom.'

I nodded gravely. 'I'll miss you both.'

Shama said in a whisper, 'We must prepare ourselves for the approaching *Say-nath'an-dar*.'

'I have heard little about this . . . *Say-nath'an-dar*.' I looked expectantly from Shama to Torr.

He smiled. 'It is the time of the *Say-naths*' arrival – they are the clan of travelling . . . you would call them "wise-folk". They follow the Ring of Tharssos and it takes them across every continent on Ashent. In each village or settlement they halt, rest a while, and settle major disputes. Their word is law – dissent means banishment. When their word has been carried through, they move on, continually following Tharssos.' He made an open-handed gesture indicating simplicity. 'In ten years they circumnavigate the planet.'

Shama still had not lifted her face from contemplation of her belly. 'But of course,' I said. 'Your child is destined to join the travelling council . . .'

Torr beamed. 'We are proud to give our first born to the *Say-nath*,' he said. 'Tharssos willing, the child will be born shortly after their arrival – any later, and we will have to wait until the next visitation.'

'Your child is due in eight days,' I stated.

'And the *Say-nath* are due in seven days. Sometimes they stay for as long as two or three days, depending on how many sittings they are called upon to attend. Often their work is over in one day, in which case . . .'

He glanced at Shama, took her hand and squeezed.

In the familiar environment of the lounge, chatting amicably to Torr and Shama, I had almost ceased to notice their alienness – even though we were discussing concepts strange to me. Only when I tried to understand their apprehension at the possibility that their child might miss the arrival of the *Say-nath*, did the fact of their profound psychological dissimilarity to human beings strike me. To human parents, the thought of having their child taken from them at birth would be anathema. Torr and Shama, on the other hand, were dreading the thought that they might be left with the child for the first ten years of its life.

During the week that followed I saw nothing more of Lorraine Lomax or her daughter. Word got round that Lomax had paid me a visit, and on the only occasion I went down to the club I was the centre of attention. Strangely enough, I felt no desire to divulge the little I had learnt about the beautiful invalid; it was as if to talk behind her back would be to invalidate the trust that Lomax had shown in me by seeking my company and telling me, albeit guardedly, about herself. As a consequence of my reticence, the inevitable rumour spread that I was having an affair with the woman, which bothered me less than I thought it might. My work was keeping me fully occupied and I had no time to worry about idle gossip.

Quite by chance, the height of the tourist season coincided with the *Say-nath'an-dar*. It was not that the visitors from Earth came to Magenta Bay to witness the alien ceremonies. *Say-nath'an-dar* was held *in camera*, a strictly aliens only affair. Although the tourists were intrigued by the events – it gave their stay on Addenbrooke that *frisson* of otherness they could talk about when they got back home – the main attraction of the area was the temperate climate and the spectacular coastal views.

At noon on the first day of the festivities I shut up shop and made my way, with hundreds of other curious humans, around the bay. We lined the coast road in anticipation, a gala-day atmosphere in the air.

That morning, the Ashentay population of Magenta Bay had quietly left the settlement to keep their rendezvous with the *Say-nath* at a port town along the coast. Now they marched back into Magenta in a spectacular torch-light procession, the wise-council leading the way. Clad only in loin-cloths, they were impressive figures, sun-browned and muscular from their arduous, never-ending trek across the face of the planet. They were of greater stature than the average Ashentay, and they seemed to emanate a certain calm assurance, an authority that even I, as a human, could not fail to notice. There were perhaps two dozen of them in total, ranging from sprightly oldsters to children of no more than four or five – and even the youngsters were possessed of a quiet dignity that had nothing in common with bravado.

When the procession reached the quayside, the *Say-nath* disappeared into the rain forest, and the remaining Ashentay produced stringed instruments and proceeded to entertain both their own people and the humans. I stayed and listened to the melodic ballads and epic poems for a while, then returned home for a drink.

The real ceremony, the *Say-nath'an-dar*, would take place the following day, when the wise-council convened to pass judgement on the major issues of the day.

I woke late, grabbed a carton of juice from the cooler and staggered out onto the verandah, hoping that the combination of a cold drink and the fresh sea breeze might do something to revive me. I was messily drinking orange juice, and naked but for a pair of shorts, when I saw the slight figure of Torr approaching along the coast road. Six Ashentay followed him, but only when they turned into the drive and paused at the foot of the steps did I recognise the tall, muscular aliens as members of the *Say-nath*.

Something in my stomach turned like a live eel.

Torr looked up at me. 'Ben Henderson, you will be present at a sitting of the *Say-nath* . . .'

I recalled what Torr had told me yesterday: that the *Say-nath* were brought in to adjudicate on major issues only.

'What's the problem, Torr?' I asked nervously.

It was a question. Torr frowned. 'The sitting will proceed forthwith. I will act as translator. The *Say-nath* have no use for the human tongue.'

Torr turned and spoke to the six, then ushered them up the steps. I stood back and watched as they took the verandah like a stage and spaced themselves in a semi-circle, sitting cross-legged and regarding me impassively. An old man and an old woman occupied the apex of the crescent, with a younger man and woman on either side, and a boy at one end and a girl at the other. The weight of unspoken accusation hung in the air. I wanted to grab Torr and shake him until he told me what the hell was going on.

Torr touched my arm. I sensed his compassion for me, which he was unable to communicate in his official position as translator to the *Say-nath*. He indicated that I should be seated before the six, and then sat down beside me.

The old man uttered a halting approximation of my name, then held out his arm, his hand palm-upwards. The five other *Say-nath* then did the same, so that their long, slim arms formed the spoke of a wheel, their piled palms the hub. Torr gestured for me to place my hand on theirs, and he completed the ritual by placing his hand on mine. The old man chanted what I took to be an oath, and the swearing-in ceremony was over.

Then he took a pouch from his loin-cloth, opened the drawstring and poured on to the floor before him a glittering pile of star-crystals. Among the gems that I had cut were several crystals in their original state. And also – I noticed with disbelief – two large uncut stones the like of which I had seen only once before, three months ago, when I had happened upon the alien with the crystal he had called a *thole*.

The six *Say-nath* regarded me unblinkingly.

The old man leaned forward and chopped a hand down into the pile of stones, deftly dividing the uncut crystals and the *tholes* from those I had worked. He drew to him the uncut crystals and the priceless gems, and pushed to me the stones I sold in my showroom.

He picked up one of the former, held it in his palm, then placed it at his forehead like a third eye. He distributed the rest of the crystals to his fellow *Say-nath*; they went through the same ritual, the same act of appreciation.

Then the old man, looking into my eyes, spoke in the quick, high tongue of his people. I could understand nothing of what he said, but the note of censure in his voice was unmistakable.

He came to the end of his speech and gestured for Torr to translate. In his soft, whispery English, Torr said, 'The *kantha-dan* crystals contain the *Shira*, the very essence or selfness, of our ancestors. Each *kantha-dan* contains a story, a life-story, that can be experienced only through *kantha-dan-akra*, deep communion. The *kantha-dan* belong to each and every Ashentay – they are as free as the essence of the ancestors they contain, and therefore are never collected as you humans might collect and hoard such treasure, but are left where everyone might happen upon them and gain from the experience of deep-communion. They were safe until you came and began to shape the stones, cut them, remove from their hearts the very essence of our ancestors and replace them with your own self. Of course, we realize that you were not to know of the sacrilege you were committing; you were acting in innocence, yet with motives of gain that seem to drive your race. Because you are human, Ben Henderson, and because you were unaware of your error, the *Say-nath* cannot see their way to punishing you.'

He paused there and spoke to the six.

The cynical, hard-bitten side of myself, which I tried to project to the community of Magenta Bay, almost laughed at such superstitious hokum; it was as if the rationalist in me, forced into a corner and resenting the *Say-nath's* accusations, wanted to kick out and deny culpability. I thought of what this would do for trade, if I advertised the star-crystals as containing the *Shira* of the Ashentay . . .

Then I recalled what little Karmel Lomax had said after holding one of the crystals I had cut. 'They're too full of you!' They were too full of my anger – and how better she thought the original, uncut crystals had felt.

I gestured. 'I see no reason why you should capture your selves, your *memories*, in this way.' It was as if I was disputing their claim so as to be free of the charge of desecration.

Torr made a gesture that eloquently illustrated his incomprehension. 'We do it because . . . because we have always done so. Through the crystals, our ancestors speak to us, teach us, guide us.'

'And does every one of you make a *kantha-dan*?'

He smiled at my question. 'Not everyone. A chosen few, those judged to have knowledge and wisdom.'

I wanted then to ask him *how*, how these simple people imbued inorganic crystals with their *Shira*, but before I could even begin to phrase my question Torr continued.

'If you refuse to stop desecrating our stones, Ben Henderson, then the *Say-nath* would have no option but to take the matter to your Planetary Governor.'

The star-crystals accounted for less than twenty per cent of my turnover. I would still be able to make a decent living without them, if I cut down on luxuries like imported whisky. I wondered how I might have responded had my livelihood depended on them; I like to think I would have agreed to their request.

'Tell the *Say-nath* that I'll stop cutting the crystals,' I said, 'and I'll withdraw from sale those I've already cut.'

He gripped my arm in gratitude and repeated my words to the council. Their expressions softened; they smiled with their eyes.

The old man spoke.

'He thanks you, on behalf of the Ashentay,' Torr said.

In a mood of considerable levity now, the arm-spoke, hand-hub oath was repeated, and the *Say-nath*, after inclining their heads to me, gathered their crystals and moved down the steps.

Torr paused at the top, then turned. I saw with surprise that tears filled his eyes, so that they resembled emeralds awash with ocean. 'I must thank you, Ben,' he began.

'I did only what was right,' I said.

'Even so, you are human. Your ways are often strange to us, but on some things we see alike.'

He took my hand in a human shake, seemed to hesitate, then said, 'Shama will birth our child at midnight, according to the *naal*. There will be celebrations at our clan dwelling-place, for the *Say-nath* do not move on until tomorrow, and so will take our child. I . . . I would be honoured, and Shama too, if you would attend the birth. You will be the first human accorded the privilege of witnessing the arrival of a *Say-na*, and the handing over of the *thole*.'

'The *thole*,' I echoed. 'The large stones I saw just now
. . .'

'They are the special *kantha-dan* of the *Say-nath*. Following the birth of a *Say-na*, they are bequeathed a *thole*
into which they will in time transfer their essence, their
selfness. These *tholes* are valued above any other *kantha-dan*,
and remain with the *Say-na* until such time as he or she
chooses an individual worthy of the honour of becoming a
thole-guardian.'

'On Earth, these stones would be priceless.'

'So too on Ashent,' Torr smiled.

He turned and hurried after the departing *Say-nath*.

I spent the rest of the day taking down advertisements
and clearing the stock of star-crystals from the showroom.
I was in the workshop that evening, stacking away the
last case of crystals, when a familiar vehicle rolled up the
drive.

I strolled out, wiping my hands on a rag. 'Lorraine – this is
unexpected.' I indicated the steps. 'I was just about to have a
drink. Why not join me —?'

She smiled. 'That's very kind of you, Henderson. I think
I will.'

Perhaps it was because I had not seen her for more than a
week, but Lorraine Lomax looked more beautiful than ever
tonight. She wore a black velvet evening dress, or rather
the bodice of one, and her dark hair was loose about her
shoulders.

She held the whisky tumbler in both hands and stared
up at the Ring of Tharssos, like a High Priestess with an
offering.

'I've heard that you've been invited to the birth of a *Say-
na*,' she said.

'Word certainly gets around.'

'Magenta is abuzz,' she smiled. 'Apparently, an Ashentay
worker down at the marina told a human, and it spread from
there. You're certainly privileged, Henderson.'

I shrugged. 'To tell the truth, I'm not looking forward to it that much.'

She seemed about to say something, then hesitated.

'Ben . . .' she said at last, and the blatant use of my first name took me aback. 'The reason I came down here tonight was to invite you back to the mansion. I'd prepared a meal before I found out about your prior engagement. Of course,' she said, 'if you'd rather join your *alien* friends . . .'

She obviously expected me to forget the birth of the *Sayna* and return with her to the mansion.

'I did promise Torr,' I said.

She shrugged. 'Very well, Henderson. I only asked.'

'Just what have you got against the Ashentay, anyway?' I said, provoked by something in her tone.

'Ben, please . . .' she began.

'Was a native responsible—?' I managed to stop myself, but too late.

She found my gaze and stared at me with stricken eyes, and I suddenly regretted my question. She nodded. 'Yes – yes, I suppose you could put it like that.' She said it in a small voice and looked away.

Which, of course, explained a hell of a lot.

I imagined a lethal implement of farm machinery in the hands of a native ill-equipped to use such things, a fatal slip, a tragedy that blighted her life and soured her view of an entire race . . .

'I suppose I was fortunate,' she went on in barely a whisper. 'There was a doctor staying at the mansion when the accident happened. He did what he could for me and rushed me to the hospital in Moresby, or as much of me as he could get there. I was clinically dead when I arrived, of course, but even then they had the resources to bring me back to life – if not to make me whole again.'

'I'm sorry,' I said. 'I didn't mean to . . .'

She shook her head. 'I haven't mentioned it to anyone in a long, long time.' She finished her drink. There were tears in her eyes. 'I really must be going. It's getting late —'

She returned to the ground effect vehicle and reversed down the drive without once looking up, and I cursed myself for so insensitively seeking confirmation of that which I already suspected.

For the rest of the evening, until just before midnight, I finished off my very last bottle of imported Scotch. I told myself that it was in premature celebration of the birth of Torr and Shama's child – but the real reason was so that I would be well anaesthetised when the time came to witness the entry into the world of the *Say-na*. I had only ever attended one other birth in my life, and on that occasion I had passed out like many a father before me.

It was eleven-thirty by the time I carefully negotiated the steps from the verandah and set off along the road from Magenta Bay. When I came to a narrow track, I left the road and stumbled into the rain-forest. The enclosing trees shut out the light of the Ring; this was the first time I had ever ventured into the forest alone on foot, and despite my drunkenness – or perhaps because of it – I was suddenly aware of the *alienness* of the place. Five minutes later I was staggering through the undergrowth, hopelessly lost, when the small figure of a young Ashentay appeared from behind a tree.

'Ben Henderson. Follow, please.'

I slurred my profound gratitude and followed him through the forest. My fear, before the boy found me, was not so much that I would become lost but that I would miss the *Say-na* ceremony and thus disappoint Torr and Shama. I experienced a surge of relief that seemed to sober me.

At last we came to a clearing occupied by a dozen low, circular tents. A corresponding clearing in the tree-tops gave a view of the Ring of Tharssos, a bright parabola in the night sky.

The boy led me through a crowd of Ashentay to a large tent, drew aside an animal-skin flap and gestured for me to enter. I ducked inside; a dozen Ashentay sat cross-legged on the ground, bathed in the roseate illumination of a hundred dancing candle-flames. Torr greeted me quietly and pulled me down beside him. Behind me, a drum beat a monotonous rhythm; someone intoned what to my ears sounded like a dirge.

'The *Say-na* is due soon,' Torr whispered. 'The *Say-nath* leave within one hour.'

Shama lay on a pile of skins before the invited audience. The brown-skinned dome of her pregnancy swelled hugely above her parted legs, bent at the knee to ease the load. She was saturated in sweat, her head turning from side to side in pain. From time to time an old woman, the *naal*, forced liquid into her mouth from a gourd.

The atmosphere in the tent was heavy with heat and sweat. I felt sick at the very sight of the pregnant girl, at the thought of the pain she must endure to void what I was sure must be twins.

Shama cried out. The old woman gestured to Torr, who rushed forward and knelt beside his wife. The tempo of the drumbeat increased. The *naal* cradled Shama's head on her lap, and Shama moaned again.

I was taken by the ridiculous urge to shout, 'Not like that!' even to rush forward and assist the delivery. They seemed to be doing nothing to ease the passage of the child. Shama screamed, a long, animal howl of pain, and thrashed about in agony.

I took what happened next to be some temporary visual aberration on my part, the result of the whisky and the stifling heat in the tent. Surely, legs could not part quite like that, or a belly split with such a rending, tearing sound of flesh and muscle and finally placenta. I gagged and closed my eyes, expecting, when I opened them again, to behold a normal birth.

A sigh of satisfaction passed through the gathered Ashentay.

The *Say-na*, the *infant*, knelt amid the remains of its mother's shattered body. As I watched, incredulous, it gained its feet with the trembling insecurity of a yearling, slipping often in the wash of spilled intestines.

Torr reached forward, sliced the umbilical cord and wrapped the mewling, upright child in furs. Then he lifted his son from the mess and carried him through the press of eager onlookers.

I leapt up and caught him by the shoulders. 'Torr! You can't leave her – if we can get her to the clinic in Moresby —'

'Shama has joined the legion of Tharssos, Ben, who watch over us —'

'This is insane!'

'You cannot hold yourself responsible for the delay until the *Say-nath* come again.'

I felt sick and dizzy from the stench of blood and faeces and the semi-digested contents of the woman's lacerated stomach.

'Let me through, Ben. My son must join the *Say-nath*!' He pushed past me and hurried from the tent, followed by his fellow Ashentay.

I turned back and started into the tent. Shama was dead, her pelvis crushed like an egg-shell and her spine truncated in the frantic struggle of the *Say-na* to gain its freedom. In the glow of candle-light, I could see that only the upper half of her body remained intact . . .

I retched.

I reached out for support as my vision misted and I found the frame of the entrance. The heat and the stink, but above all the *knowledge*, was suddenly unbearable. I flailed aside the flap of animal skin and stumbled gratefully outside.

The *Say-nath* had arrived in time to collect Torr's child. They stood in the clearing with their staffs and small bundles of possessions. Torr led his son to the old man who yesterday had adjudicated at my hearing.

All that remained, I knew, was for the final rite of *Say-nath'an-dar*. As the Ashentay watched in silence, the old man took a large stone from his pouch and passed it to the boy –

and I recognised the stone as a *thole*. The old man spoke and the crowd began a stirring chant.

Then the *Say-nath* prepare to leave, and as they said their farewells I caught sight of a small figure in their midst. She had exchanged her dungarees for a loin-cloth, and it seemed that the simple change was all it took to establish her without ambiguity as an Ashentay.

As the *Say-nath* slipped quickly into the forest, Karmel saw me, raised a hand and smiled before rejoining her people and following the Ring of Tharssos across the face of Addenbrooke.

The following evening Lorraine Lomax drove down from Barnett's Landfall and joined me for a nightcap. We drank beer and watched the sunset. Lomax's invalid carriage whirred gently beside me, maintaining her at an altitude conducive to conversation.

'Of course,' she said, 'the Ashentay are mistaken. Like all primitive peoples, they ascribe pagan superstition to scientifically explicable phenomena. The *Say-na* children are not the chosen ones of Tharssos, destined to follow the Ring and lay down the law to the Ashentay — though, of course, believing themselves chosen, they fulfil their task with expertise. The *Say-nath* are the result of a genetic anomaly which is passed through the male line and recurs approximately every three generations. Many of the abnormally large foetuses are miscarried; those that go to term become the *Say-nath*. I had the misfortune to fall in love with an Ashentay who was unknowingly just such a carrier.'

I took a long drink of beer. 'So . . . when do you leave?'

She stared at the *thole* on the table before us.

'I'm taking the flight to Earth in three days,' she said. 'I should be able to have the operation within six months.'

I took the stone and turned it over in my hand, trying to feel something, the slightest hint of warmth. Earlier, she had asked me how much she might get for it on Earth, and I had shrugged and said, 'Enough . . .'

81

'You could have left Addenbrooke long ago,' I said now, 'with Karmel.'

She stared at me. 'Like this?' And she indicated the machinery that had replaced her missing half.

'But is it worth it?' I asked her. 'The loss of a daughter for the stone, for the chance to be whole again?'

'That's cruel, Ben. The circumstances are very different. You daughter is dead – you're prejudiced. I think you would have done the same, in my position.'

I stared at the sunset and wondered if she was right.

'Will you return to Addenbrooke?' I asked at last.

She considered this. 'Oh, I should think so,' she said, 'occasionally.'

Later I sat alone on the verandah, finished my beer and tried to imagine how much Lorraine Lomax hated her daughter. I followed the Ring of Tharssos as it diminished in perspective over the far horizon, taking with it the Ashentay *Say-nath*, and I wondered just how often *occasionally* might be.

Krash-Bangg Joe and the Pineal-Zen Equation

I'm dropping acid shorts in the Supernova slouch bar when the call comes through. Gassner stares from the back of my hand, veins corrugating his mugshot. Gassner's white – fat and etiolated like a monster maggot – but my Bangladeshi metacarpus tans him mulatto. He's a xenophobic bastard and the fact that he comes over half-caste on the handset never fails to make me smile.

I like irony almost as much as I dislike Gassner.

He's muttering now, somestuff about young junkies.

'You wrecked?' he queries, peering.

'I'm fine,' I lie.

He wants me in ten. He has customers coming. Distraught parents who have evidence their daughter was butchered. 'This is big-time, girl. Some high-up in the Wringsby-Saunders outfit. Don't screw it.' I feel like telling him to auto-fellate on a cannibal personatape, but I resist the urge. Maybe later, when I have the funds to fly. He still owns me, still has his fat face stamped on the back of my hand, good as any brand.

But it's only a matter of time now.

I've been out for hours. What I did earlier needed a good hit to help me forget. My head's dead and so are my legs. I stagger through a battlescene of prostrate bodies, hanging on the shoulder of a helpful Andy *en passant*, and make it to the chute.

Outside it's night, and the crowds are beginning to hit the streets. I brazen my way across a packed sidewalk, earning taunts on three counts. I'm a telepath and a junkie – the two go together – and I have no crowd-sense. I admit everything with an insolent *yeah-yeah* to whoever's complaining and climb aboard the moving boulevard. A breeze, fresh onetime but polluted now with city stench, does its best to revive me. I ride the slide a block and alight at 3rd. Feeling better already, I dodge touts and beggars and home in on the Union towerpile.

'Bangladesh!' The legless oldster grins in my direction, dumped like garbage by the entrance. How does he do it? He gouged his eyes out yearsback and still he knows when I'm coming. Could be he's on to the scent of my hair oil, or even my crotch. His tag's Old Pete, and he's my regular. I slip him creds and he makes sure I'm stocked with gum when I see Gassner. 'Any nearer?' he asks now.

I try a probe. All I get is jumblefuzz. He's shielded. We have a game, me and him. He reckons he was someone famous, onetime, and I have to guess who. His face is certainly familiar, disregarding the absent nose and evacuated eye-sockets. He went Buddhist, yearsback. Quit the race and mutilated himself to indicate his repudiation of the modern world. I often wonder what it was that drove him to such extreme action. Maybe he was seeking enlightenment, or perhaps he'd found it. Once again I concede ignorance, pass him ten and chew gum in the upchute.

I'm feeling great when I hit the 33rd. Gassner has his office shelved this level, though 'office' is a grand title for his place of work. It's little more than a cubby filled with Batan II terminals and link-ups and however much of his blubber isn't spilling through the hatch. I enter bright, my metabolism pumping ersatz adrenalin. It doesn't do to let him see me any other way. He'd gloat if he knew how low I was at being his slave.

A metal desk-top, the bonnet of a pre-fusion automobile, pins his fat up against the floor-to-ceiling window. He's scanning case notes and his grunt acknowledges the fact that

I got in with about three seconds to spare. The only light in the place is the silver glow from the computer screen. I clamber over this and sit cross-legged in the hammock where Gassner slings his meat between shifts. Every ten seconds the chiaroscuro gloom is relieved from outside by the electric blue sweep of a misaligned photon display, strobing sub-lim flashes of 'Patel's Masala Dosa' into our forebrains.

I slip my ferronniere from its case and loop it around my head. And instantly all the minds in the building, previously mere distant flickering candles, torch painfully. I strain out the extraneous mindmush, editing the occasional burst of brainhowl from psychopathic individuals, and work at keeping my head together.

Gassner, of course, is shielded. It wouldn't be good policy for someone who employed a telepath to go about with his head open. I'm shut out, *persona non grata* in his meatball. Times are when I'd love to read my master. Then again, times are when I'm glad I'm barred entry. I read too many screwballs in the course of a day without Gassner opening up.

Seconds later Mr and Mrs Distraught roll in.

The guy is Kennedy, and he's playing it cool. I'll be lying if I call him distraught; on the Richter scale of personal upheaval he'd hardly register. He's chewing *djamba* to calm himself and he carries his bonetoned body with a certain hauteur. Or call it arrogance. Under one arm he has the silver envelope containing the evidence, and under the other his wife. She's Scandinavian, beautiful in better circumstances, but grief plays havoc with good looks and right now Mrs Kennedy is ugly. She's sobbing into a drier and I get the impression that Mr Kennedy is embarrassed by the degree of his wife's distress.

They sit down while Gassner murmurs pleasantries, then jerks a thumb up at me. 'Bangladesh,' he says. 'My assistant.'

My name's Sita, but ever since the invasion I got the national tag. Here in the West they reckon it's kinda cute. I'm just glad I wasn't born in Bulgaria.

My presence, perched aloft, surprises Mrs Kennedy. She flickers a timid smile, then sees the connected-minds symbol on my cheek. She recoils mentally; she has no wish to have her grief made any more public than she can allow. I think reassurance at her, telling her that I have no intention of prying – at least, not *too* much. There's no way I'm probing deep into the angst-ridden maelstrom of her psyche; grief and regret and self-pity boil down there, and I have my own quota of these emotions to contend with at the best of times.

As for Mr Kennedy . . . He's shielded, so I don't waste sweat trying to probe. And anyway I already know enough about him, everything I want to know, and even things his little Oslo-born third wife doesn't know.

He nods at me, his gaze coolly observant.

I give him my best wink.

And my presence here is token, now. Gassner questions them and they answer, and I probe Mrs Kennedy to ensure veracity, not that I really need to. I had the facts of the case even before she crossed the threshold.

Becky Kennedy was snatched inside an uptown gymnasium at ten this morning, her bodyguard taken out with a neural-incapacitator. Their assailant came and went so fast that the bodyguard saw nothing. Around noon the Kennedys, waiting anxiously in their suburban ranch, received a silver envelope mailed collect.

Kennedy glances at Gassner, who nods. He lays the envelope on the desk and, amid fresh whimperings from his wife, slides out a glossy photograph. I lean forward. It isn't pretty. The still shows a young girl, spreadeagled in a leotard, with a massive bullet wound in her pubescent chest. Her dead eyes stare at the camera, frozen with terror.

'No note or message of any kind?' Gassner wheezes.

Kennedy replaces the photograph in the envelope. 'Nothing. Just this,' he says, and adds, without the slightest hint of appeal in his tone, 'can you get my daughter back, Mr Gassner?'

My boss fingers the folds of fat at his neck. 'I'm almost certain we can, Mr Kennedy.'

'Within the three-day limit? She's due on the Vienna sub-orbital next month. We'd like her to make it —'

And Mrs Kennedy breaks down again. She knows that the majority of missing kids are never found, except after the three-day limit. Despite Gassner's reassurances, she can't believe she'll ever see her little Becky again.

Gassner is saying, 'The fact that your daughter's abductor sent you this photograph indicates to me that what we have here is no ordinary abduction.' By which he means that Becky might not end up as the meat in a necrophilic orgy.

'My guess is that you'll receive a ransom demand for your daughter pretty soon. My agency will handle the negotiations. On top of whatever ransom demand is made, my fee for the case is two million creds.'

Kennedy waves. 'Just get my daughter back, Mr Gassner. And you'll get your fee.'

'Excellent. I'm glad to see that someone appreciates how dangerous our line of work can be. We are dealing with criminal psychopaths, Mr Kennedy. No price can fully compensate for the dangers involved . . .'

But two million creds will do nicely, thanks . . . Two millions that Gassner needs desperately. Trade is bad nowadays, and Gassner is struggling to keep his fat head above the choppy water-level of Big-City business.

He arranges to keep in touch and the Kennedys quit. I jump down and squat by the hatch, watching them go. 'You got everything?' Gassner wheezes.

I nod. 'Everything I need.'

Gassner catches my eye as I'm about to leave. 'Hey – and if you find the body before they get the ransom demand, you know how to work it, girl.'

I wink, point a blaster made out of fingers to show that I'm on his wavelength – but his instructions worry me. Does he suspect?

'I'm flying, Gassner,' I say.

'Hey, how's Joe? I haven't seen him around.'

The bastard sure knows how to land a cruel one. 'Joe's just fine,' I lie. I pray Allah give me strength to make minestrone of his meatball. But what the hell? 'Ciao,' I call, blow him a kiss and quit.

Drifting . . .

I was drifting monthsback when I found Krash-Bangg Joe, or plain Joe Gomez as he was then. Drifting? It's a state of mind as well as a physical act. You can't have one without the other; they're sort of mutually inter-dependent. To drift, get high on whatever's-your-kick, fill your head with some sublime and unattainable goal, and hit the night. Ride the moving boulevard a-ways, alongside the safe-city civvies out for the thrill of slumming, and when their mundane minds become just *too* much, quit the boulevard and try out the mews and alleyways. Drift forever and lose track of time. There's something for everyone down there; was even something for me.

Back then I was a screwed up, neurotic wreck. My past was a time in my head I tried to forget about, and my present wasn't so strawberries-and-cream, either. A second-grade telepath indentured to a fifth-rate, one-man investigative Agency. I worked a twelve-hour shift and the work was hard: try probing a mind seething with evil, sometime. I had another ten years of this hand-to-mouth, mind-to-mind existence ahead of me, and there were times when I thought I could take no more . . . If I survived the ten years I could leave the agency, discard my ferronniere and let my telesense atrophy – but even then I'd always be aware that taken as a race we weren't up to much . . . So I had no hopes for the future and the only way I could take the present was to chew my gum and live from day to day. Even so, I neglected myself. I'd go days without eating; I was never fat, but after a stretch of working and drifting and starving I'd be famine-thin, wasted.

I suppose the drifting helped, though. It was part of the day to day routine. My goal? You'd laugh – but they say if you seek long enough, you'll find. And I found. My goal was *someone*.

I had no idea who. I sometimes kid myself I was looking for Joe all along, that I knew he existed out there among the millions and it was just a matter of time before I found him. But that's just old retrospect, playing tricks. Truth is, I was looking for a good and pure mind to prove to myself that we weren't all bad, that hope existed.

So I'd get high at the end of a shift, ride the boulevard and slip into the tributaries. On the prowl, drifting . . .

I was a familiar face down the lighted darktime quarter. I'd be given rat-and-sparrow kebabs by the Chinese food-stall owners who wanted to fatten me up. The touts, they left me alone after the first few weeks when I declined to buy. They hawked everything from themselves to pure smack, from spare parts for illicit surgery to the Goodbye Express itself – Pineal-z. The drug from the third planet of star Aldebaran that'd give you the trip of a lifetime and total you in the process. It freaked me, that hit. Onetime monthsback I was drinking shorts in a seedy slouch and through the wall I probed a jaded businessman who'd had his fill of everything and wanted out. He'd paid a cool half million for the pleasure of ending his life, and he went with an extravaganza. Subjectivewise he lived another eighty years and his pineal bloomed to show him the evolution of his kind. I tripped along with him until he died, then I staggered back to my pad. I was zonked for three days following, and for another week hallucinated Pithecanthropus and Java Man dancing the light fantastic on the boulevard. Only later did I get vague flashbacks, memories of the vast, impenetrable blackness that swallowed the oldster when the drug blew his head. It frightened me at first, this intangible nothingness I could neither experience nor understand. In time, a month maybe, I managed to push it away somewhere, forget.

Then I was back drifting again, seeking . . .

I'd black my connected-minds symbol and probe, discarding heads by the thousand one after the other as they each displayed the same flawed formulas. Some heads were better than others, but even the better ones were tainted with greed and selfishness and hate. And then there were the really bad ones, the heads that struck me at a distance with their freight of evil, that stood out in a crowd like cancer cells in lymph gland.

But worse than that were the shielded minds, in which *anything* might be lurking.

I found Joe Gomez in a bar called the Yin-Yang.

It's an underground dive with a street level entrance washed in the flutter of a defective fluorescent. Three figures were standing in the silver sometimes-light that night, and something about them caught my attention. They wore the fashionable greys of rich businessmen, and their minds were shielded. They were discussing something among themselves in a tone which suggested they had no wish to be overheard. And one of the guys had oo tattooed on his cheek.

Now what the hell were three uptown executives doing whispering outside a slum bar at four o'clock in the morning? As sure as Allah is Allah not transacting boardroom business, I reasoned.

But I was wrong. They were.

I got close and listened in on their whispers. At the same time I became aware of an emanation from the subterranean Yin-Yang. The two connected. Casualwise, I slipped past the three execs and, once out of sight, jumped the steps two by two. The emanation was the sweet music of violin over din. My quest was almost over.

But not quite. I had to get him out first.

The bar was a slouch. Felled junkies littered the various levels of the padded floor. The barman was an Andy. I asked him if the place had another entrance, and he indicated west.

Then I looked around and probed.

The guy with the harmonious brainvibes sat against the far wall, drinking beer. He wore the blue one-piece of an off-duty spacer, and I read with surprise that he was an Engineman. He was good-looking too in a dark, Spanish kind of way. And he was unshielded . . .

I glanced at the entrance. There was no sign of the executives. They were no doubt still debating whether this was the guy they intended to scrape. Obviously their telepath was a few grades below me; I knew immediately that the spacer was prime material for what they had in mind.

I projected an aura of authority and crossed the slouch. 'Joe Gomez?'

He looked up, startled; surprised at being paged by a not-so-good-looking black girl. I realized that the telepath outside would be getting all this, too. So I slipped my shield from my tunic and palmed it onto his coverall. Then I grabbed his arm and blitzed him with a burst of life-or-death urgency.

As we hurried to the far door and up the steps I caught the tantalizing whiff of flux on his body. Then we were outside and swamped in the collective odours of a dozen ethnic fastfoods. 'This way —'

I ran him up the alley and under an arch, then down a parallel thruway and up an overpass. Crowds got in the way and we barged through, making good progress. Years of drifting had superimposed a routemap of the quarter on my cortex. The exec dudes would be floundering now, cursing their lost opportunity. I'd grabbed the golden goose and I could hardly believe my luck. To be on the safe side I took him across the boulevard and up a towerpile into a cheap Mexican restaurant I used when I was eating.

Outside, the city extended in a neverending, jewelled stretch. The million coruscating points of light might have indicated as many foci of evil that night – but we were away from it all up here and I had Joe Gomez. I could hardly control my shaking.

Then it came to me how close he'd been to annihilation, and I broke down. 'You stupid, stupid bastard,' I cried.

'Look, Sita – that's your name, isn't it?' He was bemused and embarrassed; he'd caught bits of me as I rushed him out, and he knew he owed me. 'Who were those guys?'

'Who? Just your funeral directors, is who.' My tears were tears of relief now. 'They were pirates in the scrape-tape industry. I overheard them before I got your vibes —'

'So? I could have been a star.'

'Yeah, a dead star, kid. Not many ways you can be killed nowadays, but they would've killed you *dead*.'

His tan disappeared and he looked sick. 'But I thought the industry was legal? I've seen personatapes on sale in the marts . . .'

His naivety amazed me. 'The personatape side of the thing is legal. They make tapes of the famous, or how they think the famous might have been. But these pirates make personatapes of real people by squeezing fools like you *dry*. You're so good you gave me raptures, and they wanted that.' And I was already wanting to snatch my shield away from him, wanting *more* . . .

He stared at his drink. He didn't seem very convinced.

'Listen, kid. You know what they'd've done to you if I hadn't happened along? They'd've killed you and taken your corpse to their workshop. They can scrape stiffs, and they're easier to handle – don't struggle. Then these guys, these pirates . . . they'd open your skull and go in deep and scrape the cerebellum, leaving your nervous system wrung out and fucked up. They'd get more than just emotions, they'd get everything. They'd rob you of your very self just to make a few fast creds, and then dump your body. And there'd be nothing no rep-surgeon could do to put you back together. You'd be dead. The only place you'd exist is on tape and as a ghost in the heads of non-telepaths who want the sensation of experiencing other states of being without having the operation.'

92

I took a long drink then, angry with him. 'And keep that shield. I want you to stay alive. Consider it a present.'

'Thanks,' he said.

'For chrissake!' I exploded. 'Where the hell do you usually drop? Don't you know what a shield is for?'

'I work a line out of Lhasa, Kathmandu, Gorakpur . . . They're quiet cities. I never really needed a shield there. This is my first time here . . .' He avoided my eyes and gazed out at the city.

'Yeah, well – think on next time. This isn't no second world dive. This is for real. Mean City Central where you have to think to survive.'

He nodded, sipped his drink.

I cooled. 'Where you from, Joe?'

'Seville, Europe. You?'

'Chittagong, what was onetime Bangladesh. China now.'

His gaze lingered on my tattoo. Then he saw the face on the back of my hand. 'Your husband?'

I laughed. 'Hey, Mr Innocent – you never seen one of these before?' I waved my hand around theatrically. 'This guy's my boss. He *owns* me. I'm indentured to him for another ten years.'

'I never realized . . .'

'No, well you wouldn't, would you?' I glared at him, bitter. Then I smiled. I had to remind myself that I had a Mr-Nice-Guy here, who was naive-for-real and wasn't playing me along.

I sighed, gave him history. 'My parents sold me when I was four. They were poor and they needed the rupees. I was one of six kids, and a girl, so I guess they didn't miss me . . . I checked out psi-positive when I was five and had the operation. I had no say in the matter, they just cut me and hey-presto I had the curse of *ability*. I was taken by an agency, trained, and sold to Gassner when I was six. I've been reading for small cred, gum and a bed in an Android quarter slum dwelling for nine years now . . .'

Joe Gomez was shocked. 'Can't you . . . I mean,' he shrugged. 'Get out?'

'Like I said, in ten years when my indenture runs its course. This makes sure I don't do anything stupid.' I held up the miniature of Gassner, his face stilled now; it'd come to life when he contacted me. 'With this he knows where I am at all times. There's nothing I can do about it . . .'

We rapped for ages, ordered tostadas, drank. Beneath the jive-assed, streetwise exterior I was like a little girl on her first date. I was trembling, and my voice cracked falsetto with excitement.

Joe Gomez . . . He was short, dark, around twenty. He had a strong, handsome face, but his eyes were evasive and shy. It was what lived behind those eyes that I was interested in, though . . . He was pure, and I needed *pure*. I wanted to get into him, become one. I was nothing special to look at, but I was sure that if I let him take a look inside my head, gave him the experience . . . But at the same time I was scared shitless I might frighten him away.

We watched the dawn spread behind distant towerpiles.

My heart was hammering when I said tentatively, 'Where you staying, Joe?'

'I just got in. I haven't fixed a place yet. Maybe you know somewhere?'

'I . . .' There was something in my mouth, preventing words. 'You can always stay at my place. It's not much, but . . .' Sweet Allah, my eyes were brimming again.

'I don't know . . .'

'Give me the shield,' I said.

'I get it. If I don't come with you, you want your present back, right?' He sounded hurt.

'Balls. I might be other things but I'm no cheat. I want to show you something.'

He passed me the shield, a silver oval a little smaller than a joint case, and I put it out of range on a nearby table. His goodness swamped me, and I swooned in the glow. I pushed myself at him, invaded him, showed him what it was like

94

to have someone inside his head . . . Then we staggered from the towerpile and rode the boulevard to the Android quarter.

Joe was on a three-week furlough, and we spent every day together. We were inseparable, cute lovers like you see on the boulevard Sunday afternoons. The girl from Chittagong and the boy from Seville . . . I got better quick, saned-up and began enjoying life. I stopped drifting and phased out the gum. I didn't need them, now. Joe was my kick, and I overdosed.

We explored the city together. I saw life through his eyes, and what I saw was good. We tried personatapes. He'd be an Elizabethan dandy for a day, and I'd be Bo Ventura, latest hologram movie queen. Once we even sexed as Sir Richard Burton and Queen Victoria, just for the hell of it. We made straight love often, and sometimes we'd exchange bodies; I'd become him and he'd become me. I'd move into him, pushing into his autonomic nervous system and transferring him to mine. I'd experiment with the novelty of a male body, in control of slabs of muscle new to me, and Joe would thrill to the sensation of vagina and breasts. At climax we'd be unable to hold on any longer and the rapture of returning, our disembodied personas twanging back to base, left us wiped out for hours.

Then one day towards the end of his furlough Joe pulled me out of bed and dressed me in my black skinsuit like a kid. We boarded a flyer and mach'd uptown. 'Where to?' I asked, sleepy gainst his shoulder.

'I'm a spacer,' he said, which I'd figured already. He was an Engineman, a fluxer whose shift was three months in a sen-dep tank pushing a Satori Line starship through the *nada*-continuum. 'And I want to show you something.'

We decanted atop the Satori Line towerpile that housed the space museum, and entered a triangular portal flanked by Andy militia. The chamber inside corresponded to the shape of the portal, a steel grey wedge, and we were the only visitors that day. By the entrance was the holographic sculpture of a man, vaguely familiar; the scientist who discovered the *nada*-continuum and opened the way for the starships.

Through Joe I had experienced everything that he'd experienced. His past was mine, his every sensation a shared event. I'd travelled with him to Timbuctoo – and as far as Epsilon Indi. But there was one experience of his that defied my comprehension. When he entered the sen-dep tank of a Satori Line starship I could not go with him; I had no idea what it was to flux. Joe knew, of course, but he was unable to describe the sensation, unable to recall the feeling so that I might read him and understand. He likened it to a mystical experience, but when I pressed him he could draw no real analogues. To flux was an experience of the soul, he said, and not of the mind – which was perhaps why I floundered.

We walked down the ringing aisle of the space museum. At the far end, on the plinth and cordoned by a low-powered laser-guard, was a trapezoid of blackness framed in a stasis-brace. What we had here, according to the inscription, was a harnessed chunk of the *nada*-continuum.

It did nothing to impress a sleepy Bangladeshi, until she saw the expression on the face of her lover. Gomez was a goner; even transfer-sex had failed to wipe him like this. 'Joe . . .?'

He came to his senses and glanced over his shoulder at the entrance. Then he vaulted over the laser-guard and lifted me quickly after him. 'This is it, Sita. Take a look.'

After a time the blackness became more than just an absence of light. It swirled and eddied in a mystical vortex like obsidian made fluid. I too became mesmerised, drawn towards a fathomless secret never to be revealed.

'What is it?' I asked, stupidly. I leaned forward. Joe held me back. He warned me that the interface could decapitate me as neat as any guillotine.

'It's the essence of nothing, Sita. That which underpins everything. It's Heaven and Nirvana and Enlightenment. The ultimate Zen state . . .'

His voice became inaudible, and then he said, 'I've been there . . .' And I recalled something – the ineffable blackness I had known monthsback. My mind reached out for something just beyond its grasp, a mental spectre as elusive as the wind . . . Then the spell was broken.

Joe laughed, pulled himself away and smiled at me. He jumped back over the laser-guard and plucked me out. We held each other then, and merged. His period of furlough was coming to an end. Soon he would be leaving me, drawn away to another rendezvous with the *nada*-continuum. I should have been jealous, perhaps. But instead I was grateful to whatever it was that made him . . . *himself*.

Hand in hand we ran through the chamber like kids.

Allah, those three weeks . . .

They had to end, and they did.

And it happened that Joe died a fluxdeath pushing his boat through the Out-there beyond Star Groombridge. That which had nourished him kicked back and killed him, with just three days to go before he came home to me.

I quit Gassner's and drop to the boulevard, my head full of Becky Kennedy and her loving parents. As I leave the towerpile a shadow latches on to me and tails, keeping a safe distance. I ride the boulevard to the coast.

Carnival town is a lighted parabola delineating the black bite of the bay. I choose myself a quiet jetty away from the sonic vibes and photon strobes, fold myself into the lotus position and wait.

Overhead, below a million burning stars, big starships drift in noiseless, clamped secure in phosphorescent stasis-grids. Ten kilometres out to sea the spaceport pontoon is a blazing inferno, with a constant flow of starships arriving and departing. Joe blasted out from here on his last trip, and for weeks after his departure the dull thunder of the ships, phasing out of this reality, brought tears to my eyes. Back then I came out here often, sat and contemplated the constellations, the stars where Joe might've been. Now I stare into space and try to figure out just where the accident happened.

A noise along the jetty, the clapping of a sun-warped board, indicates my shadow has arrived. I sense his presence, towering over me. 'Spider,' I say. 'Sit down. I've been expecting you.' And I have – he's one of the few people I can rely on to help me.

Spider Lo is a first-grade telepath and he works for the biggest Agency in the West. He's about as thin as me, but twice as tall. He earned enough last year to buy himself a femur-extension, and I was the first to admit he looked really impressive riding the boulevard, especially in a crowd. He's a Chink, and I should hate him for that, but he's a gentle guy and we get along fine.

'Gassner sent me, Sita.'

'That much I figured.'

'He told me to make sure you did your stuff. To me, it doesn't look like you're doing that out here . . .'

He hesitates, watching me. 'I'll let you into a secret, Sita. Gassner's in big trouble. Business is bad and a few of the bigger Agencies are going for the takeover. They'd buy Gassner out for peanuts and employ him as a nothing button-pusher. As for you – you'd be taken on by whichever Agency buys. You'd be on longer shifts for less pay. You're a second-grader, remember . . .'

I let him mouth-off. His *secret* is no secret at all. He's telling me nothing I don't already know. I let my lazy posture describe apathy, and stare at the stars.

Spider tries again. 'This case is worth two million to Gassner. It would mean solvency for him, and who knows, even a rise for you. But you're blowing it —'

'And won't Mr Gassner be angry with me,' I say.

'Sita . . . this is the biggest case you've ever had to crack. You don't seem to be trying . . .'

Languid, I give him a look, long and cool. 'Maybe I don't need to try,' I say.

'Sita . . .' His Oriental features pantomime despair.

'I'm serious, Spider. Hasn't it occurred to you that maybe the reason I'm lazing around here is because I've got the case wrapped up?'

His eyes glint with quick respect, then suspicion.

'No shit,' I say. 'I know where Becky Kennedy's meat is hidden.'

'You just this minute left the office, Sita.'

I shrug. 'How would you like to earn your Agency the two million riding on this case?' I ask him.

He tries a probe. I feel it prickle my head like a mental porcupine in a savage mood. But my shield is up to it.

'You don't have to probe, Spider. I'm honest – I'll tell you. Your Agency can pick up the creds from Kennedy when you find the body and deliver it to the resurrection ward —'

'But Gassner . . .' Understanding hits him.

'Yeah,' I say. 'You've got it.'

Spider looks at me.

'Why you doing this, Sita? If Gassner folds, you get transferred, and that won't be a picnic for you —'

'Listen, Spider. I'm getting out of it altogether. No more probing for this kid after tomorrow.'

'You're not —' Alarm in his voice.

I laugh. 'No, I'm not. I'm getting out and I want to see Gassner sink . . .' But there's an easier way than this to tell him.

I take my shield and toss it to him. He catches it, holds it for a second, then throws it back. That's all it takes for him to read what I'm planning. And he reads everything: my love for Joe and the reason I need big money, what I did yesterday and why I did it. He reads what I want him to do, and he slowly nods his head. 'Very well, Sita. Fine . . .' We finalise the arrangements, and then slap on it. We sit for a while, watching the starships and chatting, until Spider's handset calls him away on a case. He cranes himself upright and strides off down the jetty like someone on stilts.

I stay put a while. Above the city a hologram projection, like a stage in the sky, is beaming out world news. I watch the pictures but can't be bothered with the subtitles. Only when the business review comes on do I take an interest. After five minutes the takeover bids are flashed up. Multi-Tec International today made bids for a dozen small-fry – one of them, I learn, Gassner's Investigative Agency. But the bid didn't make it and Gassner is still independent. I smile to myself. By the time I finish with Gassner he'll be wishing he never bought me, all those years ago.

I leave the coast and ride back into the city. I stop off at a call booth and get through to the Kennedys, using the teleprinter to make the demand. Then, instead of going straight to the Union towerpile, I make a detour to take in the cryogenic hive-complex, uptown. I ride the chute to the seventh level and squat beside Joe's pod. If I concentrate I can just make out his thoughts, deep down and indistinct. Even diluted, crystallised and fragmented by the freeze, his emotions are still as good and pure as always. I tell him that soon it'll all be over, and he responds with a distant, mental smile.

I'm tearful when I leave the hive and ride across town.

After I heard about Joe's death I began drifting again.

I got back on the gum and stopped eating and hit the darktime quarter. When I wasn't working I got high and drifted without sleep for nights, probing, seeking . . . It was impossible, of course. What I was seeking I had found and lost, and there could be no substitutes, however good. There were no more Joes, and it was no good telling myself that there had to be. It was too soon after his death and I was still too close to him to accept anyone else.

Then I got it into my head that Joe was still alive. I thought I could feel his brainvibes in the air, as if he existed somewhere in the world and was trying to get through to me. I concentrated and struggled to contact him, to prove to myself that he was still alive. Crazy, I know . . .

But I was right.

100

It was a month after the accident and I was beginning to lose hope. I spent more and more time tripping on acid shorts and trying to forget. I reckoned that if maybe I could lose my identity, then the pain wouldn't be so bad.

Joe called a couple of nights later.

I was laid out on my bunk, coming down after a week of crazy, crazy nights drifting and tripping. My head was alive with vivid nightmares and Joe played a starring role.

When his face appeared on the vidscreen I knew it was a hallucination. 'Sita!' it shouted. 'It's me – Joe!'

I giggled. 'I know you're dead, Joe. You died Out-there. You can't kid me . . .'

'Sita . . .' His arms were braced on either side of the screen, and his head hung close. It looked like Joe, but there was something wrong with the geometry of the features. They were too clean-cut and perfect to be Joe's, even though they resembled his. Some effect of the acid, obviously . . .

'Sita, please – listen!' He was near to tears. 'I know I died a fluxdeath. But they got me out in time. They saved me. They put me back together in a Soma-Sim and —'

'Where are you?' But I didn't believe. I was still hallucinating. Joe was dead, and what I saw on the screen was a phantom of my imagination.

'That's why I called. I need your help. I'm at the city sub-orb station. I just got in. I need your help . . .' He looked over the screen, then behind him. When he stared at me again I saw that he was swaying, holding the set for support.

I crawled across the bunk and sat on the edge. I could not bring myself to believe, however much I wanted to. If I rested all my hope on what turned out to be cruel illusion . . .

'Joe . . . What's wrong, Joe?'

'They're after me, Sita. The pirates. They almost had me. I got away. Please . . . come and get me.' He grinned then, a wry quirk of the lips I knew so well and loved. 'I can't move. They hit me and I can't move. I managed to get this far . . .'

101

I staggered around the room and collected my clothes. I struggled into the bare minimum required for decency and dropped to the street. I hailed a flyer, gave the destination and collapsed in the back seat. I knew there'd be no Joe when I got there; already our dialogue was becoming dreamlike. It was too much to hope that I could save him a second time . . .

At the station I told the flyer to wait and stumbled into the crowded foyer. I wasn't wearing my ferronniere and the absence of brainhowl was a relief. The call-booths were ranked at the far end by a Somalian fast-food joint. I pushed through the crowd and collapsed against the first crystal pod. The caller inside gestured me away. I staggered from booth to booth, my desperation increasing when each one turned out to be empty. With three to go and still no sign of Joe I gave up and went berserk. I crashed against them one after the other, flailing at the doors with my fists. The last door remained stubbornly shut, as if pinned by a weight on the inside. I peered over the privacy screen and my heart went nova. Joe had slipped to the floor with his cyber-legs folded beneath him at crazy angles. He grinned when he saw me and reached out his arms . . .

I managed somehow to get him into the flyer and back to my pad.

Once inside he collapsed on the bunk, the Joe Gomez I knew and loved, but *different*. The only part of him that had survived the fluxdeath was his brain, and the rest of him was a power-assisted Krash-Bangg Somatic-Simulation with all the sex bits and the latest Nikon optics. It was impossible to tell that the body was a Soma-Sim; the surgeons had been faithful to Joe's old appearance, if anything making him even more good-looking than the original version.

I thought maybe I was still hallucinating . . .

'They were waiting at the port,' he said. 'They waited till I got in from the medic-base and they shot me, Sita. But I got away . . .' And he indicated his leg.

There was a hole in his thigh big enough to contain my fist. Charred strands of microcircuitry fuzzed the circumference, and the synthetic flesh had melted and congealed in dribbles like cold wax.

'It doesn't hurt,' Joe reassured me, peering down. 'I don't feel a thing. It's just that I can't walk.'

'We'll get you fixed up,' I said.

'You've got a spare half million?'

'Surely the Line?'

He laughed. 'They took all my savings to put me in this.'

'We'll find some way,' I said. 'Can't you go back?'

His hand moved to touch the hole, with just the faintest whirr of servo-motors. 'The Line's fired me, Sita. I'm in no condition to flux and I'm out of a job . . .' Tears were beyond the expertise of 21st-century cyberneticists, or Joe would have cried, then.

'Can you remember anything about the attack?' I asked.

'Not much. Three guys piled out of an air-car and called out to me. When I began to run, they opened fire —'

'Did you get the flyer's plate?'

'I was too busy trying to survive, Sita.'

I probed. I relived the attack and saw the same three guys I'd seen outside the Yin-Yang. The subconscious mind forgets nothing, and the quick glance Joe had taken at the air-car had lodged the plate code in his head. I memorised the code and came out. It was a slim lead, but perhaps a valuable one.

Joe reached out and pulled me to him. 'You haven't said how good it is to have me back, Sita.'

'No?' I opened up, and we merged. Beyond his relief at being with me I saw a dark shadow in the background, a sharp regret that he would never flux again. He was like a junkie deprived his fix, and the withdrawal symptoms were craving and melancholia. I shouldn't have felt jealous, but I did.

The following day I decided that my pad was not a safe place for Joe. Too many people had seen his arrival, and all it would take was for the scrape-tape pirate's telepath to send out a chance probe in the vicinity.

I had a contact in the cryogenic-hive complex uptown, and Joe agreed that this would be the best place for him until I came up with the creds to buy the services of a cyber-surgeon. I had a few ideas I wanted to think over during the next couple of days. I installed him in the hive, then left for Gassner's office.

I told my boss I was using the Batan II to check detail on the current case, and instead tapped into the city plate file. I found the number of the flyer Joe had seen, and I was in luck. The flyer was a company vehicle belonging to the Wringsby-Saunders Corporation. I looked them up and found they were into everything, but their biggest turnover was in the personatape market . . .

So I dropped to the boulevard and rode uptown.

The Wringsby-Saunders Corporation had a towerpile all to themselves, a hundred-storey obelisk with a flashy WS entwined and rotating above the penthouse suite.

I marched in, exuding bravura.

I roamed. I was looking for company personnel with faces that matched those I carried around in my head. I took in every level and a couple of hours later found what I wanted. A tall executive left his office and strode along the corridor towards me. He wore silvered shades and an arrogant expression. He was shielded, of course – as he was on the last occasion I had encountered him. In the defective fluorescent lighting outside the Yin-Yang bar . . .

The glow-tag on the door of his office told me: Martin Kennedy. He was the marketing director of the personatape division, one of the top jobs in the Corporation. And not satisfied with a director's fat salary, Kennedy dirtied his fingers with illegal scrape-tape dealings. Some people . . .

Over the next few days I neglected my duties for Gassner and followed Kennedy. It was my intention to blackmail him; his superiors at Wringsby-Saunders would not be amused that one of their top executives was dealing in death.

Then something happened to make me change my mind. There was a better way of extracting what I wanted from Kennedy, one that did away with the risk to myself.

It came to me as I watched him arrive home one evening and meet his daughter in the drive. It was one of the few occasions when he was unshielded, and I learned that the only pure and unsullied emotion in Kennedy's head was the love he had for his daughter, Becky.

Next time I found Kennedy unshielded I slipped him the sly, subliminal suggestion that Gassner's Investigative Agency was the best in town, specializing in murders, kidnappings, missing persons . . . The first place he'd think of when he found his daughter gone would be Gassner's.

Then I turned my attention to Becky and checked her movements. She had her own bodyguard and he escorted her everywhere. Well, almost everywhere. He was a big, ugly bastard, but I wasn't going to let him stand in my way at this stage of the game.

I decided the best place to strike would be in the gym she used every Tuesday morning. I joined up for the classes and obeyed all the instructions like a good girl, despite the protests from my drug-wrecked body. I arrived early Tuesday morning and watched Becky at her calisthenics while her minder did the same, only with more interest in how she filled her leotard in all the erogenous-zones-to-be.

I was right behind them when they left the free-fall chamber. I'd taken the precaution of putting the chute out of action and barring the communicating doors. We were quite alone.

I hit the bodyguard with the neural-incapacitator and he dropped like a sack of wet sand. Then I did the same to Becky before she got a look at me. While the guy was still jerking his beef on the floor I dragged Becky along the corridor and into the service chute.

I'd prepared myself for this part of the operation all week. I'd told myself over and over that this was not murder, that before the three days had elapsed little Becky would be patched up and resurrected and as good as new. If not better. Inside a fortnight she'd be back working out at the gym, her death a thing of the past. Even so, as I pulled the trigger of the pistol I had to close my eyes and think of Joe . . . Then I photographed the corpse and concealed it behind a sliding panel. The next chute inspection was due in a week. I'd done my homework and checked.

I left the gym and mailed the developed print to the Kennedys. Then I made for the Supernova and drank acid shorts to help me forget.

Hours later, the call from Gassner came through.

I cross town and head for the Union towerpile. 'Bangladesh!' the cackle greets me. Old Pete the Beggar grins toothless along the sidewalk. I slip him ten and he lays gum on me. I'm high by the time I hit the foyer.

Spider Lo has done his stuff. He sits with Kennedy in the ground floor bar, done out in the deco of a starship. I hoist myself onto a highstool, businesslike.

Kennedy gives me the inscrutable look through his silvered shades, but the empty glasses at his elbow belie his cool. 'I'd like to know what's going on?' he asks me. 'This . . . this gentleman apprehended me outside and claimed to be working with you on the case. I hope you've found my daughter —'

'Do you have the crystals?' I ask.

Kennedy hesitates, then lifts a valise onto the table. He opens it to reveal two sparkling crystals burning within the leatherette gloom. They're for real. The substance locked inside them glints like powdered diamond. I take the valise.

'The Gassner Agency has been taken over,' I tell Kennedy now. 'As such, it no longer exists. Mr Lo here represents the Massingberd Agency. You will pay his Agency upon completion of the case.'

'My daughter?'

'By the time I deliver the crystals, your daughter will be in the safe care of the city hospital.'

Kennedy nods his understanding. Spider Lo pushes papers across the table and Kennedy signs. 'Mr Lo will take you to the hospital, Mr Kennedy.' I shake him formally by the hand, but his shield deflects my probe.

We move outside and Spider and I slap palms and go our separate ways. Little Becky Kennedy will be alive again in a short while. Thirty minutes ago Spider rushed a medic-squad to the gym to retrieve her corpse, and soon she'll be respiring normally in the resurrection ward, the attack edited from her memory, looking forward to whatever it is little girls look forward to nowadays. Her sub-orbital trip to Vienna, maybe.

I ride the boulevard, one last time. In case Kennedy suspected anything and put a watch on me, I dodge clever. I alight on 5th and take a devious detour through the downtown quarter, lose myself in crowds and backtrack numerously. Then I hire a flyer and mach uptown to the cryogenic-hive.

After the formalities of payment and after-care instruc-tions, I decant my shining knight from his sarcophagus and assist him to the flyer. His head is hardly awake yet, barely thawed from the cryogenic state, and it's his power-assisted Soma-Sim that walks him from the ziggurat.

I think love at him to help the thaw.

I programme the destination of Rio de Janeiro into the flyer, but before we set off there's the small matter of my indenture to sort out. I fly to the Satori Line towerpile, Joe immobile beside me. I leave the flyer on the landing pad, drop to the twentieth level and enter the museum.

I have to wait a while before a rich family decide they've had their fill of wonder, and when they leave I leap over the laser-guard surrounding the shimmering shield of the *nada*-continuum.

I stand mesmerised, regardless of the danger should anyone enter and find me here. Before me is the ultimate, the primal state we all aspire to – the only thing ever to be wholly beyond my ability to grasp.

My contemplation is interrupted by a glow at the end of my arm. My hand tingles. Gassner's miniature portrait becomes animated. I hold up my arm, as if shielding my eyes from the *nada*-continuum, and stare at him. 'What do you want, Gassner?'

'Sita!' he cries, and he uses my real name only in times of stress. His regular pallor is suffused now with the crimson of rage, and he's sweating. 'Sita – where's Kennedy? I thought you —'

'I didn't crack the case, Gassner. Spider Lo got there first. Kennedy owes the Massingberd Agency, not you.'

'Sita!' He's almost in tears. 'Get back here!'

I smile. 'I'm sorry, Gassner. I'm through. I've had enough and I'm getting out. Goodbye —'

He panics. He knows that without a telepath he's nothing. 'You can't, Bangla —'

I can, and the *desh* is lost as I thrust my hand into the *nada*-continuum/reality interface. The satisfaction of getting rid of Gassner dilutes the pain of losing my hand; my tele-ability repels the frenzied communications shooting up my arm and keeps the agony below the tolerance threshold. The wrist is neatly severed when I stagger back, the stump cauterized and blackened. I jump the barrier and stumble through the chamber.

The hologram of the scientist stands beside the portal. Pedro Fernandez, discoverer of the *nada*-continuum and opener of the way. He seems to be smiling at me, and I know the smile. I give him a wink as I leave.

Joe touches my arm as I climb into the flyer and take off. We bank over the city and head towards the ocean. I probe him. His head is slowly coming to life, warming as if to the sunlight that shines through the screen. I read Joe's need, his craving.

Above the city, canted at an angle, the hologram screen pours morning news over a waking world. Did the Gassner Agency surrender to the take-over bids that must surely come now? Come on, an ending like that would be just *too* storybook. I can only wait until we reach Rio and find out then.

Meantime, I hope.

Weakly, Joe says, 'You get the creds?'

I open the valise and shake the crystals into his lap.

'Pineal-z,' I tell him, and I open up and let him have the experience I had monthsback when I tripped on Pineal-z and lived.

'It's Pineal-z or me, kid,' I tell him. 'Enlightenment or love. Take your pick.' And I withdraw, close up. I don't want to influence his decision and I don't want to eavesdrop on his infatuation with something I can never hope to understand.

Old Pete? Yeah, he kidded me not. He *was* someone famous, onetime. He was probably the most famous person in the world. He was Pedro Fernandez yearsback, discoverer of the *nada*-continuum and opener of the way.

I know for sure now that Old Pete is good, behind that shield of his . . .

I glance across at Joe. He's staring at the crystals in his hand, weighing the experience he had and lost against whatever I can give him. He drops the crystals back into the valise, looks at me. 'We'll sell them when we get to Rio, Sita. Find a cyber-surgeon to fix me up and get you a new paw . . .'

Enlightenment, or love? Perhaps they're one and the same thing.

Tears fill my eyes as I fly us away from the city and into the sunrise, one-handed.

Pithecanthropus Blues

24th May, 2060
Proxmire Industrial Solar Satellite

It began as a tickle in the backbrain, just like the first time. The cerebellum is a difficult place to scratch, and I was reduced to holding my head in my hands and yelling at the top of my voice. The neighbours on all five sides began complaining and I had to quit the cubby. I took the radial slide out to the arcing crystal membrane of the dome, darkened now in night-phase. I stepped on to the perimeter causeway and began walking.

The tickle was a constant chatter now, no longer just tactile but *audible*. It was as if the two hemispheres of my head were conversing in tongues, or rather in grunts. Then I became aware of a very real *presence* in my head, of an identity taking over my brain. This was how it had happened before. Soon, I knew, I'd find myself *elsewhere* . . .

I passed the hatch of a slouch bar in the deck, raised like the conning tower of a submarine. Strobing lights and music throbbed out, along with the sound of voices and laughter. I wanted to climb down there and talk to people, to establish the reality of my identity through social contact. But I knew that would be a mistake. The last time this had happened, two nights ago, I had returned to my senses to find myself naked and chin deep in an H_2O effluent conduit on the flipside of this solar spinning top. The last thing I wanted was to go under drunk.

I blacked out.

As before, I had the sensation of swimming in some neutral medium. I was in darkness and thrashing around and shouting for help. Gradually, with a sense of relief I suspected was ill-founded, I returned to consciousness. I felt the reassuring physical form of a human body assume substance around my shattered psyche. I almost whooped for joy – surely *anything* was better than the sensory deprivation I had just undergone. Then some vague recollection of my last experience made itself known to me. I opened my eyes, and I was no longer aboard the Sol orbital satellite.

Anyone born on Earth might have called this paradise. To me, conceived on Venus and a Spacer ever since, it was purgatory. The clear blue sky went on for ever without the reassuring confines of a dome, and on all sides the land stretched away with nothing more substantial than scrub and sun-parched trees between me and the distant horizon. To someone accustomed to overcrowded orbital agglomerations, the sudden sense of infinity was overwhelming. My head spun with agoraphobia.

More disconcerting than the geographical dislocation, however, was the fact that I was no longer in my own body. Ridiculous as it may seem, the lean, hairless body of my former self was no more. In its place was the squat, hirsute frame of a being one step above the ape. My arms hung down to my bowed knees in a manner both negligent and thuggish. I was naked. I tried to protest, but all that came out was a plaintive scale of grunts.

I had been this way before. I recognized the body by the parallel claw marks on its belly and the missing left big toe. That first . . . *seizure* . . . had lasted mere seconds before I was returned to my own body. I had retained but a hazy recollection of the interlude, the alien landscape and the even more alien body. I had managed to convince myself that the experience was the flashback effect of certain pharmaceutical substances partaken of during my

111

time as an Engineman for the Canterbury Line. Which still might be the case . . . But I doubted it. There was something very real about the way I inhabited this proto-human form beneath the open, searing sun . . .

For the first time I became aware that I was not alone. A hundred metres ahead of me was a small band of short, trotting creatures; it was some minutes before I realized that I, or rather the body that I inhabited, was one of their number. There was something about their diminutive stature, their hairiness and the way they almost *skulked* across the plain, that lent them the aspect of animals. One of their number turned, grunted and gestured at me to hurry; and there was something at once reassuring in the familiarity of the human gesture, and frightening in the fact that this identified me unmistakably as one of *them* . . .

Warily, I began shambling in pursuit. The absence of the big toe gave me a wild, swaying gait. I approached the band but kept my distance. They jogged across the plain with the stealth of the hunters I assumed they were. They carried rocks and lengths of wood in such a fashion as to suggest they had discovered their application as weapons. I alone was unarmed.

After what I judged to be about ten minutes we came to a gorge or rift in the land. Here the flat, scorched plain came to an abrupt end, and fell away in a deep, steep-sided valley. A river bisected the valley bottom, and the land on either side was lush and green.

The creatures – I could not bring myself to call them men, though the evidence was mounting that they were indeed just that – crouched on the lip of the escarpment in attitudes of wariness. They took cover behind sparse trees and infrequent boulders, peered into the valley and from time to time pointed.

As I scanned the valley bottom I made out the subject of their interest. Beside the river, in a green meadow of knee-high grass, a group of figures – as humanlike as my compatriots – lay about or sat watching the water. They too were naked, small and hairy. I tried, and failed, to find in them some difference, some evidence that they were somehow *less* human than my band, to excuse what I sensed was about to happen.

At a gesture from our leader – a tall creature with a monstrous, flattened face – the band charged *en masse* down the steep incline, yelling and waving their clubs.

And I lost consciousness.

I experienced the familiar sensation of being afloat in darkness, of struggling towards some unseen point of safety. One by one I felt my senses return – and last of all my sight. I was in my own body again, but naked, and wading waist-deep in the freezing waters of an effluent conduit. Par for the course, this; last time, I had managed to creep back to my cubby without being seen, and I endeavoured to do so again. I waded from the wide steel trough and ran naked through the darkened industrial sector of Sol City, fear and dread pounding in my head like migraine.

26th May, 2060
Proxmire Industrial Solar Satellite
The day following the 'seizure' I skipped work – I just couldn't bring myself to leave the cubby. I lay on my back and stared at the ceiling, six inches above my nose. Eventually I could stand no more: there was something about just lying and waiting for the first hint of backbrain tickle that was more horrific than the actual experience. The following shift I went to work. I thought that the familiar routine of the job might take my mind off what had happened to me. But I thought wrong.

I worked as a coffin-engineer for Sol Funeral Services Inc, and while I'd rather have worked on bigships or shuttles, coffins were easy and the money was good. I did a six hour shift each 'day'. The first three hours I spent in the control room, a cosy bleb that adhered to the turning collar of the station and provided a constant view of Sol burning outside.

113

From here I loaded coffins into the breach by remote control and, with the service over and the mourners gathered by the viewscreen, I pressed the button that sent the jet-powered coffins on graceful trajectories towards the big fire. Once out of sight, the coffin ejected its passenger into the sun and turned for home. The second half of my shift I spent repairing and servicing the coffins I'd sent out earlier, tuning the jets, spraying the casks with new coats of silver paint burned off on each run, and in general readying the coffins for their next trip.

That 'morning' I sent three casks on their way, and in the 'afternoon' I tinkered around with them in the service bay. I usually took pride in my work, enjoyed the manual labour of replacing faulty jets and test firing the coffins on a quick orbit of the satellite, but today my heart wasn't in the job. Visions of my time among the proto-humans returned to me, and I could concentrate on nothing for fear of that first, insidious tickle that would prefigure another seizure.

I was considering whether to check off sick when Anton, my boss, gave me the excuse to leave. His thin, high voice summoned me to the Chapel of Rest. 'Hey Chester, boy. Get yourself down here and take a look at this . . .' Now Anton is sick – it's a combination, I suppose, of being reared in the subterranean hives of Ganymede and spending half a lifetime in the business of death. From time to time he'd summon me to the nether regions of the complex to show me what he considered a particularly interesting corpse.

I took the down-chute to the Chapel of Rest and found him in the preparations room. Sickly organ music played. Anton stood beside an open cask, garbed in the black cloak and top hat of the Morticians' Guild.

He looked up when I entered. He frowned. 'You look ill, Chester. Is something bothering you?' He gave me the swift appraisal usually reserved for sizing up a new corpse.

'I'm fine,' I lied. 'What is it, Anton?'

114

He gestured towards the cask. 'Not a pretty sight, Chester.'

Anton had an aptitude for the understatement. The body, that of a man in his fifties, had met a violent end. I clutched the edge of the cask for support.

'What . . . what happened to him?'

'In my opinion,' Anton said, 'he was eaten alive.' He pointed to the thigh bone. 'Observe the teeth marks. Much of his entrails are missing – ditto a large proportion of his brain . . .'

I managed a feeble chuckle. 'Eaten? On Sol station?'

Anton looked at me. 'And why not? For the past week the bigship *Hanumati* has been docked here, refuelling before its run to the Out-there. Haven't you noticed all the boosted-animals in the bars and night clubs? Obviously one of these, a boosted leopard or tiger, suffered a computer malfunction and reverted to type. I always said that augmentation was unnatural. And now look . . .' He gestured again at the body.

I refrained from doing so. 'I don't feel so well,' I said, and slipped to the floor in a cold faint.

When I came to my senses, Anton was slapping my face back and forth with a clammy hand. 'I thought you looked rather pale, Chester. Take the day off. And a word of advice – see a medic.'

I took my leave of the funeral parlour and wandered home in a daze. Sight of the corpse had served to focus my mind on the fact of my own mortality – and on my singular predicament. In the cubby, I lay tossing and turning in a torment of indecision. If I did take Anton's advice and consulted a medic, then my worst fears might be confirmed. On the other hand, there was always the chance that my 'seizures' had a perfectly innocent psychological explanation. A trip to the medic might put my mind at ease.

I decided to make an appointment first thing in the morning.

27th May, 2060
  Proxmire Industrial Solar Satellite

The clinic was the tallest building on the satellite. It stood at the exact centre of the residential hemisphere like a giant spindle. Dr Lassiter's penthouse consulting surgery was a great glass bauble that hung metres below the apex of the dome and commanded a three-hundred-and-sixty-degree view of the surrounding city.

Lassiter himself was a tall, dignified man in his late nineties. He sat between the wings of a large v-desk and joined his fingertips before his long nose. He turned from the screen on his desk and regarded me.

Already I had been thoroughly examined and questioned by a Robodoc, and I had expected to be diagnosed by the same. The fact that the Robo' had seen fit to refer me to a human medic, and a top specialist at that, suggested that something was very wrong indeed.

I quaked.

'I see that you have been suffering *seizures* as you call them, Mr Carnegie,' Lassiter said softly. The man had a honeyed larynx. 'Perhaps you would care to explain the nature of these seizures . . .?'

I did my best to describe the physical symptoms of my displacement, the terrible sense of disorientation I experienced as a result.

'And you've suffered these on two previous occasions now?'

I nodded.

'Tell me, for how long did the first attack last?'

I shrugged. 'A matter of seconds.'

'And the following attack?'

'About one hour.'

Dr Lassiter nodded. 'I see.' He murmured into a microphone and regarded the ceiling.

'Can you recall if, preceding these attacks, you heard *noises* in your head?'

'Yes – a tickle at first, and then . . . grunts. Then I black out and come round again . . . elsewhere, in a different body.'

Dr Lassiter nodded sympathetically.

He glanced at the screen on his desk. 'I see that you worked as an Engineman. How long were you in this employment, Mr Carnegie, and when did you leave?'

'Ten years,' I answered promptly. 'And I left six months ago. I was made redundant when all the Lines decided it was more profitable to employ boosted-animals instead of Enginemen.' I shrugged. 'Does it matter?'

The Doctor chose to ignore me and murmured again into the microphone.

I waited until he finished, then cleared my throat. 'Do you know what's wrong with me, Dr Lassiter? Am I imagining all this, or —'

'I'm afraid that your imagination has nothing to do with this, Mr Carnegie. And yes, I do know what is wrong with you . . .'

I waited.

'You are suffering from the rare and particularly unpleasant syndrome of Ancestral Persona Exchange . . .'

I mouthed the last three words like an idiot, then echoed: 'Unpleasant . . .?'

'Ancestral Persona Exchange strikes one in every eight hundred million people, Mr Carnegie. Stated simply, you find yourself in the body of a far distant ancestor, in your case a proto-human from prehistoric Earth – and he, for the period of these attacks, finds himself inhabiting your body. Very disconcerting for both of you, I don't doubt . . .'

I gestured feebly. 'But there is a cure? You can do something for me?'

Dr Lassiter glanced at his buttressed fingers. 'I'm sorry . . .'

'You mean – you can't prevent this? At any time of day I'm likely to find myself in the body of this prehistoric ancestor, without warning, and there's nothing you can do to . . .?'

I stopped, there.

117

Dr Lassiter was regarding me with sad eyes.

'I'm afraid it's somewhat more serious than that, Mr Carnegie. Soon, on the occasion of your fifth attack – if you go the way of the other cases we have observed — you will remain forever in the body of your proto-human ancestor.' He lowered his gaze. 'I'm sorry, Mr Carnegie . . .'

He murmured that he would refer me to a therapist, and that she would be in touch soon. He expressed his sympathies with such professionalism that I knew they had been offered many, many times before. I took the down-chute to the street and wandered home like a zombie.

Ancestral Persona Exchange . . .

'Oh, my God . . .' I cried.

I was going APE.

That night, the inevitable happened. The backbrain tickle began as I lay in my bunk, pondering my fate. Too afraid to move, I closed my eyes and tried not to scream. The cerebellum itch became unbearable. Next, I thought, the grunts – then I find myself in the dark, neutral medium of non-being an instant before the transfer. But I was wrong. In place of the grunts I sensed the apeman attempt to articulate – he shaped his grunts into the semblance of latter-day English. *Where am*? he thought-asked. *Who you*? I sensed his confusion and felt pity for him.

But before I could question him as to how it was that he had managed to communicate with me in my own tongue, I slipped into utter blackness and struck out blindly for the safety of physical reality – even if it was in this case the reality of a million years ago.

I sensed myself settle into the apeman's body – and then I knew how he had managed to question me, for I was doing the same thing now. I had a limited understanding of the grunt-language used by these people. I was aware that the apeman's name was Gna, and that among this band of proto-humans he was regarded as something special – exactly why, though, I did not know. To some vestige of

118

Gna still lingering in his own head I asked: *Who are you people? Where are we?* But before he could frame a reply he passed into my own body uptime and I came to my senses in his.

I opened my eyes and found myself seated in the shade of a tree some way from the main body of the tribe. Many of them were stretched out asleep and snoring; others attended to their partner's nit population. A few youngsters chased around in play, for all the world like baby chimpanzees.

A huge red sun hung above the treetops, and something that I had experienced only once before moved in from the west: a wind. This one was hot and discomforting, like a blast of heat from a furnace. Evidently we had eaten; my hands were bloody and my belly full. My gaze fell to my body and I had to admit that I was a hideous specimen, even by prehistoric standards. I was four-feet-nothing of fat hairy ape – and I stank. I teetered on the verge of slumber and pondered my misfortune.

Dr Lassiter had told me that, on the occasion of my fifth transference, I would remain here . . . stranded for good! I tried to look on the bright side and work out the advantages of living in this prehistoric era. But as far as I could see there were none. In fact, of all the possible times in Earth's past to which I might have found myself transported, this one had to be the most hellish. The environment was totally alien to me; the citizens of this time were little better than animals – and of all my ancestors I had had the mischance to find as my exchange partner, fate had deposited me in the overweight body of a geriatric cripple.

I was philosophising thus in the sultry dawn of planet Earth when I was visited by a member of the opposite sex. She squatted before me and bared her fangs in what might have been an amorous smile. She had teeth like tombstones, bad breath and dugs that dropped to her knees. She grunted at me, and I knew that this was the prehistoric equivalent of a pick-up. She turned on all fours and presented herself, and the prospect did not appeal. I realized, then, that this might

119

be the fateful encounter that produced the genetic line that would culminate, in the year 2030, in the birth on Venus of one Chester Carnegie. Perhaps, if I abstained, I might never be born. All the more reason for chastity, I thought. I grunted that I had migraine. The female became angry – but I was saved her wrath by a cry from across the clearing, and my partner-who-almost-was scampered off.

The tribe had gathered and were staring at the setting sun. As the fiery ball touched the rim of the horizon, the tribe prostrated themselves on the ground in obvious obeisance. I stared, amazed. Sun worshippers, yet!

Minutes later, as the sun disappeared and pulled night in its wake, I was further amazed when each member of the tribe approached me, genuflected and deposited at my feet some small gift or token: clubs of wood, nuts and berries, gobbets of meat and small rodents. They retreated across the clearing and watched me as I regarded the offerings. I went through the limited knowledge of this era I had picked up from Gna in the transfer, but came up with nothing that might explain this.

I was cautiously sorting through the revolting oddments and wondering how to respond – the tribe was still watching me intently – when I was saved by the familiar sensation of approaching oblivion. Seconds later I blacked out and returned to my own time.

28th May, 2060
Proxmire Industrial Solar Satellite

As this was my penultimate day in civilized times I decided to give work a miss. Besides which, I had influenza. I had come to my senses the night before in the industrial sector, wet, freezing, and, as always, stark naked. Only the late hour prevented my being seen as I sprinted like a madman back to the cubby-stack.

I remained in my cubby all day and attempted to reconcile myself to my fate. I made a printout of the daily newsheet, but the current events only made me aware of what I was leaving. There had been another murder on the satellite; the authorities had tagged every boosted lion, tiger and panther who had left the bigships at the dock. On Earth, food riots had erupted in America, again. Titan and Europa were at war in a dispute of spatial territory . . .

And, in cubby 101, Chester Carnegie was slowly going APE.

Towards midnight the screen above the hatch bleeped and I accepted the call. A panda-faced girl peered out. 'Chester Carnegie?' she asked. 'The guy who's going APE?'

'Who the hell are you?' I yelled.

'Your therapist,' she smiled. 'Hincty Little-O'fay.'

'Is this some kind of sick joke?' On the fur of her forehead I made out her serial number, and as she turned her big panda head I saw the microphone implant at the back of her neck. She was a call-girl.

'No joke, Chester. You want to find out *why* you're going APE?'

'You know?' I exclaimed.

'Meet me in the *Carotid Fix* slouchbar in fifteen minutes,' she said. 'I'll be a dolphin.'

I was there in ten.

The *Carotid Fix* slouch serviced the spaceport quarter, a mixed bar with one wall looking out across the system. Aliens, humans and boosted-animals drank together or got their fixes alone and jugularwise. A bigship Captain sat cross-legged on the floor, discussing Einstein-Fernandez physics with a tiger and a slow loris. Mood music bubbled, Martian tablas and Lyran waterpipes. I found an elevated booth and five minutes later Hincty Little-O'fay strode in.

She was the most beautiful dolphin I'd ever seen.

Her body was human-female and well-proportioned, but from the neck up she was pure bottle-nose. She slipped into the seat across from me. 'I'll change if you prefer,' she said. 'Some human customers like fauna, though.'

She touched the back of her head and the dolphin disappeared. She was a cute white kid, maybe twenty.

'Of course, I can be anything you want. Subdermal laser fibre-optic capillaries. You like?'

'Just what the hell kind of therapist are you?' I asked.

She tossed her head. 'I was hired by the Canterbury Line when Dr Lassiter informed them you were going APE.'

'The Canterbury Line? I don't see . . . ?' I was confused, to say the least. Why would my old employees hire a call-girl to act as my therapist? 'You said you knew why I'm going APE?'

The cyborg barman hovered over to us and Hincty Little-O'fay ordered a cyberpunch – a Gibson with helium. The goldfish bowl before her bubbled from the bottom up. She sucked through a straw, nodding and making big eyes to halt my impatience.

'Yeah,' she squeaked, smiling at me. 'You were once an Engineman for the Canterbury Line, right? Well, a few months ago they discovered that a number of their Enginemen were going APE. They found out why, and started drafting in boosted-animals to do the work instead.'

'So why am I . . . ?'

She pulled a face. 'Well . . . hate to be the one to tell you this, Chester – but the Line kept a lot from you Enginemen. Like when you put yourself in those thingy-tanks to flux —'

'Sensory-deprivation —'

'Yeah, sen-dep tanks – to flux, to mind-push the bigships through the *nada*-continuum . . . Well, while you were in there on a three month stint, it wasn't technically *you* who were mind-pushing the bigship —'

'Then who?'

'You see,' Hincty gestured with spread figures, 'when you tanked yourself, the ship's computer interfaced with your neo-cortex, accessed your DNA and brought forward one of your Pithecanthropan ancestors from the Pleistocene Period to inhabit your head and mind-push the boats. Apparently, these little ape guys were closer to the. . .' she screwed her face up and peered at something written on the palm of her hand. 'Sorry, Chester – you're my first patient, see. They were closer to the Essential Elemental Quiddity of the Primal Cosmic Null-state of the *Nada*-Continuum . . .' She squinted at me. 'That make any sense to you, Chester?'

'I think I get the gist,' I answered. 'Pithecanthropus man can mind-push bigships better than us humans.'

'Yeah.' Hincty shrugged. 'Guess that's what it boils down to. So for the three months you were tanked, you inhabited some basement of your subconscious while this apeman did the work. Now . . . in quite a large percentage of Enginemen, something went wrong on a cellular level. Many of you underwent terminal Ancestral Persona Exchange.'

'So that's why six months ago all the human Enginemen were made redundant and the boosted-animals got the jobs?'

'That's why, Chester.' She looked relieved that she'd managed to get to the end of the explanation.

'You said I was your first patient?' I asked. 'Just what kind of therapy can you give me that might help my condition?'

She glanced around the bar, wrinkled her nose at the music. 'Not here, Chester. How would you like to come back to my place?'

Before I had time to reply she pulled me from the *Carotid Fix* and along the perimeter walkway. She owned an expensive cluster of bubble rooms barnacled to the inner curve of the dome. She took me by the hand and led me through to the bedroom. She opaqued the walls for privacy, stepped from her wrap and put her arms around my neck. 'I can be any race or colour you like,' she breathed into my ear as she lowered me to the bed. 'Just speak your instructions into my occipital microphone.'

I felt like asking her if she could transform herself into a Pithecanthropan – after all, I'd have to get used to it. But, somehow, the thought did not appeal. I'd have the rest of my life to sample the dubious pleasures of proto-human love-making.

'So this is the Line's idea of therapy,' I said. 'A sop? A few hours of ecstasy to compensate for a life-time of hell . . .'

Hincty Little-O'fay was unzipping my overalls. 'Not at all, silly. You see, I can cure you, Chester.'

'Huh? You can?'

She whispered how.

Three hours later, as Hincty slumbered gently beside me, I felt the first twinges of the transfer in my head. I rolled from the bed, dressed quietly and left.

I was going APE for the very last time.

My trans-temporal dialogue with the apeman Gna was extended on this occasion. The familiar thought-grunts became a definite presence, and in the darkness of my head arrived the question: *Where-is-this?*

The good old twenty-first century, Gna, I replied.

I-don't-like.

Can't say that I'm too enamoured of the Pleistocene Period, either.

Huh?

Just hang on in there, boy. With any luck this'll be the last time we pass this way. Au revoir!

I opened my eyes and found myself on a scorched African plain. I was among the merry band of hunters again, trotting towards the gorge. We came to the escarpment and dropped into postures of surveillance. Down below, though further along the valley bottom this time, another tribe of proto-humans disported themselves beside the river. On a signal from our leader we charged. I contrived to trip and allow the others to pass me, then hung back and witnessed the slaughter from a safe distance. The valley people stood little chance against this armed and ferocious onslaught. They looked up, seemed frozen for a second, then scattered. The halt and lame were dispatched first, and then a couple of youngsters caught unawares waist-high in the river. The carnage was over in seconds. The survivors scurried whimpering along the valley and out of sight, and my tribe assumed the immemorial attitudes of triumph; they beat their chests and *yi-yipped* at the tops of their lungs.

We were joined minutes later by the non-combatants of the tribe. Some fifty in all, we gathered around in a rough circle while two males slit the carcasses with stone cutting instruments and removed the heads. These were passed around the tribe and, through a hole stove in the cranium, the brains were scooped and slurped. I declined my share and passed the head to the next apeman. Then the lights were distributed, the choice tidbits going to the warriors and the children. The feast began in earnest only when the limbs were severed and apportioned. I managed to refuse all offers without arousing suspicion – my fellows were too bothered about getting their share to worry about me.

Later, the repast over and only a pile of picked-clean bones scattered like jackstraws to indicate the fact of the carnage, the apemen stretched out in the grass, belched and scratched themselves and slumbered.

I found a tree at some remove from the crowd, sat and gave thanks that this was my last visit to this barbaric age. The prospect of salvation made the fact of what had happened just about tolerable: certainly the thought of a lifetime among these people would drive me mad.

At sunset the tribe roused themselves and, in single file, walked into the river and waded chest-high downstream. As the sun disappeared below the distant horizon, they submerged themselves in what was obviously a post-prandial rite of purification.

I stared at the ceremony with sudden and sickening realisation, followed by nausea, and I thought of Gna, in my body in the twenty-first century, and the hideous murders he had committed in the name of survival and tradition.

I had been in this time for many hours – certainly the longest period I had endured in the Pleistocene – when I was visited by the apewoman with designs on me. She swiped at my crotch in play and breathed the reek of dead flesh over me. I thought of Hincty Little-O'fay, still a million years unborn, and blessed her, my saviour.

The apewoman wrestled me to the ground, straddled me and bounced, gibbering with delight – and I was saved further indignity by the darkness that came down rapidly and carried me away. Goodbye, Pleistocene! I yelled-grunted to my ancestors. Hello twenty-first century!

29th May, 2060
Proxmire Industrial Solar Satellite

I shivered in my cubby for hours, naked and freezing from Gna's last purification dip in the effluent conduit. I felt bloated and ill from the last meal my body had taken. What action, I wondered, might the authorities take if they discovered that 'I' was the phantom cannibal of the Proxmire satellite? I was grateful that the police were concentrating their attention on the boosted-animals. With luck, I'd remain undiscovered for a while longer. I had only a matter of hours to go before I met Hincty Little-O'fay for the final part of my cure.

Perhaps I should have felt a modicum of guilt at the grisly ends that the innocent citizens had met, but I didn't. After all, technically I had nothing to do with their deaths, even if my body *was* physically involved. Gna had done the deeds, and he was only acting out his inherited and environmental imperatives for survival. If anyone was to blame it was the people at the Canterbury Line for summoning forth my cannibal ancestor in the first place.

At noon I left the cubby and took the radial slide to Hincty's bubble pad. My arrival before the diamond hatch alerted sensors which activated a blast of jazz throughout the domes. I waited. Hincty didn't answer. I stepped back and peered into the transparent rooms above me, but there was no sign of the kooky little call-girl. Perhaps I'd made a mistake, and we'd arranged to meet at the *Carotid Fix* slouchbar instead. I took the walkway to the spaceport quarter.

There was no sign of her in the slouch, either. I found an empty booth and ordered a drink. I'd give her one hour, then return to her place. I was jumpy. Last night Hincty had explained the final part of the cure – and I didn't like the sound of it one bit. She'd finally convinced me that this was the only way I could be saved, and I'd agreed to go along with her scheme. It was either that or spend the rest of my time impersonating Gna.

One hour later I was still alone, and more than a little drunk. I was climbing from the booth when I became aware of an insistent itch in my head . . .

Gna, coming through again!

'Apollo!' I yelled at the top of my voice.

I ran from the bar like a madman.

'Hincty!' I cried.

I sprinted back to her pad and rapped on the hatch. She still wasn't home. And I could feel Gna, assuming identity in my head. There was only one thing for it: I would have to go through with the 'cure' without Hincty's help.

I took a down-chute to the flipside, sprinted along the walkway towards the glowing neon that proclaimed: Sol Funeral Services Inc. Anton was powdering a corpse when I flew through.

'Chester, where've you been?" he cried after me. 'You're fired!'

'I resign!' I yelled over my shoulder as I pushed through the swing door to the despatch parlour.

Gna began grunting.

There was a coffin in the breach, like a torpedo ready to be fired. I swarmed up the ladder to the control room, pressed buttons and flipped switches in a frenzy, then dived back into the parlour. Anton came through the swing door, then stopped. 'Chester? What the hell!'

'Bye, Anton,' I said, diving aboard the coffin. 'I'll explain everything, in time . . .' I pulled the lid shut and held on as the ram punched the coffin into the chute and the jets caught and fired. The coffin rattled like a toboggan as it shot from the breach. Through the faceplate I could see the Proxmire Satellite moving slowly eastern, and Anton's puzzled face watching me go.

My scalp prickled with the heat of the sun.

Chester? Gna thought-grunted at me.

Hi there, old man, I replied.

What-you-doing?

It's the only way I can stop myself going back to your time, Gna. I have to kill myself. Hincty was going to help me die, but . . .

Huh?

The coffin hurtled towards the sun.

You see, Hincty Little-O'fay is having my baby. She took a . . . *hmm* . . . sperm sample last night, and by now she'll be impregnated –

Chester . . .?

It's quite simple, I explained. The Canterbury Line hired Hincty and arranged it all. They owed it to me. When my baby is born, the technicians of the Line will utilise the same technique they used to bring you forward when I was in flux, and install my persona – my genetic identity – in the baby. I'll have a new life in a new body in my own time. O happy days!

Chester . . .

There was something about his tone . . .

I could feel the casing of the cask begin to heat up. I sweated. Through the faceplate I watched a sunspot flare.

Hincty-Little-O'fay? he asked. *Small-white-hairless-female?* That's her, Gna.

She-followed-you-from-her-place, he told me. *She-wanted-us-do-it-again-to-make-sure*.

And? I asked.

And . . . I-ate-her-Chester.

No!

I hardly had time to register the terrible fact that I was leaving my own time for ever, then I felt myself falling, blanking out. The coffin opened up; the body of Chester

128

Carnegie was ejected head first into the sun, and I slipped into brief oblivion.

Circa One Million BC
  Somewhere in Africa

Of course, I'd rather be growing up in the twenty-first century as Hincty Little-O'fay's child – but even life in the Pleistocene Period is preferable to death. Poor Hincty . . . And poor Gna. He was the one who introduced sun worship to these people, by the way, so there was something ironical in the means of his end. As he mind-pushed bigships from star to star, he developed a reverence for the burning balls of fire that were his destination – and on his return to his own time he conceived a simple form of sun theology.

I am the High Priest of these people . . .

Already I have revolutionised their lifestyle. I've invented fire, the wheel, sartorial decency and crop plantation; next I'm working on their morals. I'm trying to dissuade them from cannibalism and promote good neighbourliness.

But I need help – I can't do it all alone. And besides, the conversation around here is limited. I need someone with whom I can chew the fat over old times.

That's why for the past five years I've been spending all my spare time chiselling these stone tablets with the account of my arrival here. There must be other ex-Enginemen who went APE before the Line discovered how we might be saved. I'm leaving these tablets at various places far and wide on my travels – and what I suggest is that we get together to improve the lot of both our Pithecanthropan friends and ourselves while we're at it.

I belong to the tribe with the grass skirts and the wheel-barrows. We summer by the Great Pachyderm Lake in the shadow of the two peaks. Drop by any time. I'm known as Gna – but if you come in shouting, 'Chester!' you'll find me.

I'm the ugly little brute with the missing big toe and six kids on my heels all day . . .

The Girl Who Died for Art and Lived

I knew Lin Chakra, the famous hologram artist, for two brief days in spring. Our acquaintance changed my life.

I first met her at the party held by my agent to celebrate the exhibition of my crystal, *The Wreck of the John Marston*. The venue was Christianna Santesson's penthouse suite in the safe sector of the city. The event was pure glitter and overkill; big-name critics, artists in other fields, government officials and foreign ambassadors occupied the floor in urbane groups. With *The Wreck* I had, according to those in the know, initiated a new art form. Certainly I had done something that no one else had been able to do before.

The crystal stood angled on a plinth at the far end of the long room, a fused rectangular slab that coruscated like diamond. Earlier, there had been a queue to experience the work of Santesson's latest find. And, when the guests had actually laid hands on the crystal, they were staggered. The critics were pretty impressed, too, and that pleased me. I wanted to communicate my experience of the supernova to as many people as possible, allow them to *live* the last flight of the *John Marston*. Critical acclaim didn't always guarantee popular success, but I was sure that the originality of my art would catch the imagination of the world.

This was the first social gathering I'd attended since the accident, and I was uneasy without Ana.

As the party wore on, I eased my way to the bar and drank a succession of acid shorts. With diminishing clarity

I watched the guests circulate like the polychromatic tesserae of a kaleidoscope, and tried to keep a low profile. This wasn't too difficult. The press-release had been brief and to the point. I was described as the sole survivor of an incredible starship burnout, but Santesson's publicity manager had failed to mention the fact that I had no face. Now there was a clique of artists here from the radioactive sector of the city who had taken over the select towerpiles deserted since the meltdown of '67. These people wore fashion-accessory cancers, externalized and exhibited with the same panache as others might parade pet pythons or parakeets. One woman was nigrescent with total melanosis, another had cultivated multiple tumours of the thyroid like muscatel grapes on the vine. I spotted one artist almost as ugly as myself, his face eaten away by some virulent strain of radioactive herpes. They were known in art circles as the Strontium Nihilists, and tonight I was taken as just another freakish member of their band. The observant guest might have wondered, though, at the steel socket console that followed the contour of my dented cranium, or the remains of the occipital computer that had melted and fused with my collarbone.

From my position at the bar I watched Christianna Santesson as she moved from group to group, playing the perfect host. She was a tall blonde woman in her early seventies with the improved body of a seventeen-year-old and a calculating business brain. Her agency had a virtual monopoly of the world's greatest artists, and when I joined her stable Santesson had never lost an opportunity to press me for the secret of the fusion process. She told me that she had people who could produce mega-art on my fused consoles, but I wasn't selling.

I was on my fifth acid short when a white light like the nova I'd survived blinded my one good eye. I raised an arm and called out. Silhouetted in the halogen glare I made out the hulking forms of vid-men toting shoulder cameras. Then I became aware of action beside me. Christianna Santesson was being interviewed. The front-man fired superlatives at the camera, stereotyping Santesson as the Nordic Goddess of the art world and myself as The Man With A Nova In His Head. He moved on to me, and I was blitzed with inane questions to which I gave equally brainless replies. Things like how I wanted the world to understand, and how I did it all for my dead colleagues.

Then the painful glare moved away, leaving the bar in darkness. The vid-men dashed the length of the lounge, the spotlight bouncing like a crazy ball. It appeared that the far entrance was now the focus of attention. The party-goers turned *en masse* and gawped like expectant kids awaiting the arrival of Santa.

I thumbed the lachrymose tear-duct of my good eye. 'What the hell?' I managed. 'I could have done without that.'

'Daniel,' Santesson said, her Scandinavian intonation loading her words with censure. 'I had to have them in to record the arrival of Lin Chakra.' And she smiled to herself like a satisfied stage-manager.

Seconds later Lin Chakra entered the spotlight, a diminutive figure surrounded by a posse of grotesques. And I experienced a sudden lurch in the pit of my stomach. Chakra hailed from the same subcontinent as a dead girl called Ana Bhandari, and her resemblance to Ana was unbearable. But then every Indian face sent pangs of grief through me.

Chakra lived in the radioactive sector, though she seemed unaffected by cancer, and compared with the hideousness of her hangers-on she emanated a fragile Asian beauty. She wore black tights, a black jacket, and a tricorne pulled low. Her face between the turned-up collar and the prow of her tricorne was an angry, inverted arrowhead as she scowled out at the assembled guests.

She walked across to my crystal, the cameras tracking her progress. I found it hard to believe that this was being piped live into half the homes on the continent.

She stood on the lower step of the plinth and played her hands over the crystal spread. Visually, it was not impressive, an abstract swirl of colour in the pattern of a vortex; interesting, but nothing more. It was to the touch that the crystals gave out their store of meaning, transforming the object from a colourful display into a work of art. Now, Lin Chakra would be experiencing what I had gone through in the engineroom of the *John Marston*.

She took her time, the guests watching her with silent respect, and soaked up the emotions. She lingered over a certain section of the slab, and came back to it again and again to see if the single crystal node still read as true in the light of cross-reference with other emotions. She was being diligent in her appreciation of this newcomer's work.

Then she backed respectfully from the plinth, found Santesson and engaged her in quiet conversation. My agent indicated me with a slight inclination of her head; Lin Chakra's frequent glances my way were like sudden injections of speed.

Then she joined me at the bar. She hoisted herself on to a highstool and crossed her legs at the knees. 'I like your crystal,' she said in a small voice.

Seen closer to, her resemblance to Ana was less marked. Ana had been beautiful, whereas Lin Chakra was almost ugly. She had risen from the oblivion of a low-caste Calcutta slum, and her origins showed. Her lineage consisted of Harijan lepers, char-wallahs and meningital beggars. Physically she was a patchwork of inherited genetic defects, with a misshapen jaw and pocked cheeks, the concave chest and stoop of a tubercular forebear. But like her compatriots of the radioactive sector, she carried her deformities with pride, the latest recipient in a long line of derelict, hand-me-down DNA. And yet . . . and yet she wasn't without a certain undeniable charm, a frail attraction that produced in me a surge of the chivalrous and protective instinct that some people call affection.

When she spoke she looked directly at me, using my misplaced remaining eye as the focus of her attention, and not staring at my shoulder as others were wont to do. My injuries were such that some people found it hard to accept that the slurred, incinerated mass of flesh had once been a face.

Our conversation came to a close. She slipped a single crystal into my hand and climbed from her stool. She mingled with the crowd, then pushed through the shimmer-stream curtain to the balcony.

In my palm the crystal warmed, communicating. The millions of semi-sentient, empathic organisms gave out their record of Lin Chakra's stored emotion message. The alien stones were sold on Earth as curiosities, novel gee-gaws for entertainment and communication. No one before had thought of using the crystals as a means of artistic expression. Once invested in a crystal, an emotion or thought lasted only a matter of minutes, and as artists created for posterity the crystals had been overlooked as a potential medium.

Then, quite by accident, I had come across the method by which to change the nature of the crystals so that they could store emotions or thoughts forever. Hence my sudden popularity . . .

A guest, fancying his chances, parted the curtain and stepped on to the balcony. He returned immediately. 'She's gone.'

I moved unnoticed from the bar and slipped into the adjacent room. Lin Chakra was waiting for me on the balcony. She had leapt across, and now sat on the rail hugging her shins. I paused by the shimmer-stream curtain. 'Hey . . .'

'I have a fabulous sense of balance,' she reassured me.

'I get vertigo just thinking about the drop,' I admitted.

'An ex-Engineman shouldn't be afraid of heights,' she mocked, jumping down and leaning against the rail on her elbows.

Behind me, pressure on the communicating door made it rattle.

She glanced at me.

'I locked it,' I said. 'As you instructed. What do you want?'

'I really meant what I said about your crystal. I like it.'

'It's crude,' I said. 'Honest in what it portrays, but incompetently executed. A kid with six months' practice could do better.'

'You'll improve as you master the form,' she told me.

I would have smiled, but that was impossible.

'A lot of people would give both arms to know how you fuse those crystals,' she said now. 'Do you think you can keep it to yourself forever?'

I shrugged. 'Maybe I can,' I said, and tried not to laugh at my sick secret.

Lin Chakra nodded, considering. 'In that case, would you contemplate selling a crystal console already fused, so that other artists might create something?'

'So that's why you're here tonight. You want a crystal?'

'I came,' she said, 'to see your crystal. But —'

'Forget it,' I snapped. 'I don't sell them.'

'Don't you think that's rather selfish?'

I laughed, though the sound came out as a strangled splutter. 'I like that! I'm the one who discovered the process, after all. Aren't I entitled to be just a little selfish?'

She frowned to herself, turned and stared into the night sky, at the stars spread above the lighted towerpiles. A long silence came between us. 'Which one?' she asked at last.

I stood beside her and found the Pole star, then charted galactic clockwise until I came to the blue-shift glimmer of star Radnor 66. A couple of degrees to the right was Radnor B, where the accident had happened. The star no longer existed, and the light we saw tonight was a lie in time, the ghost of the sun before it went nova. In fifty years it would flare and die, reminding the people of Earth of the time when a small cargo ship from the Canterbury Line was incinerated, with the loss of all aboard but one.

I pointed out the star.

She gazed up in silence, and as I watched her I was reminded again of her frailty. I wanted suddenly to question the wisdom of her living in the radioactive sector. She seemed so fragile that even something as innocuous as influenza might kill her; but that was ridiculous. No one died nowadays from flu, or cancer. The freaks in the penthouse were merely exhibitionists; as soon as their pet cancers showed the first signs of turning nasty they would be excised, their owners given a clean bill of health. And anyway, Lin Chakra seemed cancer free.

Her request interrupted my thoughts. 'Tell me about the accident,' she said.

I stared at her. 'Wasn't the crystal enough?'

'I haven't experienced everything,' she said shrewdly. 'And I want to hear the way you tell it.'

'For any particular reason?'

'Oh . . . let's just say that I want to clarify a point.'

So I gave her the full story.

It had been a regular long haul from star Canopus to Sigma Draconis, carrying supplies for the small colony on Sigma D IV. The *John Marston* had a crew of ten; three Enginemen, two pilots, and five service mechanics, the regular complement for a small boat like ours. After the slowburn out of Canopus we phased into the *nada*-continuum with one of my colleagues in the sensory deprivation pod. We were due for a three-month furlough at the end of the run, and perhaps that was what gave the voyage its air of light-heartedness. We were in good spirits and had no cause for concern – certainly we could not foresee the disaster ahead. When one of the pilots pointed out that we could save five days, and add them to our furlough, if we jumped the flight-path and cut through a sector of space closed to all traffic, we put it to the vote. Five of us voted for the jump, four were against the proposition, and one mechanic abstained.

The prohibited sector was the size of Sol system, with an unstable star at its centre ready to go off like a time bomb. The star had been like this for centuries though, and I thought that the chances of it going nova just as we were passing through were negligible . . . if I thought about it at all. So we changed course and I took the place of the Engineman who had pushed us so far – the only reason I survived the accident. I was jacked-up, laid out and fed into the pod. The last thing I remembered was the sight of the variable sun just outside the viewscreen, burning like a furnace.

I didn't even say goodbye to Ana. But how was I to know?

'When I regained consciousness I found myself in the burns bath of a hospital on Mars. Three months had passed since the supernova.'

Lin frowned. 'But if you didn't actually experience the nova, how were you able to. . .?'

'Hear me out. I'm getting to that.'

The star had blown just as the *John Marston* was lighting out of the danger zone; any closer and the boat would have been cindered. As it turned out, the ship was destroyed with the death of all aboard – or so it was thought at the time. The salvage vessel sent into the area reported that only fragments of wreckage remained, and that one of these fragments was the engine-vault. It was duly hauled in, and the salvage team was amazed – and horrified – to find that I had survived.

If that was the right word to describe the condition I was in. I bore little resemblance to the human being who had entered the pod. Although the engine-vault had saved my life, the flux had kicked back and channelled a blast of nova straight into my head. My occipital computer had overloaded and melted, forcing my skull out of shape and removing flesh and muscle from my face. I suffered ninety-five percent burns and only the null-grav effect of the pod had saved me from sticking to the side like a roasting joint . . . I was lucky to be alive, the medics told me more than once. But in my opinion I was far from lucky; I would have gladly died to be free of the terrible guilt. The one thing for which I was thankful was the fact that I could not recall the accident or the death of Ana and my friends. But I should have known . . .

The dreams began a few weeks later.

My computer had recorded the entire accident, and from time to time what was left of the machine, the still-functioning memory that interfaced with my cortex, bled nightmare visions into my sleeping mind. I saw the star go nova and the ship disintegrate and the crew, my friends for years, die instantly. Ana's brief cry of comprehension as the nova blew would echo in my head forever.

When I'd finished, Lin Chakra gripped the rail and stared down at the ground effect vehicles passing back and forth like luminescent trilobites. 'Your pain doesn't come through on the crystal,' she said at last.

'It isn't supposed to. The *Wreck* is a statement of fact, a documentary if you like, to show the world what happened. I'm working on other crystals to show the agony caused by the tragic decision . . . Why? Is that what interests you? The agony?'

She glanced at me, and gave her head that typically Indian jog from side to side that might have meant either yes or no. I never realized that the gesture of a stranger could be so painful. 'Partly,' she said. 'And partly I'm interested in death.'

I nodded. That was understandable. In a world where death was a rare occurrence, it had become an even more popular subject of artistic enquiry, an even greater source of inspiration.

'The death of my colleagues was almost instantaneous,' I told her. 'Mercifully they didn't feel a thing.'

'Oh, I'm not talking about their deaths,' she said. 'It's yours that interests me . . .'

I was glad then that my face could no longer register expression; she would have seen my shock. I was shocked

138

because my decision to die had been a private one, and I had no idea that I'd allowed it to come through on the crystal. Then I recalled the way she had lingered over a particular node on the console.

'You read it?' I asked her.

'Very slightly. I almost missed it at first, like everyone else. I don't think you meant to show it, but it's there, buried beneath all the other emotions but just about discernible.'

I remained silent. I had spoken to no one about my decision, and the fact that Lin Chakra knew made me uneasy. Then her question came. 'Why?'

I had to think for long minutes before I could begin to explain myself. My decision had been a matter of instinct, a feeling that what I planned to do was somehow right. Now, when I came to explain this need, I feared I was cheating a genuine conviction with a devalued currency of words. 'I want to die because I survived,' I told her. 'I had no right to survive when the others died. I can't get over the guilt . . .'

'I don't understand.' She looked at me, her face serious between the V of her collar. 'Maybe you want to end your life because you can't stand to go on as you are?'

Again my face failed to show the emotion I felt – anger, this time. 'I resent that! That would make my decision to die a petty thing, self-pity masquerading as heroics. And anyway, I needn't remain like this. The best medics could fix me a new face, almost as good as new, remove the computer. I could live a normal life despite the fact that Ana's cry would be in my head even when it was no longer there . . . I'm sorry I've failed to justify my decision to you, but to be honest I don't feel that I have to.'

'There is one way you can do that . . .'

'I don't see —' I began. Then I did.

She took a small box from her tunic and flipped open the lid. Inside, a fresh crystal sparkled in the starlight. 'Take it,' she said. 'Concentrate on why you feel you have to die.'

'I don't see why I should justify my need to you —'

'Or perhaps you're unable to justify it to yourself.'

So I snatched the crystal and gripped it in my fist, hearing again Ana's scream as she passed into oblivion. And again I experienced the gnawing guilt, the aching desire to share her fate. The crystal soaked up the fact that I had had the casting vote on whether or not we should take the short-cut. I had voted for it, and by doing so had sent Ana and my colleagues to their deaths.

Ana had voted against the jump.

When it seemed that I'd wrung moisture from the crystal – my hand dripped with perspiration – I passed it back to Lin Chakra. She held the hexagonal diamond on the flat of her palm, staring at it with large brown eyes.

Without a word she slipped the crystal into her tunic.

'The medics give me another six months if I don't agree to a series of operations,' I said. 'In that time I should be able to finish quite a few crystals. The last one will be an explanation of why I feel I have to die . . .'

We talked of other things until Chakra said she had to go.

'Why not come over to my studio tomorrow evening?' she asked. 'The work I'm doing now might interest you.'

With reluctance I accepted the invitation and we left the balcony. She unlocked the door to the party room, and the glare of the spotlight was on her again. I could hear the front-man yammering questions.

Lin pushed through the crowd. Our first meeting was over.

I arrived back at my slum dwelling at dawn, and from across the studio an empty crystal console beckoned me. I began work immediately, spurred by my conversation with Lin Chakra. By telling her of my intentions I had reminded myself of the short time I had left in which to complete the crystals. In six months I would be dead; until our meeting, that had been almost an abstract notion. The fact was definite now, substantial. I had work to do, for myself and for my dead colleagues, and I had no time to waste.

The first step in the production of a crystal, even before the choice of subject matter, was the preparation of the thousand or so individual gems. I arranged the console on my workbench and set about the fusion process. I had chanced upon the method to do this almost by accident a few months earlier. Like most people, I had kept crystals and toyed with them occasionally. I found that the stronger the emotion infused into a crystal, the longer it remained. Superficial emotions or simple messages were gone in seconds; but love and hate lingered for long minutes . . . Now, from time to time, the remains of the computer that linked with my cortex gave me nightmares, blinding images of the nova chasing the ship. And the sheer terror that these nightmares produced in me . . . I was sure that if I could soak a few crystals with this fire-terror, it would last long enough so that people might gain an appreciable insight into what I had gone through.

So the next time I awoke with the inferno raging inside my head, I was ready. I had jacked the leads into my skull-sockets – the same I had used as an Engineman to achieve the state of flux – wound the wires around my arm and attached the fingerclips. I could have simply held the crystals, but I wanted to gain the maximum effect. When the nightmare began I fumbled for the racked crystals beside my mattress and played a firestorm arpeggio across the faceted surface.

The result was not what I had expected; instead of impressing my terror on the crystals, I had unknowingly fused them into one big diamond slab. Not only that, but when I experimented with these transformed crystals later in the day I found that the emotions I discharged – my love for Ana, as ever – remained locked indelibly into the structure of the gems.

I had worked at the technique of bringing about the nightmare at will, and *The Wreck Of The John Marston* was my first effort. Christianna Santesson had snapped it up and signed me on practically seconds after first experiencing it. According to her, I was made.

141

Now I fused the largest console I'd ever done and began transferring the emotions and images that were in my head. I recreated the atmosphere of the flight before the tragedy, the camaraderie that existed between the crew members. Further on in the crystal I would introduce the accident as a burst of stunning horror. To begin with, I committed to crystal the times I had made weightless love to Ana, relived again the sensation of her sturdy little body entwined with mine in the astro-nacelle. Ana was a Gujarati engineer with a shaven head and bandy legs covered with tropical ulcers the shape of bite marks. We had met when she was assigned to the *John Marston*, and we had been lovers for two years before that last flight.

The sun was going down behind distant towerpiles when I realized that I'd gone as far as I could for this session. I was drained and emotionally exhausted. I had worked all day without thought of food and drink; the task had sustained me. I took an acid short from the cooler, dragged myself across to the foamform mattress and collapsed. I was drifting into sleep, and into certain dreams of Ana, when the call came through.

I crawled to the screen and opened communications. The picture showed a large studio with a figure diminished in the perspective. Lin Chakra stood with her back to the screen and turned when it chimed. 'So there you are. You took so long I thought you must be out.'

'I very rarely go out,' I told her.

'No?' She walked towards the screen and peered through at me, her expression as stern and unsmiling as ever. 'Well how about tonight? Remember what we arranged yesterday? I'd like to show you some work I'm doing.'

I considered. I had enjoyed the novelty of her company yesterday, and talking to her had proved an inspiration. I nodded. 'I'd like that,' I said. She gave me directions and I told her I'd be over in thirty minutes.

I rode the moving boulevard to the end of the line and took a flyer the rest of the way. The pilot dropped me by

142

the plasma barrier that covered the radioactive sector, and I paid him and stepped through the gelatinous membrane.

The difference between this sector and the rest of the city struck me immediately, and impressed itself on every sense. The air was thick and humid and the quality of light almost magical. The sun was setting through the far side of the dome, transmitting prismatic rainbows across the streets and buildings, many of them in a state of ruin softened by the mutated vegetation that had proliferated here since the meltdown. I walked along the avenue towards the intersection where Lin Chakra lived. The roar of the rest of the city was excluded here, but from within the sector a street band could be heard, their music keeping to the hectic tempo of a geiger counter. There was an air of peace and timelessness about the deserted streets, and it seemed to me the perfect place for the artist to reside, amid the equal influences of beauty and destruction.

'Dan . . .!' The cry came from high above. I craned my neck and saw Lin Chakra waving at me from a balcony halfway up a towering obelisk.

I counted the windows and took the upchute to her level.

'In here,' she called from one of the many white-walled rooms that comprised the floor she had entirely to herself. I walked through three spacious rooms, each containing holograms like a gallery, before I found her. She was pouring wine by the balcony. She turned as I entered. 'I'm glad you could make it,' she said.

I murmured something and stood on the balcony and admired the view, to give me something to do while I tried to surmount the pain I felt at meeting her again.

She seemed a different person from the woman of last night, and more like Ana. She wore a short yellow smock, and her thin bare legs were pocked with the tight purple splotches of healed tropical ulcers.

As she invited me to follow her, I realized that she was ill. Her hands shook, and her breath came in ragged, painful spasms.

We moved from room to room, the contents of each charting Lin's development from small beginnings through her apprentice work to her more recent and accomplished holograms. She had two main phases behind her; the dozen pieces she produced from the age of fifteen to eighteen, and a triptych called *Love*, which she brought out from the age of eighteen to twenty. These had deservedly earned her world recognition. She had done nothing for more than a year now, and the critics and public alike were eager for the next phase of her work to be released.

She took me into her workroom overlooking the arching membrane of the outer dome. The contents of the room were scattered; hologram frames and benches in disarray, indicating the artist in the throes of production. Three completed holograms stood against the wall, and others in various stages of completion occupied benches or were piled on the floor.

'These three are finished and okay. The others . . .' She indicated those on the floor with a sweep of her hand. 'I think I'll scrap them and release these three later this year.'

I stared into the three-dimensional glass sculptures. The imprisoned images were grotesque and disturbing, grim forebodings and prophesies of darkness. I was horrified, without really knowing why. 'Dying,' I whispered.

Lin Chakra nodded. 'Of course. The ultimate mystery. What better subject for the artist who has done everything else?'

I moved to the next hologram. This one was more graphic; inside great baubles and bubbles of glass I made out the shrunken image of Lin herself, her small body contorted in angles of pain and suffering. 'You . . .?'

'I contracted leukaemia six months ago,' she said. 'The medics give me another three.'

'But why the hell did you come here?'

'To give myself the opportunity to create art out of death, of course.'

144

'And when you've finished you'll go for a cure . . .' I began.

She averted her gaze, stared at the floor.

'You can't let it kill you, Lin!' I cried. 'You're still young. You have your life ahead of you. All your art —'

'Listen to me, Dan. *I have done everything.* I've been everywhere and experienced everything and put it all into holograms and there is nothing else for me to do.'

'Can't you simply . . .' I shrugged. 'Retire? Quit holograms if you've said all you can?'

She was slowly shaking her head; sadly, it seemed. 'Dan . . . You don't understand. You're no artist, really. Not a true artist. If you were you'd understand that artists live for what they can put into holograms, or on paper or canvas, whatever. When that comes to an end, their lives are finished. How can I go on when I have nothing more to say?' She stared at me. 'Death is the final statement. I want to give the world my death.'

'Does Santesson know about this?' I asked her.

She nodded. 'I told her, of course. She's an artist, Dan. She understands.'

I moved around the studio in a daze. At last I said, 'But these holograms aren't your death, Lin. These are your dying.'

Her eyes brimmed with tears, and she nodded. 'Don't you think I realize that? Why do you think I've scrapped all these?' She flung out her arm at the half-completed holograms. 'They're imperfect, Dan. Impressions of dying, that's all. These three are the closest in dying that I've come to death . . .'

I thought of Ana, who had died when she had most wanted to live. Lin's slow suicide was an affront to her memory, and it was this knowledge that burned in me with anger. 'You can't do it, Lin.'

'You don't understand!'

I'd had my fill of pain and could take no more. I left her standing by the entrance and without a word took the down-chute. The music had stopped and I walked quickly through the empty streets towards the safe sector of the city.

For the next couple of days I remained in my studio, drank acid shorts and stared morosely at the crystal I had started but could not finish. My old need to create art from the tragedy of the *John Marston* was overcome by apathy; it was as if what Lin Chakra was doing had reminded me that nothing, not even art, could ease the agony of my being without Ana.

Lin called repeatedly, perhaps in a bid to explain herself – to make me understand. But I always cut the connection the second her face appeared on the screen.

I considered killing myself before my time was due.

A few days after my meeting with Lin I stood before a crystal I'd completed months before. It failed as a work of art, but as a statement of my pain and my love for Ana it was wholly successful. I ran my hand over the crystals, reliving again the experience of being with her; reliving the horror of her absence.

Next to the crystal I had placed a laser-razor . . .

Christianna Santesson saved my life.

The screen chimed and I ran to it, intending to scream at Lin Chakra that I resented her intrusion. I punched the set into life.

Santesson smiled out at me. 'Daniel . . . How are you?'

'What do you want?' I snapped, venting anger on her.

'Business, Daniel.' She chose to ignore my rudeness. 'Your crystal is showing very well. I'm delighted with the response of the public. I was wondering . . . How would you feel about producing a sequel to exhibit beside it?'

Her commercialism sickened me.

I told her that that was out of the question – that in fact I'd stopped working.

She frowned. 'That's unfortunate, Daniel,' she said; then, with an air of calculation, 'I don't suppose you've considered telling me how you produce your crystals, Daniel? After all, you did promise that you would, one day . . .'

I nodded. 'One day, yes.'

'Then perhaps I could persuade you to sell me one single fused console, instead?' There was a look of animal-like entreaty in her eyes.

I laughed as something occurred to me. 'Very well, I will. But I want a million credits for it.' I'd show her that I could play her at her own game.

To my surprise she smiled. 'That sounds reasonable, Daniel. You have yourself a deal. One million credits. I'll pay it into your account as soon as the crystal is delivered.'

In a daze I said, 'I'll do it right away.'

She smiled goodbye and cut the connection.

Later, I wired myself up and arranged a crystal console, induced a nova-nightmare and channelled the firepower into the alien stones. As always it took immense concentration and energy to sustain the power required to fuse an entire console, and I was exhausted by the time I finished. I sealed the slab in a lead wrap and hired a flyer to take it to Santesson. Then I returned to my studio and sprawled across the foamform. All thoughts of pre-emptive suicide had fled; with the million credits I had visions of offering Lin Chakra the stars – literally buying her passage aboard a starship to give her that which she had yet to experience. I slept . . .

I dreamed of Ana. We were making love in the astro-nacelle, our bodies joined at the pelvis and spinning as the stars streaked around the dome. Ana moaned in Hindi as orgasm took her, eyes turned up to show only an ellipse of pearly white. Our occipital computers were tuned to each other's frequency, and our heads resonated with ever-increasing ecstasy. Around our spinning bodies cast-off sweat hung weightless like miniature suns, each droplet catching the light of the genuine suns outside. Then, with a surreal rearrangement of fact common to dreams, the nova blew while I was still with Ana. She burned in my arms, though I remained strangely uninjured. Her flesh shrivelled and her bones exploded, and through our computer link she screamed her hate at me.

The horror pushed me to a shallower level of sleep, though I didn't awake. I tossed and turned fitfully, and then began to dream a second time. Again I was in the astro-nacelle, and again I was making love – but this time not to Ana. I held Lin Chakra to me, distantly aware of this anomalous transposition, and she stared in wonder at the starlight wrapped like streamers around the dome.

It was dark when I awoke. I had slept for almost twenty-four hours. Through the slanting glass roof of the studio, star Radnor B winked at me. I got up feebly and staggered across to the vid-screen. I called Lin Chakra, but she was either out or not answering; the screen remained blank. I paced around for an hour, going through the contents of my dreams. Then I tried to reach her again, and again there was no response. I decided to go to her place, dressed and left the studio.

I walked through the deserted streets of the radioactive sector and rode the upchute to her suite. I called her name as I passed through the large white rooms, but there was no reply. The words I had rehearsed were a jumble in my head as the time approached for me to use them. I think I realized that she would refuse my offer, point out quite simply that she could have bought the experience of starflight herself, if she had thought it might afford her new insights. In the event I had no need to make the offer. I entered her room.

I found Lin on the floor.

Her naked body lay in a pool of her own blood. Choking, I dropped to my knees beside her. She had taken a laser and lacerated her left wrist almost to the point of amputation. She appeared far more beautiful in death than ever she had in life, and I knew that this was because of the expression on her face. I realized then that during all the time I had known her I had never seen her smile.

148

I cried something incomprehensible, lifted her body into my arms and began to rock, repeating the name, 'Ana . . .' over and over.

A few weeks later I met Christianna Santesson at a party.

I had completed a dozen crystals since the first, and they were showing quite well. My last crystal had been an admission of the guilt I felt at consigning my colleagues to death, an expiation that stood in place of my own death. I hoped that soon I would be able to leave the psychologically crippling subject of the *John Marston* and move on to other things. Perhaps in fifty years I would be able to watch the nova of star Radnor B without the pain of guilt.

I had hired the services of a top medic and he had removed the computer and rebuilt my face. I was still no beauty, but at least people could look at me now without flinching. The scars still showed, physical counterparts of the mental scars that would take much longer to heal.

Christianna Santesson did not recognize me.

As I stood beside her in a group of artists and critics, I could not decide if she was evil or supremely good. My attitude towards her was ambivalent; I passed through phases of wanting to kill her and wanting to thank her for saving my life a second time.

Someone mentioned Lin Chakra.

'Her death was such a tragic loss,' Santesson said. 'But she will live on in her work. Her final trilogy, *Dying*, will be out this summer. I had arranged for her to make a definitive statement on the subject, but the piece was stolen soon after her death. As I was saying —'

I left the party early and returned to my studio.

The crystal lay in the centre of the room, sparkling in the starlight and still covered in blood. Lin had even titled it before she killed herself: *The Death of Lin Chakra*. I knelt before the console and passed a hand across the faceted surface. Agony and pain saturated each crystal, and in total they communicated the awful realization that everything she had ever known was drawing to a close with the inevitable approach of death. Lin had achieved her final artistic goal; she had successfully transferred to crystal her ultimate experience. Soon, as she would have wished, I would give her masterpiece to the world, so that everyone might learn from Lin Chakra's bloody death how fortunate they were to be alive.

The Inheritors of Earth

Wooton Hall, Surrey
30th January, 1884

My Dear Charles – the end is in sight.

Parnell is dead, the Valley People are safe at last, and the constables are at the door and will force entry at noon. Not that this last detail bothers me: by noon I will be far away from here, leaving only mystery and destruction in my wake. The future holds strange and bizarre wonders in store for me; though none so strange, I'll wager, as the many events I have experienced of late.

I am sitting at the desk in the conservatory, hemmed in on every side by the veritable jungle of your dear Mama's tropical plant collection, neglected and rampant these last twelve years since her passing. Before me on the desk lies the journal I have kept for the past month, which will serve as a short account of how I came to find myself on the threshold of this new Golden Age.

I have much to explain; you are likely wondering, Charles, how it came about that your father disappeared so abruptly and successfully from the face of the Earth, and if you read on you will not be disappointed. I well realize that as a father to you I have left much to be desired, and for this I am sorry. As for the ultimate act of desertion: I can but ask you to read my account of the affair, and beg your understanding.

From the Personal Journal of Clarridge Wooton.
21st December, 1883

An extraordinary day by any standards!

My natural impatience urges me to set down forthwith an account of the drama enacted tonight in the *Coach and Horses* – but much happened before this little incident, and to put it in its proper context I must first record the other events of the day.

One month ago I took my correspondence with Tesla, the Croatian, one step further by formally inviting him to come to England and work at Wooton Hall as my research partner. This morning I received his reply, and much to my disappointment it was in the negative. Tesla informed me that he was busy with his own research, and anyway intended in the not too distant future to pack his bags and set sail for the United States of America. He thanked me for my kind offer, and hoped that our correspondence would continue.

This should have been enough to plunge me into a grim mood for the rest of the day – I had set my heart on the idea of a partner in this venture, and Tesla had seemed the ideal man – but, as things turned out, it had the effect of spurring me to greater effort. My experiments went well, and my work progressed further in one day than it had in the whole of the previous week. I have no wish to detail these experiments in this journal, for, such is the competitive nature of my work, if I did make mention of them, and my journals fell into the wrong hands, I should be ruined. Suffice it to say that my quest to develop Alternating Current this afternoon took a step further towards completion.

At around six I was at work in the ballroom when Saddler called my name and rattled the double doors in some agitation. I unlocked the doors and asked him what the deuce was the matter. He told me, whereupon I pulled on my topcoat and hurried after him, out of the Hall and across the snow-covered grounds.

In the final margin of snow, before the dry ground of the woods, lay the remains of the stag that had made its home in the estate for the past three years. It had been skinned, butchered, and its carcass carried off; all that remained was its fine, proud head and magnificent antlers, its chestnut pelt and legs splayed awkwardly across the blood-soaked snow.

I commented to Saddler that it was a damned inefficient poacher who had done this deed. The antlers and pelt would fetch a significant price in the right market, much more than the meat, which was the only part of the animal that had been taken. I had often watched the majestic beast from the window of the ballroom, and I was grieved to see it reduced to such an ignoble end. I instructed Saddler to attend to the disposal of the remains, and returned to the Hall.

After a substantial dinner of jugged hare, I decided to take a turn around the village and call in at the *Coach and Horses*. The night was pitch black when I set out, without moon or stars to light the way, which was appropriate in the circumstances, for, despite the success of my experiments that afternoon, my thoughts had taken a somewhat melancholy turn. The arrival of Tesla's letter and the discovery of the dead stag, though not in themselves incidents of great moment, together combined to overshadow the results of my work. One part of me cursed the other roundly for submitting to such introspection, but to no avail: by the time I reached the tavern and ordered a whisky at the bar, my thoughts were on the past.

The tavern was full; two coach parties, *en route* from Dover to Birmingham, had stopped for the night and had found, in the abundance of fine ale and the proximity of Christmas, an excuse to celebrate. The main bar was full of drunken roisterers; I was in no mood to join in the revelry – I required comfort and quiet in which to contemplate my thoughts – and I was about to take my drink into the back snuggery when the publican caught my attention. 'Wouldn't if I were you, sir,' said he. 'There's a ragamuffin stranger in yonder with his nigger mate. They have the room to 'emselves on account of the stink . . .'

I took his advice and remained at the bar, my whisky and a pile of coins before me. Despite the noise, I followed the maudlin track of my thoughts and considered the passing of Catherine. To state that since her death I have thrown myself into my work with greater vigour and single-mindedness of purpose would be to commit a falsehood – for I have always approached my work with these attributes. However, I do spend more time now with my work, and where before I might have talked over any problem with my wife when disappointments and setbacks came my way, this option is no longer available to me, and I find myself in the distressing condition of both despairing of my work *and* grieving anew at the loss of Catherine.

As I stood to attention at the bar and stared into my drink, a mere three hours ago now as I write, I contemplated Tesla's letter, and then what Catherine might have said to me, on looking up from her embroidery. 'You should not let his refusal worry you, Clarry. There will be other talented men along in time, eager to pool their knowledge with the scientist that history will come to recognise as a genius . . .'

Then, as her ghostly words echoed in my head, my reverie was interrupted by the arrival beside me of a tall figure, who cleared his throat and began: 'Excuse me, sir . . .'

A sudden silence came down on those drinkers grouped around me; I sensed a stirring of interest. Hard on the man's hesitant preamble came the strong, though by no means unpleasant, reek of naphthalene and camphor. I turned and regarded the man from head to toe.

I was immediately taken aback by his appearance. He was perhaps fifty, tall and stooped. His head was balding, though the little hair that he did have was long, grey and unkempt. His face was thin and had about it, despite the stubble and the dark patches around the eyes, a look of intelligence and sensitivity; this last impression was heightened perhaps by a pair of circular gold spectacles that perched upon the point of his nose.

It was not his face, however, that struck me as singular, so much as the mode of his dress. He wore a thick, knitted jersey of the kind seen on sailors, and a ripped frock-coat one size too small. A pair of tight green breeches clothed his lower half, though these barely covered his knees and left exposed a thin length of shank as pale as tallow.

He spoke again. 'You are Clarridge Wooton?' he asked. His tone was educated – I thought I detected a slight Edinburgh accent – and certainly at odds with his appearance. He had the habit of prefacing his statements with a gentle, almost apologetic cough, and hesitantly pushing his spectacles up the incline of his nose.

We now had the undivided attention of half the tavern.

'I am, sir; and to whom do I have the pleasure of speaking?'

He smiled diffidently. 'Parnell, Alexander Parnell, sir.' We shook hands, and his grip was surprisingly strong, despite his appearance of frailty. 'I have read all your published papers in the scientific journals.'

Curiouser and curiouser! The man with the appearance of a ragamuffin first speaks in cultured tones, and then claims to have read my published papers, which to the layman would make little sense at all.

'I admire the work you are doing to broaden the frontiers of scientific understanding, especially as regards electrical Alternating Current . . .'

For a brief moment I was speechless. Quite apart from my astonishment at the content of his statement, its manner of delivery struck me as odd. It was as if he were calculating the effect of every word, as if he were afraid of offending me or losing my attention; there was a hint of desperation in his manner that baffled me – as did his knowledge of the term Alternating Current.

'You cannot have this knowledge merely from reading my papers,' I began.

Parnell cleared his throat hesitantly. '*Ahem* . . . I too am a student of electrical science,' he said. He relocated his

155

spectacles before his eyes with a soiled forefinger. 'I hope you don't think it impertinent of me, but have you thought of . . .' And here he made a suggestion pertaining to the method of my experimentation, which cut to the quick of certain difficulties I have faced of late and suggested an immediate remedy.

By now we had lost our audience of attentive listeners; they had returned to their drinking and merry-making, and while these mindless frivolities whirled around us I stood stock still and stared open-mouthed at my benefactor. Presently I gathered myself and took Parnell by the elbow. 'This is no place to discuss such matters,' I said above the din. 'Perhaps —'

'The snuggery is vacant,' said he. 'We can talk in there.'

I collected my whisky and followed him into the calm of the back room; immediately I was assailed by a noisome stench – not of old clothes and camphor, which was perfume by comparison – but of a body odour of such overwhelming unpleasantness that I almost gagged. Parnell seemed quite unaware of the smell.

He ushered me to a table by the fire and I beheld for the first time Parnell's strange partner.

My first impression (following the smell, of course) was that the creature was not a man, as I had imagined, but a young woman – if such a delicate phrase might be used to describe so unappealing an individual. Parnell took his seat without so much as an introduction, and only when my gaze remained steadfastly on the girl did he consent to mutter a grudging: 'Oh, this is my . . . companion, Arondel.'

She was no nigger, as the publican had said, but of some other far-flung race instead. Her skin colouration was not black but a deep, burnished copper, the like of which I imagined she might have in common with the American Red Indian. It was not her tan, however, or even her odour that held my rapt fascination, but the nature of her physiognomy and her manner.

Her face was broad across the brow and cheeks, her thrusting jaw underhung. This might suggest that she was ugly, though such is not the case. Her face was striking in its difference to any other I had ever seen, though of its kind I thought that it exhibited a certain handsomeness. Her expression was somewhat mournful, this emphasised by a pair of large brown eyes.

Her manner, as she sat on the wall-bench, with her arms spread along its back, intrigued me. She was relaxed with an abandon I have seen in no other. From time to time she scratched herself with such negligence that I knew she could not be civilized as we understand the meaning of the word.

Only now, as I enter this into my journal, am I reminded by her mannerisms of nothing so much as an ape in a menagerie. Her mode of dress seemed to point this up, for she wore a blue-checked frock of such feminine design as to appear absurd on a body so simian.

With difficulty I dragged my gaze away from the girl – she had given my arrival the merest flicker of interest – and regarded Parnell, who was rubbing his hands together with vigour before the roaring fire.

'Have you considered my suggestion?' he asked now.

For the next hour we traded talk of a technical nature, and I became convinced that I had made the acquaintance of a kindred spirit who was, in my narrow sphere of interest, as knowledgeable, if not more so, than I.

To say that he intrigued me would be an understatement. The very nature of his appearance contrasted with the fact that he was well-educated and intelligent. Added to this, he spoke with a marked clipped intonation, in short sentences, as if he had spent a long period abroad and was re-educating himself in the proper use of the mother tongue. And then, of course, there was the singular fact of his choice in female company . . .

Towards the end of the hour, Arondel reached across to Parnell, gripped his upper arm in short, strong fingers and spoke to him in what can only be described as grunts. In return Parnell issued a brief cannonade of similar noises.

'Is she well?' I enquired.

'As ever,' he sighed, 'she is hungry . . .'

'They do a pleasant line in ham and turkey suppers,' I said.

He glanced up at me. 'I have hardly the price of an ale apiece.'

'In that case allow me to buy you your suppers in payment for the conversation you have supplied tonight.'

He made a token protest, though I guessed that he was as hungry as his companion. I left the snuggery and minutes later returned with two laden platters. Parnell attacked the meal with relish, though with the manners that might be expected from a man of learning – by which I mean that he used both knife and fork. Arondel for her part dispensed with such etiquette and picked through the food with her fingers. Those morsels of meat which she found to her liking she popped quickly into her mouth and chomped, while the potato and turnip she left until last, then chewed with reluctance and obvious dislike. She held her tankard in both hands and slurped noisily, spilling a trickle of ale down her chin.

I was about to broach the delicate subject of Parnell's present circumstances, and Arondel's origins, when he happened to look up from his empty plate and glance through into the main bar, which I had seen him do a number of times during our conversation. Now his gaze remained fixed on the crowd in the other room; his eyes widened and he turned pale.

He grabbed Arondel's shoulder and grunted, whereupon the girl let out a shriek and attempted to hide herself beneath the table.

'Parnell?' I exclaimed.

'We must run,' said he. 'The fool has found us again! Arondel!' He stood and pulled the girl to her feet.

'Parnell! Would you mind explaining —?'

'I'll be in touch soon, Wooton, and perhaps next time I shall ask for more than just a meal – we might even come to some arrangement,'and with this cryptic parting shot he took the squealing girl by the hand and opened the rear door of the snuggery. It was a wild night. Snow fell unceasingly and the ground was covered in a deep, luminescent mantle. It was hardly the weather in which to throw out a dog – and yet, I noticed, Arondel was barefoot. Parnell yanked the girl after him, and the last I beheld of the pair was Arondel's skirt dancing about her ankles as they disappeared into the swirling snow.

Less than a minute later a young man appeared in the doorway from the main bar. He was no more than eighteen, well dressed and sporting a large handle-bar moustache. He took a deep breath and made an expression of disgust. 'Evidently they passed this way,' he said in a high-pitched voice.

I warmed myself by the fire and affected disinterest. 'They?' I enquired innocently.

'Parnell and that infernal girl!' he snapped, pacing to the door and throwing it open. He peered into the night, cursed and turned to me with an expression of rage. 'What did Parnell want from you?' he asked. 'I know he was seen talking to you in there.'

'I hardly see why I should answer to the likes of you,' I began.

The young man glanced at the evidence of the empty plates on the table. 'I warn you, sir,' said he, upbraiding me with a pointed finger. 'Parnell and the girl are dangerous. Stay well clear of them if you value your life and sanity!' With this he bounded outside and through the snow, and I swear that it was not my imagination, or the amount of alcohol I had consumed, that witnessed the young man pull from his belt a pistol and brandish it high as he pelted yelling into the darkness.

I remained before the fire for long minutes, my pulse hammering in my ears, then gathered my wits about me and made my way back to the Hall. On the way I kept my eyes peeled for Parnell and the girl – or their bodies. But the night was still and silent and I came upon no evidence of violence as I hurried home. I locked myself in the ballroom, and, before I managed to convince myself that the events of the evening were nothing more than a dream, feverishly set down the many and varied incidents of the day, which account I have now brought to a close.

23rd December, 1883
No sign of Parnell and the girl these past two days.

This afternoon I went into the village and made discreet enquiries concerning the pair. I drew a blank in most cases, but the vicar reported that two disreputable-looking characters answering to their descriptions had sought refuge from a snowstorm in the church two days before, and what is more had enquired as to my address. The vicar had thought it wise to withhold this, though he did mention that some nights I could be found in the main bar of the *Coach and Horses*. (That worthy also invited me to partake of Christmas dinner at the Parsonage this Sunday – a service he performs annually for all the waifs, strays and solitary types in the parish. Needless to say I declined his kind offer, excusing myself on the grounds of pressure of work.)

Speaking of which, I have been busy applying Parnell's theories to my experiments. They show every sign of bearing fruit; but, as ever, I need more materials. I have sent off an order to my supplier in Southampton, and I should receive delivery shortly before the New Year. Without doubt Parnell is a genius, which makes all the more mysterious his ragamuffin appearance, his impecunious condition, and his choice of female company. I am living in hope of another meeting with him soon.

No sign, either, of the young man with the pistol. I recall his warning – that Parnell and the girl are dangerous – with a certain scepticism. Parnell seemed to me the very model of all that is sane and rational, even if Arondel was somewhat unconventional. If I should judge anyone as dangerous, it would be none other than the young man himself.

25th December, 1883

Awoken early this morning by Saddler who rapped on the bedroom door and, upon receiving no reply, opened it and called: 'Mr Wooton . . . sir!' He apologised for waking me so early – but I had visitors. 'A gentleman of reduced circumstances, and a . . . a rather odd-looking creature.'

I hurried downstairs and found the strange couple in the library.

Parnell was doubled up by the hearth, toasting his out-stretched palms before the flames. He was all a-shiver like a man with ague, his complexion a ghastly hue of grey. He had lost a shoe on his travels and his foot, bereft of sock, was blue with cold. A battered grey travelling case stood beside him in a puddle of melting snow.

Arondel, for her part, was curled up in a corner, hugging her shins as if in a futile efort to warm herself.

'Parnell!' I cried. 'What a sight for sore eyes on Christmas morning!'

He looked up and smiled wanly. 'Christmas morning? I'm sorry, had I known I wouldn't have bothered you —'

'Bothered me? I've been anticipating your arrival for days! You are my guest – you look as though you could do with a good meal, a bath and a comfortable bed!'

'But surely, as it's Christmas . . . won't you be enter-taining guests, your family?'

'I do not usually celebrate the occasion,' said I. 'My son, Charles, is spending the holiday with relatives in Brighton.'

At this juncture Arondel, crouched between the window and the bookcase, began a pitiful whimpering, for all the world like some animal in pain.

Parnell glanced from me to the girl. 'She was attacked by a dog last night,' he said. 'It nipped her arm rather badly.'

I told Saddler to bring food, and iodine and bandages, and he returned minutes later with the medicaments on a tray.

I advanced cautiously upon the girl with an outstretched hand, as I might to some injured beast, which, if I was honest with myself, was as much as I considered her to be. The stench that hung about her person was, if anything, stronger now than it was two days ago. She whimpered anew and attempted to worm her way further into the corner, staring at me in fright with those massive, chestnut eyes. 'Tell her that I mean her no harm, man!' I snapped at Parnell. 'Inform her that I can ease the pain.'

From his position by the fire, Parnell grumbled a fluent series of grunts. Arondel glanced from Parnell to me, and her expression softened. She proffered her injured arm. I cleaned the mess as best I could and bound her forearm with a clean bandage. All the while Arondel whimpered to herself, a pitiful mewling sound on the verge of tears. Despite the climate without, she was clad only in a thin cotton frock, and this was ripped and torn in places, revealing immodest areas of her compact and mature body. She wore no undergarments, and this fact, along with Parnell's eclectic fashion in dress, led me to consider the fanciful notion that they had started out naked somewhere and had picked up whatever garments came to hand along the way.

Ten minutes later they were seated upon an old chesterfield, which I had Saddler bring in from the hall and place before the fire, and were eating as heartily as they had the other night.

'The man you were running from,' I said, 'questioned me briefly in the tavern. He claimed that you were dangerous, and when he set off in pursuit he was armed with a pistol.'

Parnell looked up briefly from his plate of lamb with mint sauce. 'Dangerous, us? Do we look dangerous, Wooton? If anyone is dangerous it is young Wells. The man is a maniac —' His teeth chattered with the chill that had taken hold of his slight frame.

'What complaint does he have to hound you so?' I asked.

'One picks up enemies along the way,' Parnell replied. 'Let's just say that he once misunderstood something I confided to an acquaintance of his, and from that day he has seen me as supremely evil.' He fell to eating again and would say no more on the matter.

Arondel sat cross-legged upon the chesterfield, eating the food with her fingers. She gnawed at the meat and threw the stripped bones into the fire, where they sizzled and popped.

I poured myself a whisky, and after a lengthy interval I cleared my throat. 'For a man of obvious learning, Parnell, your circumstances fail to do you justice . . .'

He laughed. 'My circumstances are at rock-bottom, sir. I am penniless, without a formal abode, family or friends . . .'

'Can't you obtain work? The Scientific Institutes are eager for men of your ability —'

'I must admit that I do not seek work, as such. I have tried at various places to find that which I seek —'

'And I am your last resort?' I enquired.

He looked surprised.

'I know that you came to the village to look me up,' I said. I recounted what the vicar told me the other day.

He nodded. 'Since arriving in this . . . this country, I have visited various scientists and men of learning – even, mistakenly, Wells's friend – but none have been able to assist me. Then I came across your papers and learnt that you were a man of independent means . . .'

I stood with my elbow on the mantelshelf and regarded him. 'You mentioned the other day that we might come to some sort of arrangement?'

He smiled. Already, with a good meal inside him and a blazing fire by which to warm himself, he seemed re-animated. He was still soiled and unshaven, but this was nothing that a hot bath would not put to rights.

'Indeed I did,' said he, 'an arrangement which, I think, will benefit us both.'

Although I was curious I insisted that, before we discussed business, I show them to their rooms in the west wing. I was concerned that our conversation should take place when Parnell was more comfortably disposed. I escorted them from the library and through the Hall.

This was the first time I had observed Arondel walk for any significant distance, and I was struck by her utter lack of deportment; it seemed as though this, along with every other hint of sophistication, was absent from her make-up. She padded along silently, her upper half thrust forward and her arms dangling by her sides. The way she regarded the paintings on the walls, the chandeliers and light fittings, the way she *mooned* at these, suggested to me the scant intellection of a cretin.

Since my first meeting with Arondel, I have pored over all the geographical journals in my possession. I have come across numerous photographic plates depicting people of a similar skin-coloration to Arondel, and others of her muscular build, but not one have I discovered with even the slightest facial resemblance to the girl's heavy, out-thrust features. She is even more of a mystery to me than is Parnell.

I showed them to their bed-chambers and adjacent bath-rooms. I filled the tubs, and while Parnell bathed and Arondel dipped a reluctant finger in the steaming water of her bath, I equipped each with a wardrobe of clothes; Parnell with spare items of my own, and the girl with dresses and undergarments which had once belonged to Catherine.

Almost two hours later – it had taken that long for Parnell to scrub himself clean, and for Arondel to wait until the water was almost cold before she chanced to submerge herself – they entered the library. Parnell was a new man: gone was the disreputable vagabond of old, and in his place stood the very personification of a society gentleman in a smoking jacket and cravat. He had removed the stubble from his chin, and, though dark smudges still underlined his eyes, some colour had returned to his cheeks.

As for Arondel . . . would nothing transform the girl from the savage she so manifestly was, into a personable member of society? My wife's gown served only to emphasize the creature's gauche manner, her stumping gait and coarse features. I had supplied stockings and house-slippers, but she had foregone these, and her broad, bare feet were an incongruous sight indeed beneath the delicate lace hem at her ankles. In one detail only was Arondel changed: no longer did she smell.

I poured our drinks – water for the girl – and we sat by the fire and exchanged polite conversation for a while. I do not pride myself on an encyclopaedic knowledge of current events, but it is phenomenal when compared to Parnell's ignorance. I can only guess that his sojourn abroad was to some remoter than remote region where news was hard to come by.

At length, he coughed diffidently into his fist, pushed his spectacles to the bridge of his nose and drew from an inside pocket several sheets of note-paper.

He passed them across to me. 'I dare say you might find these of interest.' I noticed, as I took the sheaf from him, that his hand trembled.

At first I gave each page a cursory glance, and then, some inkling of the import of these jottings dawning on me, I began again at the first page and fell to reading them in earnest.

Parnell gestured. 'Forgive me if they are a little difficult to read in places – I had to make them on the run, as it were.'

I shook my head in wonderment. What I had before me, in these symbols, diagrams and explanations, would revolutionize the project I was working on.

'But this is incredible,' said I. 'Of course, I cannot accept . . . Why, man, the knowledge contained herein would put you ahead of the field – no one else would be in the race.' I thrust the sheaf back at him, but not without a certain regret. 'Take them. Do your own experiments —'

Parnell shook his head, his diffident smile widening. 'I assure you, I have no need of the knowledge these notes contain, or the results of any experiments arising from them.'

I glanced down at the symbols scattered across the pages, and then back to Parnell. His smile seemed frozen on his thin visage, as if terrified that I might refuse his offer. I recalled his attitude of barely suppressed desperation at our first meeting.

'You mentioned an arrangement of some kind,' I said. I waved the papers. 'But how can money pay for this – if it *is* money you require in return?'

He made a sour grimace. 'Not as such, my friend —'

'Then what else . . .?'

'To begin with I would like the assurance of board and lodging for Arondel and myself.'

'Granted, of course. You can remain here for as long as you wish.'

'That should be no more than a few weeks. I can envisage my experiments lasting no longer —'

'Experiments?'

He waved this aside. 'Also, I would need a suitable area in which to conduct my work.'

'The conservatory is free,' I said. 'I used it for a time, before the size of my generators necessitated the move into the ballroom.'

'And then there is the small matter of the materials.' He rooted once more in an inside pocket and produced a single piece of paper, which quivered as he passed it to me.

I read the list aloud. Many of the items were of an electrical nature which I have already in stock; others were common enough and could be obtained through my regular supplier at no great cost. Still other items were neither common nor cheap. 'A twenty-four-carat diamond?' I enquired.

'Absolutely necessary – essential – to my work. Without it I could not even begin to – to . . .' and he stuttered into silence.

I nodded, and calculated the expense of these materials. They would add up to quite a tidy sum, but the information I was receiving in return was worth, in my estimation, many times the total of the final bill I would be required to foot.

'Can you obtain everything listed?' Parnell asked. 'I was not sure as to whether . . .?'

'There should be no problem, my friend, though it might be a good few days before they can be delivered.'

'Then – then you will . . .? I appreciate the great expense involved, but the eventual benefits you will gain from my calculations, if put into practice —'

'I think this calls for a toast,' I interrupted, refilling our glasses.

He stood, and there were tears in his eyes. 'This is quite the finest Christmas present I have ever received,' he declared.

I laughed and waved the papers. 'The same is true for me, also. To our mutual success,' I announced. 'And merry Christmas!'

'To our success!' Parnell echoed.

For the rest of the day we drank and discussed the work I was doing; Parnell's knowledge, as evidenced by the notes he had made, was years in advance of present theory. I tried to guide the conversation to the subject of his past, but Parnell was adept at evading such enquiries that might involve holding forth on his own achievements. I even asked him bluntly what line of research was his speciality, but he said that one condition of his success was absolute secrecy. 'I spoke too freely of my work on one occasion in the past,' he said, 'and now Wells haunts me the length and breadth of the country.'

So absorbed was I in our conversation that I was hardly aware of the fall of darkness and the approach of midnight. By this time Arondel had moved from us and was seated cross-legged upon the window-seat, staring out into the night.

Parnell spoke to the girl in her language of grunts. She turned from the window, and for the first time I witnessed her smile; her lips parted to reveal astonishingly white teeth. This expression of happiness so transformed her rather obtuse and dour visage that I almost brought myself to believe that she was not the ignorant savage I assumed her to be. She fired a rapid series of glottal barks at Parnell, who laughed.

He turned to me. 'I have told her that we will be staying here for a while, that we are safe from Wells and that, thanks to you, I can begin my work. She is pleased by this. She wishes me to give you her personal thanks.'

At this, it was my turn to laugh. 'You make her sound almost civilized,' I commented.

'Oh, but she is civilized, Wooton – in her own way. Don't be misled by the sound of her language or her absence of the manners we think of as important. It is wrong to assume that because certain peoples cannot communicate with us, and because their ways are strange to us, then they are our intellectual inferiors. This is not so.' While Parnell was lubricated by the wine and thus inclined to talk, I determined to find out more about the girl.

'Tell me, Parnell, how old is Arondel?'

'By her method of reckoning,' he said, 'she is fifteen winters old. But you must understand that where she comes from the winters are longer than ours.'

I was pondering this mysterious reply, and was about to enquire as to exactly where she came from, when Parnell yawned and regarded the carriage-clock on the mantelshelf. 'It's late,' he said, 'and I have had a long day. Thank you for your hospitality.' He stood and bowed formally from the waist. He grunted at Arondel, who responded without turning from the window.

'She says she is not tired.' Parnell smiled, thanked me once again and took his leave.

For long minutes then I regarded the strange girl. She seemed quite unaware of me; she was contemplating the full moon with a wistful expression, and it occurred to me quite suddenly that it was likely the only object in our environment – this opalescent satellite – that was common to her own far-flung place of birth, wherever that might be.

Before I withdrew from the room, I said: 'Good night' softly to her, and to my surprise she turned and smiled at me, before resuming her contemplation of the moon.

Hours have elapsed since I began this entry, and as I sit here in my workroom, surrounded by the stilled contraptions of my own invention, my head is a-buzz with questions. Many concern the girl Arondel, and Parnell, and the reason Wells might want to do them harm . . . But my main and most immediate query is simple. As Parnell has furnished me with blueprints which, when put into practice, will bring the wonder of electrification to all the isles – then what possible invention of importance can he himself be planning to work upon?

7th January, 1884
Since Boxing Day I have been working like a man possessed, with little time to spare for Parnell and the girl. My research is going well, and already Parnell's notes have yielded results. My study was interrupted, however, when his supplies arrived on the third day of this month. We spent the morning supervising the workmen in the unloading of the various crates and trunks, and the positioning of them in the conservatory. That same morning the diamond merchant arrived from London and delivered the stone in person. I hurried forthwith to Parnell and presented him with the diamond. He held it on the palm of his hand before his long nose, the faceted gem catching the winter sunlight that slanted through the glass roof. Around him stood a dozen crates and cases, some unpacked and others as yet unopened; the potting table was strewn with sheets of paper like an autumn fall of leaves. I enquired as to whether he needed any help unpacking and setting up the equipment, but he assured me that he had everything in hand, and when I left the conservatory he locked the door behind me.

We have slipped into a regular working routine. We rise early, though not together, and partake of a cooked breakfast alone in the dining room. I consume a substantial meal at this point so as not to be bothered with lunch at mid-day; breakfast usually sees me through until seven, at which time, weary after so much physical labour and mental effort, I retire to my room, take a bath, and arrive downstairs for dinner at eight.

This is the only occasion of the day which we spend in each other's company, if one excludes the evenings when we sometimes take a drink in the library. After a full day of work we have hearty appetites, and it is usually not until the port that we begin to discuss our work in earnest: or should I say that *I* begin to discuss *my* work? Parnell rarely vouchsafes anything appertaining to his own experiments, and then only to confirm that all is going well, or that he was visited by a problem earlier which he has now overcome. At any rate, the time is filled with the various questions and doubts that I place before my benefactor, which he answers promptly with good humour and great expertise.

As for Arondel, she consumes her meals in silence – that is, without conversing with Parnell; though it is true that she accompanies her eating and drinking with much sloshing and gurgling. She seems sullen of late, though perhaps I do not know her well enough to comment on her day to day demeanour, as all her moods are strange and alien to me. In general, I have noticed that Parnell and the girl hardly trade words, and to sit through their silence during a meal one is forced to speculate anew as to the precise nature of their relationship.

Although the girl does not smell to the degree that she did at our first meeting, she has yet to take a second bath, or to change from my wife's gown that I presented to her almost a fortnight ago. On more than one occasion at the table, busy with my food and tired after much work, I have caught a peripheral glimpse of Catherine's dress and given myself quite a turn, only to look up with shock and sadness at the blunt and primitive features of Arondel.

One more point before I turn in: the girl has no use for a bed. She seems to sleep wherever she finds herself when tired. Often I have come down in the morning to find her curled and snoring on the cold marble floor of the hall, or in the library or dining room. Indeed she spends much of the day asleep, for all the world like some nocturnal animal.

10th January, 1884

Last night I lay awake for hours, staring out at the stars through the open curtains and wondering if there might be a time, in the not too distant future, when the night-time land of the British Isles would be illuminated like a reflection of the starlit heavens.

I was still unable to sleep a while later when I heard the unmistakable sound of bare feet on the parquet floor outside my door. I sat up in bed and listened; the footsteps moved along the corridor towards the staircase. On impulse – and I am unable to state even now if that impulse was genuine curiosity, or fear that Arondel might be up to mischief – I slipped from bed and pulled on my dressing-gown. I opened the bedroom door and peered down the length of the corridor; Arondel's tousled mop of hair was disappearing down the stairs. I followed on tiptoe. By the time I reached the top of the stairs, the girl was at the bottom and trying the door, though invisible in the shadow of the hallway. Finding it locked, she padded towards the library; all I saw of her, as her dark form passed the foot of the stairs, was the glint of something silver in her grasp. I moved down the stairs to the library and peered inside; she had succeeded in opening the window – I recalled that she had watched me perform the operation the other night – and now she climbed out. I followed.

Only then, as I stood before the Hall and beheld the girl in the silver glow of the gibbous moon, did I realize that Arondel was naked.

I considered leaving her to her sport and returning at once to my room, as was only proper; and I might have done just that had the young girl in question been any other than Arondel. Yet there was something so natural in what she

171

was doing, as she skipped through the moon-silvered night, so elemental and shameless that to observe her could in no way be considered wrong.

Garbed in pyjamas and dressing gown, I was still chilled to the bone; yet Arondel as naked as she was seemed unaffected. She moved with a grace I would never have expected, and as I watched her caper and gambol around the snow-covered grounds I realised that this was the first time I had seen her in the context of a natural setting. Of course, in the sophisticated environment of the Hall, and the familiar precincts of the Coach and Horses, she would appear as a coarse savage; yet here, at liberty where she belonged beneath the stars, the fact that she was in her element made her seem almost beautiful.

Then she stopped and held a pose as still as the statue behind which I crouched, and for a second I assumed she had seen me; then I noticed, at the far end of the lawn, a deer come stepping from the woods. My gaze returned to Arondel, and already she had moved quickly to position herself upwind of the beast. She crouched and advanced on the deer from behind, the flash of silver no longer in her hand but gripped between her teeth. I wanted to show myself and shout out so that the animal might escape, yet at the same time I was hypnotized by Arondel's movements, fascinated by the simple economy of action that would lead to the inevitable death of the deer.

It was over in a matter of seconds. Almost before Arondel was upon it, the deer started and fled – but too late. She leapt and landed astride its back and reached forward, gripped its head in both hands and twisted with one vicious, neck-breaking wrench. The animal hit the ground with a grunt of expelled air, and Arondel lost no time in stripping the hide from the carcass. She left the head and the hide where they lay on the lawn and dragged the meat into the wood.

I crouched behind the statue as she emerged from the trees and paced towards the Hall with the long, arm-swinging strides of a huntress. A matter of feet from me she squatted on the steps and answered the call of nature with all the grace and unconcern of a beast of the field, and in the stark light of the moon I saw that her brown, muscular body was streaked and glistening with blood. She rose and walked up the steps and slipped through the library window, and I found myself in a state of great agitation, to my shame then and embarrassment now as I record the episode in my journal.

This evening, as we sat around the dining table, Arondel was once again an awkward savage-girl, picking through her food and finding nothing to her satisfaction. I decided that she must have gone into the woods earlier and eaten her fill of the meat she had hunted in the early hours.

Later, we repaired to the library and sampled the brandy. Arondel left us, sat upon the window-seat and stared out into the darkness. Parnell had maintained an abstracted silence during dinner, as if contemplating some intricate problem concerning his work.

For some time I had been contemplating the mysterious character Parnell refered to as Wells; now I decided to broach the matter with him.

I cleared my throat. 'This fellow Wells,' I said. 'Just who the devil is he, anyway?'

Parnell stared into the fire and considered my question. 'Wells will be a famous writer one day,' he said. He looked up and corrected himself. 'That is, he *is* a famous writer.'

I thought nothing of this at the time – instead despaired at Parnell's economy in conversation – but now that I come to contemplate the matter, with the hour on midnight and the Hall quiet around me, I am reminded of another exchange ten days ago, as we waited, the worse for wine, to see in the New Year. I had happened to mention Nikola Tesla, and Parnell had murmured something to the effect that the man was a genius never recognized in his lifetime. 'A Van Gogh,' were his exact words, 'of scientific research.'

Which strikes me as exceedingly strange, for the fact of the matter is that Tesla is not yet thirty, and is at the start of his scientific career.

11th January, 1884

Before dinner this evening I was approached by a deputation from the staff, headed by Saddler. They were diffident,
and it was some minutes before I could elicit the reason for
their presence. Saddler proceeded to mutter that several of
the servants had been shocked by the state of dress of the
young lady I was presently entertaining as a house-guest.
She had been seen on a number of occasions running naked,
in full daylight, around the kitchen garden. They would not
normally have bothered me, but just the other day Cook had
taken quite a turn . . .

I told them that I would deal with the matter forthwith.
I proceeded to the conservatory, where I guessed I might
find Arondel, and paused before the door; it was ajar, and
beyond it I caught sight of Parnell and the girl, engaged in
a loud altercation of grunts and cries. Such was the spectacle
of the confrontation that it wholly absorbed my attention.

Arondel was in a state of semi-undress; the bodice of
her gown was ripped down the front, revealing her chest.
I did my utmost not to stare, though the sight of the girl
so disrobed caused me no small degree of discomfort. She
had Parnell backed up against a bench, and as I watched she
grasped his hand and pressed it to her breast, whereupon
she grunted again and cried out in encouragement. As for
Parnell, he snatched his hand away and turned his back on
the girl; he stanchioned his arms on the bench and, head
bowed, spoke in deliberate tones, though what he said was
lost to me. His words had the effect of wrenching from
Arondel a pitiful cry; her bosom was heaving, and her eyes
smouldered. Tearful at being thus spurned, she fled sobbing
towards the door, and I was forced to beat a hasty retreat, my
pulse loud in my ears.

Arondel was absent at dinner this evening; Parnell was
silent and distracted, and I thought it best not to enquire as
to the whereabouts of the girl.

12th January, 1884

This morning, on my way to the ballroom, I happened to notice Arondel seated by herself in the herb garden. All that was visible above the lavender was her head, as she chewed a shoot of grass and stared vacantly into space. Recalling the complaints of yesterday, I stepped outside, intending to rebuke the girl for her breach of manners. Only when I was almost upon her did I notice that she had divested herself of her gown. I halted in my tracks and stared. Instead of taking fright and endeavouring to cover herself, she smiled up at me in such a way as to make quite obvious her thoughts. Only then did I notice the tears on her cheeks, and, torn between comforting her and chastising her for such indecency, I turned and ran to the ballroom, where I locked the door securely behind me.

My dear Catherine! Forgive me the thoughts I entertain now . . .

13th January, 1884

Truly I am going mad!

Until this day I considered myself the sanest of individuals, a rationalist and a man of science! My head ruled my heart, and my intellect was in full possession of the facts of the universe so far discovered. But no longer! In a few short hours all this has been turned upside-down. My intellect is assailed by notions at once bizarre and threatening, my heart won by the unlikeliest of partners. I am a man besotted! I look at the date at the head of this page and, such is my mental torment, give credence to the ridiculous assumption that the events of today – a Friday – have been managed by the wicked hand of fate . . . or the Devil!

But where to begin? It seems appropriate that my earliest recollection is that of the explosion.

At noon I was busy at work in the ballroom. About me, generators hummed and moaned like souls in torment; at the far end of the room great arcs of electricity leapt from point to point and cast eerie illumination like amethyst lightning.

I was at my desk, and beginning to write up the morning's experiment, when a thunderous detonation shook the very foundations of the Hall. 'Parnell!' I cried, leaping to my feet.

I hurried through the Hall to the conservatory, where I hammered upon the door and called out Parnell's name repeatedly. My initial emotion was one of anger that he had more than likely destroyed expensive scientific apparatus, as well as the conservatory; then, as my efforts elicited no response from within, I worried that Parnell had destroyed himself into the bargain. I paused to listen, but heard only silence from behind the door. I began pounding and crying out again, and this time received a reply.

'Wooton! Cease your jabbering, man. All is well!' Whereupon he opened the door and stared at me.

'Parnell – what on Earth . . .?'

Although he had opened the door, he had wedged himself in the opening so as to disallow my entry and inhibit my view. 'Parnell?'

'I have everything under control, my friend —'

'Do you intend to let me in and assess the extent of the damage?' I enquired.

'There has been no damage,' he assured me. 'The report you heard was the natural result of opening the interface.'

'The interface? Are you going to explain exactly what it is you're working on? After all, I feel it only right —'

'We have an arrangement, Wooton. One of my requirements is secrecy, the need to work unhindered —'

'I am hardly hindering you!' I cried.

I peered over his shoulder into the conservatory, but all I could make out were a few shattered panes of glass – contrary to his claims that there had been no damage – and the litter of his scribblings on the floor.

'For the last time, will you allow me in – or at least tell me what it is that you are working on?'

'I'm afraid that's impossible, Wooton.' And before I had time to reply he closed the door and locked it in my face.

I walked back through the Hall in a quandary. It crossed my mind that Parnell was working on something akin to, but far in advance of, my own inventions. That would explain his reluctance to let me into the conservatory, and his marked reticence. The more I considered this, the more it seemed the only explanation. He had fobbed me off with designs and experiments which he knew to be outmoded beside his own; and behind my back, using materials I had purchased for him, he was attempting to beat me at my very own game.

As my experiments were over for the day, and all that I had to do was to write them up, I decided – oh, what a fateful decision! – to retire to my room, take a bath, and there further contemplate my suspicions.

As I strode along the corridor to my bed-chamber, I happened to notice that the door to Parnell's room was ajar. On impulse I glanced inside, and noticed, on the bed, the old grey case he had brought with him on Christmas day.

I paused, and something alien to my nature took hold of me then. Whether it was due to my new suspicions concerning Parnell, or something else, I cannot say. I entered the room and stepped lightly towards the bed. The case was closed, but not locked. I opened it, peered inside and beheld an old scarf, a pack of playing cards, a crust of bread and something that looked like a small pocket diary. This last I took out and stared at the date embossed in gold on the cover, and then I opened it and read a few lines, and stared once again at the cover. Then, at a sound from the adjoining room, I dropped the diary back into the bag and managed to convince myself that what I had seen was a trick of my eyes.

From the other room came the sound of a grunt, and I made out: 'Par-nuh?' – Arondel's approximation of Parnell's name.

Before I could make my retreat, she appeared at the communicating door; in one hand she held a gobbet of raw meat, and her chin was streaked with rivulets of blood. All I could do was stare at her as she stood in the doorway, stare blatantly like a man enchanted or terrified, for Arondel was naked.

When she noticed the direction of my gaze she tossed aside the meat, then pressed bloody fingers to herself and called out an urgent, appealing grunt.

Perhaps fearing that I might flee as I had the day before, Arondel attacked me and wrestled me to the floor, and only through main strength was I able to overcome her and pinion her arms beneath my knees. I pressed a forefinger to her lips, and held out a calming hand as I climbed from her. She watched me with massive, staring eyes. Passive, like a child, she did not resist as I picked her up and carried her to the bed. I pulled off my necktie, my shirt, my trousers, kicked off my shoes . . . and, at last, naked, I paused before falling on her like a demon. Again Arondel attacked me, and the noises she made belonged more to the jungle than to the bed-chamber.

Later, as we lay exhausted on the bed, I reviewed what had come to pass, and why what had happened seemed to me so perfectly natural, while with Catherine those many years ago such acts had seemed unnatural, hardly sanitary. The reason, no doubt, lay in my partner this time. Arondel felt no guilt; she had performed a perfectly natural function with the same abandon as when the other night she had danced naked beneath the stars and killed the deer . . .

Only when I dressed and slipped from the room did the first wave of guilt and regret sweep over me like nausea. My desire satisfied, I began to see our union, in the cold light of rational perspective, for what it was. Arondel was little more than an animal, a brute savage, who had inveigled me into the act to sate her own desires. Then I was assailed again by another wave of guilt, for I knew that I was attracted to the girl despite myself, and that it would not be long before I desired again to acquaint myself with the pleasures of her body.

Later still I was overcome with sickness as I considered what Parnell might say when I informed him – which I felt

178

it only right to do – what had passed between Arondel and myself.

For long minutes I paced up and down outside the conservatory, working myself into a sweat, before I squared my shoulders and knocked upon the door. Parnell whipped it open almost immediately. 'Wooton, I thought we'd had this out once already?'

I stood before him like a stuttering fool, wringing my hands in agitation. The words I had rehearsed to explain myself would not come.

At last I managed: 'Parnell – I must see you.'

His eyes narrowed. 'Are you well?'

'Hardly!' I took confidence from his enquiry and pushed past him, much his annoyance. I paced to the centre of the floor, surrounded by fronds of tropical vegetation and humming machinery, to which, I must confess, I paid little attention, such was my confusion.

'Parnell, I have a terrible confession to make!'

He decided to make light of my presence. He picked up a screwdriver and busied himself with some gadget upon the potting-table, affecting disinterest. 'A confession?'

'I entered your room . . .'

He shrugged. 'But the Hall *does* belong to you, Wooton,' he said with heavy sarcasm. 'Walk in wherever you please!'

'You fail to understand. You see, on the way to my own room, I happened to notice that the door of your bedroom was open. I saw your case upon the bed, and something came over me. I went inside – you must understand that I was not myself at the time. I opened your bag and inspected its contents . . .'

Parnell peered into his machine and frowned.

'There's more. As I was doing this, Arondel came in from her room. She was . . . she had not a stitch of clothing about her person. The sight of her so divested caused me no little agitation. We . . . that is, I —' I broke off and gestured wildly. 'I hardly know how to explain this —'

Parnell looked up. 'You slept with her?'

179

'I slept? *Slept?* What I did can hardly be considered sleeping!'

Parnell smiled to himself. 'Rather, you *made love* to her . . .?'

I shrugged abjectly. 'Such it might be termed in Gothic Romances,' said I, 'though there was little love in our coupling. Parnell, I hardly know what possessed me!'

Parnell's attitude seemed to soften; he smiled sympathetically. 'I should think that Arondel possessed you, Wooton. She has the sexual proclivities of a mink.' He returned to his contraption and grimaced as he attempted some troublesome procedure with the screwdriver.

I gestured. 'Well . . . ? Is that all you have to say —'

'What more is there to say?'

'I should have thought that your initial reaction would be one of anger, seeing as I —'

'Anger?' He wore a mystified expression.

'I have little notion as to the relationship between Arondel and yourself, but you can hardly be pleased that I . . . I —'

'My dear Wooton,' Parnell said, straightening and holding the small of his back, 'there is nothing between Arondel and myself. We found ourselves in each others' company purely by chance, by accident if you like. You have my blessings, take the girl if you wish. Personally, after the first time, I found her body odour something of a disincentive.'

'You mean to say that . . . that you two have . . .'

'It would be difficult to resist her advances for a whole year,' he replied, 'which is how long we have been together.'

I strode to the end of the room, my head in a spin. I think I secretly wished that Parnell had rebuked me for taking advantage of the girl – or at least poured scorn on my choice of bed-fellow; who knows, such a response might have dampened the fire of passion within me!

Only then, my thoughts still in a whirl, did I notice that which had so occupied Parnell over the past week and more – and I recalled the diary I had discovered in his case.

At the far end of the conservatory stood an intricate

arrangement of brass rods in the configuration of an elong-
ated hexagon, not unlike the outline of an upright coffin;
this was situated on a plinth, and next to it was a series of tall
levers, some dozen in total, which brought to mind nothing
so much as the levers in a railway signals box.

I cleared my throat hesitantly. 'This is quite a spectacular
mechanism,' said I. Parnell, as I had expected, ignored
me.

I continued, hardly able to believe the implications of my
question: 'It is, I take it, a similar device to that which
brought you here?'

'I beg your . . .?' He looked dumbfounded.

'I found the diary in your bag,' I confessed.

He stared at me, his expression neutral. He seemed to
be calculating just how much he should tell me, now that
I knew his secret.

'The principle is similar,' he muttered in reply. 'But the
application quite different.'

'This defies everything I have ever conceived on the
notion of time,' I said. So many questions crowded my mind
that it was almost a minute before I could bring myself to
articulate: 'But why here? Why did you come to my time?'

He looked at me, weighing the screwdriver in his palm.
'Part of our arrangement, Wooton, was that I should have
my privacy. You have already ridden roughshod over that
agreement – why should I tell you any more than you already
know?'

'For that breach of trust, please forgive me. I admit I
was in the wrong, and apologize. But I implore you to
tell me more. Your secret shall go no further than this
room.'

He threw down his screwdriver, strode over to the
machine and stared at the hexagon of brass rods, his arms
folded in contemplation. At last he turned to me and said:
'Do I have your word of honour that you will repeat none of
this?'

'My word of honour as a gentleman!' I exclaimed.

Parnell nodded. 'Very well, Wooton, since you know so much already, I cannot see the harm in telling you more. To answer your first question: I no more intended to land myself in this benighted age than I intended to fly to the moon. It was an accident that stranded me here – though it might have been worse. Even my knowledge of temporal principles would have been next to useless had I found myself in, say, the sixteenth century. But I am beginning at the wrong end of my story. Take a seat, though I do not intend to be long with this explanation; I have much work to complete over the next few hours . . .'

I drew up a straight-backed chair and settled myself to hear his discourse, which I set down here as best my memory will allow.

'In 1995 I was – or will be? – the senior research partner of a team set up at Cambridge to look into the possibility of Temporal Transportation – time travel, if you like. Five years later, on the eve of the millennium, we had developed the first working model of the time machine: one year later we were ready to send a living subject through time. We wanted to look into the feasibility of a project funded by a group of anthropological archaeologists – we were to send the first time traveller back thirty-five thousand years. In the grand old tradition of scientific research, we drew straws to see who would be the first traveller in time; and I lost. The machine, unlike this example, was a mobile carriage. One May morning in the year 2001, I climbed aboard the carriage and began my journey back to the prehistoric age – the precise reason for this undertaking need not concern us here. I survived the journey intact, and upon my arrival stepped forth and began my exploration. The land was shrouded in a dawn mist, the ground underfoot hard with frost. The island of Britain at that time was in the grip of a winter more terrible than anything we have experienced. I was outfitted accordingly and well equipped with supplies to last me weeks, though we had decided for the sake of safety to limit my stay to just twelve hours.

In the event I remained in that frozen age barely one hour.

'My first task was to locate the inhabitants of this time, and in this it could be said that I attained only partial success – for the inhabitants of this time located me. I was skirting the fringe of a coppice when a short figure clad in skins burst through the cover before me and yelped. The native sprinted away across the open ground, and through the foliage of the coppice I made out the belligerent forms of savages, armed with stone axes and clubs, in hot pursuit. It was obvious that if I wished to survive their attentions, then I too should take to my heels. This I did, following the small figure, which I now made out to be that of a girl. She made for the only other cover in the vicinity, the spinney in which I had concealed the time machine. Before she dived into the cover of the trees, though, she fell victim to a boulder which hit her on the head and laid her unconscious. She was within a matter of feet from the time machine. To this day I don't know exactly what moved me to save her – the small tragedies of life and death in this age were of no concern to me – but some human impulse drove me to drag the girl aboard the carriage, jump into the saddle and move us forward a matter of days. That was the plan, at any rate. Instead, I found myself the target of a barrage of stones. Many hit the machine itself, wreaking havoc on the delicate instrument panel; others found their intended target – myself. Fortunately I did not succumb to this onslaught – I pushed the levers forward, only to find that I had no control over the vehicle! For brief seconds I found myself flying through the neutral grey medium of elapsing time, the nausea that this promotes filling my throat with bile, before we fetched up in some unknown era. There was an explosion, the carriage turned and threw us from our seats. I must have lain on the ground in a daze for some time, before I brought myself to wonder exactly *when* we were. Only when I picked myself up, staggered to a nearby road and beheld a passing brougham did I realize that we had crash-landed in the Victorian era. I returned to the carriage and the girl. The time machine was a mess of tangled wreckage, its forward section fused into the very molecular substance of a chalk cliff face. My supplies had been lost in time, and my only possessions were the clothes on my back – which would serve to draw attention to me in this age. Also, I now found myself the guardian of a strange prehistoric girl; she came to her senses by degrees and from the outset regarded me as her saviour.

'That was almost a year ago, Wooton. I managed to find us clothing and work – otherwise it would have been the poorhouse for us. Between odd jobs, I made the round of all the famous scientists of the day, in a bid to gain a sponsor. But to no avail – until now, that is. Thanks to you, Wooton, I am saved.'

I was speechless for a time. 'Truly an incredible story,' I managed at last. 'And this,' I gestured at the contraption at the end of the room, 'this is the portal through which you will return to your own age?'

'An improvement on the carriage,' he laughed. 'There is very little danger that it will crash. In three or four days I will be home . . .'

The hour is late. I am tired and confused – I have had a long and exacting day – though having set down the incidents herein I feel a little more composed than when I began. One thing still troubles me, though. Before I left Parnell, I enquired of him: 'If you are from the future – and I don't doubt for one minute that you are – then . . . how can I phrase this?' I cleared my throat. 'Am I known in your own age as the man who brought electrification to the land?'

Parnell frowned. 'That's an odd thing, Wooton,' said he. 'Although I consider you well-nigh a genius – your research was going along the right lines even without my help – there is no record in my time of your pioneering work.'

Alas! If it is not enough that tonight I should find myself beset by sensual fantasies concerning the strange prehistoric girl Arondel, that my knowledge of physics should be revealed as minuscule by the revelations of the future, it is clear now that all my work, all my endeavour, will come to nought.

14th January, 1884
Arondel came to my bed in the early hours of this morning. At first, as I lay rigid, she did but lie against me and pass an arm across my chest. My initial impulse was to show her the door; yet something, some visceral pang of longing, would not let me do this. Although I told myself that I would later regret my concupiscence, at the time I was powerless to resist my urges, and I took Arondel with all the abandon I had shown the day before. Thereafter I passed a fitful, guilt-filled few hours before dawn.

When I awoke I did so with a start, and pulled away from the girl as if prolonged contact might infect me with some harmful contagion. I dressed quickly, hurried from the Hall, and took myself on a vigorous march across the countryside, the episode in the bed-chamber uppermost in my mind.

Two hours later I paused outside the Coach and Horses, and on impulse plunged inside and ordered a whisky. I took it into the back room, the very same where I had first made the acquaintance of Arondel, stared into the fire and contemplated my predicament.

There could be no denying that I was attracted to Arondel's physical aspect, notwithstanding the fact that once I had found her strange and unappealing; more worrying still was that, despite myself, I longed to be beside her, if merely to bask in the enchantment of her uncivilised mien, her wild female spirit.

I ordered another drink and admonished myself for entertaining such nonsense. The girl was a rude savage, I told myself, and it was not her primitive nobility that attracted me, but the promise of the pleasures of her flesh! What would my dear Catherine make of such indiscretion on my part? It was bad enough that she would have mocked my attraction to the prehistoric girl in the first place, worse still that she might have discerned in that attraction more than the mere desire to gratify my animal instincts.

But no! I dared not even admit this to myself. I downed a third whisky, departed the tavern and made my unsteady way back to the Hall.

Arondel was peering through the library window when I returned, and upon seeing me she dashed into the hallway and stood looking at me from a distance of some five yards. I detected a certain hesitation in her manner, and joy also – as if she were unsure whether to greet me as she wished. Which was just as well, for, despite the sight of her, the very aura of primitive feminine power she seemed to emanate, my mind was still aswirl with self-admonition and guilt. My heart beating in my chest, my throat constricted by I know not what emotion, I pushed past her and all but ran up the stairs to my bed-chamber, whereupon I locked and bolted the door and sat upon the bed in a state of profound despair.

17th January, 1884
For the past three days I have taken to locking myself in the ballroom while I worked – or rather *tried* to work – and at night securing myself within my bed-chamber. Further, I partook of meals at irregular hours, so as to avoid the attentions of the girl. I told myself that time, the great healer, would work its balm on the wound of my moral weakness, that if only I avoided Arondel physically then she would soon disappear from my thoughts. Would that were so!

It seemed that my desire grew as a direct consequence of her absence, increased with the duration of our parting. In a bid to expunge her from my mind, today I barricaded myself in the ballroom and immersed myself in my work. I embarked upon a series of experiments which I had put off until now, as I judged them too advanced. My reasoning was that the degree of thought and concentration required to make a success of them would quite fill my mind and leave little room for other considerations . . .

To little avail. Arondel dominated my thoughts to the point where I made a series of fundamental mistakes and miscalculations, and at the end of the day the experiments lay in ruins, the state of my mind in little better repair.

This evening I returned to my room and paced its length in a delirium, as Arondel pawed at the door and pitifully moaned my name. I shut my hands over my ears, cried out loud, and knew that if this continued then I must surely go mad.

In due course, as I paced, something struck me with such force that I wondered why I had not considered it sooner.

It was not so much my desire that I feared, but something more. I was beset by a feeling of guilt at the thought that, if I again surrendered to my desire, then in time Arondel might replace the memory of Catherine in my affections. Yet, I asked myself, how might this be so? How might someone as rude and slovenly as Arondel ever win my heart? It occurred to me that my fear, and the suppression of my desire, was thus unfounded . . .

In a bid to prove to myself that my affection for Catherine could survive the desires of the flesh, I strode to the door and flung it open.

Arondel had scrambled to her feet at the sound of the key in the lock, and now she stood on the threshold and regarded me timidly.

My heart gave a surge at the sight of her. She was at once powerful yet pathetic, an embodiment of maternal virtues clad in the tattered remnants of my wife's dress. I opened the door further, and she stepped inside and sat upon the bed with her eyes downcast.

Hesitantly I took my place beside her, then reached out for her hand. I raised it to my lips and kissed her toughened knuckles. Strangely, I experienced no overwhelming desire then – merely a profound nervousness, as if my heart were bursting within my chest, and this frightened me more than did my previous excesses!

Arondel gazed at me, her expression unreadable, though I detected in her large brown eyes something warm, trusting.

I shook my head. 'You are causing me great pain,' I confessed.

She had no way of comprehending my words, and her slight frown, as if of puzzlement, indicated this.

'Oh . . . Arondel!' I began. 'What stroke of fate brought you here to me? I should really wish that Parnell had never happened upon my time – but I find this impossible. How can you begin to understand the restrictions that govern my conduct?' I stared down at her and I realised, then, that I was weeping.

Arondel gave a start, her expression one of sadness, and brushed my cheek with her fingers. She tried to draw me to her in an embrace designed to do more than merely comfort, but I restrained her. I indicated the bed, then lay down with Arondel in my arms as she stroked my head and made soothing sounds in her throat. For perhaps one hour we lay like this, and I was too overcome with a profound sense of peace and gratitude to dwell upon my guilt.

When at last Arondel slipped into a gentle slumber, I disengaged myself from her embrace, crossed to my writing desk and began this painful entry.

I well realise that, despite my earlier protestations otherwise, I desire more than just her body; after so long without the balm of intimacy I feel an undeniable affection towards the girl, and this realization causes me no small amount of soul-searching.

19th January, 1884
My dearest Catherine . . . forgive me!

This morning I awoke fully dressed, and climbed from the bed before Arondel could alter that state of affairs. After breakfast, I decided to take a turn about the grounds. I set out alone, but I made no move to prevent Arondel from following me, and I was secretly gratified when she did.

For the duration of our walk I could hardly keep my eyes from my young companion.

I showed her around the estate, explaining in my own language the various sights of interest. She could not understand, of course, yet she paid grave attention as if wishing with all her heart that she could. At length, she saw the humour inherent in the situation, whereupon she began to mock me: she strode around rather stiffly, indicating this and that with an outstretched arm and mouthing gibberish in a passable imitation of my tone, before breaking down and laughing out loud. How my heart warmed to her!

Like everything else about the girl, her way of showing affection is unique. Often it came over me to take her hand in mine, yet when I did she pulled away as if she resented the restriction my hold imposed upon her. As if to compensate for this, she would dart away on some errand of her own, only to return and present me with a gift: a pine cone, a large snail, a burnished pebble . . . How can I begin to describe to you, Catherine, the joy these simple gifts, and Arondel's motivation behind their giving, brought forth in me?

This evening we repaired to the Hall for dinner, and shortly thereafter a dreamy look came over Arondel's gaze. Upon finishing her trifle she held out her hand and proceeded to lead me, like a lamb to the slaughter, up the stairs to my bed-chamber.

It is midnight and I am writing this by the light of a candle, Arondel asleep on the bed. From time to time she chuckles in her sleep, and this prompts the observation that she seems to me much happier of late, that since our union she is of a much brighter disposition altogether. This, of course, begs the question of what the simple prehistoric girl sees in my person to bring her such happiness? I can only propose that in me Arondel has happened upon an individual who, denied twelve years of intimacy, is prepared to treat her with kindness and affection for perhaps the first time in her life; certainly for the first time since her arrival in my age. Arondel is young, and she sees in me someone whom can fulfil the roles of both a father and a lover.

Arondel has been my constant companion for the past two days. On the morning of the 20th, I awoke to find myself holding her in my arms. We were naked, and I had but a faint recollection of the events of the night before, together with a residuum of guilt I told myself I should not feel, but which nevertheless I did – and which I now fear will be with me for the rest of my days.

In the morning sunlight that streamed into the room, I contemplated the sleeping girl. I touched her tangled hair and the line of her blunt visage. Needless to say, I no longer beheld her as ugly; I was able to ignore the criteria of female perfection set down by my own society, which states that women should be dainty of form, fine of feature, and view Arondel with a degree of objectivity. What I beheld beneath the superficial information of her awkward appearance, as she slept in my arms, was something of her animus, her alien spirit and maternal strength.

We partook of breakfast on the bed, after which a strange impulse took me and I escorted Arondel to the bathroom. I ran a tub of steaming water, invited her to climb within, and indicated that she should wash herself. Then I arranged the vials of my wife's perfumes and powders, and it was while I was doing this that I cursed myself. Startled, Arondel looked up from her ablutions, her expression quizzical.

Forthwith I pulled her from the tub, half washed, and wrapped her in a towel. 'What in God's name am I doing to you?' I exclaimed.

Why, I wondered, as I paced the bed-chamber and Arondel dried herself, was I trying to change her? I could foresee the end result: a wild prehistoric girl fettered in the cumbersome costume and restrictive social customs of contemporary times. How could I even contemplate doing this to her, when one of the things that had drawn me to

Arondel was her *difference* – the very fact that she was a wild female spirit untamed by the petty conditions and restrictions that govern 'polite' society . . .?

As a sop to common decency I bade Arondel wear a maid's shapeless gown, and the rest of the day we spent, as yesterday, walking around the grounds of the Hall. I took the opportunity to try to teach her the rudiments of the English language, and Arondel instructed me in the meaning of her own strange tongue.

At dinner, which we partook alone – Parnell was working late in the conservatory – I watched her eat, and wondered what my acquaintances at the Club would make of all this. I pride myself on reporting that it was but for a moment that I was bothered by the thought of their reaction. I could well imagine what noise the incongruity of our union would provoke from the likes of Bartholomew and Frobisher, Travers and Ashbury . . . Yet verily their reaction would be different if only they could look upon my soul and behold the gladness therein!

Following dinner, Arondel once again escorted me to my bed-chamber . . .

This morning – the 21st – I resumed my work. Following breakfast we repaired to the ballroom, and for the rest of the day Arondel watched me work, with wide eyes and much hiding behind furniture as I caused great bolts of electricity to leap across the room like startled demons.

It might be thought that the information imparted by Parnell the other day – that my name will not be known to posterity – would prove something of a disincentive, but such is not the case. I initiated this line of research fifteen years ago with no guarantee that I might ever succeed, still less that the outside world would learn of my endeavours. Only in recent years have I paused to consider that perhaps I would go down in history as a benefactor of mankind, that I might be lauded in my lifetime by the famous and the powerful. What folly! Parnell's information caused no little bruising of my self-esteem, but I see this now as the vanity it so obviously was. If my short liaison to date with Arondel has taught me anything, it is that the opinions and prejudices of my peers count for little beside the fulfilment of one's own ambitions and desires. I am driven now by the need to discover the secrets of the universe about me, to satisfy my own curiosity and complete as best I can that which I began.

23rd January, 1884

Wells turned up at the Hall this afternoon.

I was engaged in the task of stripping down a capacitator at the time, with Arondel in attendance, when we were interrupted by a knock upon the door. By the time I had unlocked it, Saddler was standing to attention some way along the corridor. 'You have a caller, sir. A young man by the name of Wells.'

'Wells?' I exclaimed. 'Fetch my coat!' I returned to the ballroom and impressed upon Arondel, as best I could in the few words common to us, that she must remain where she was. 'Wells,' I said, significantly. Her eyes widened and she nodded her understanding.

By the time I reached the main entrance, Wells had his back to the Hall and was inspecting the grounds. The young man was attired in tweeds and green knee-stockings, the uniform of the cyclist. I remained in the doorway and cleared my throat.

Wells turned. 'Wooton – I must see you.' His face was red from the effort of pedalling; his boneshaker was propped against an ornamental flower urn at the foot of the steps.

'What on Earth do you want?' I thundered.

'I need to see you about Parnell —'

'Are you still armed? I have no truck with armed men.'

A look of confusion crossed his face. 'Oh, you mean this?' From the flap of his tweed jacket he produced an imitation pistol carved from wood. 'I merely meant to threaten Parnell —' he began.

'Your argument with him must be great if you go to such lengths —'

'Is he still here?' he asked eagerly.

'Parnell and the girl left some time ago,' said I, and indicated the drive. 'Perhaps you'd care to tell me of your quarrel with him while we take a walk?'

We descended the steps and struck out down the drive. Snow had fallen again during the night, covering the countryside for as far as the eye could see. The oaks at the end of the drive were laden and creaking with the burden, and, as we passed by, two magpies racketed from cover and flew into the grey sky.

At last Wells said: 'How much did Parnell tell you, Wooton? Did you know that he was a Time Traveller?'

'He told me that much in a bid to enlist my aid,' I said.

'And I trust you refused to supply him with the requisite materials?'

'I . . . could not afford much of what he wanted,' I said. 'The rest was unobtainable.'

'Rumour in the village is that Parnell is working with you —'

'For a week or two he did assist me in my experiments. I gave him board and lodging for a while. He took his leave a fortnight ago —'

'And his destination?'

'London, I believe.'

We turned to the right and walked along the lane that encircled my property. 'Did he by any chance mention you the reason for his going back to prehistoric times?' Wells asked now.

'He was vague on the issue,' I replied, then enquired of the earnest young man at my side: 'Why, did he mention his motives to you?'

'I have yet to meet Parnell,' said Wells. 'I heard his story from an eminent scientific friend of mine, whom Parnell had approached with his plea for aid. My friend informed me of the reason for Parnell's trip back to the prehistoric era, though the former considered it something of a joke. However, I took the trouble of travelling up to Cambridge and locating the chalk pit in which Parnell, the girl and the time machine crashlanded. There I found the remains of a strange contraption, which convinced me of the veracity of his story. When I heard that he was doing the rounds of the scientific establishment in a bid to build a new machine and return to his own time, and from there continue on his dangerous mission, I decided to prevent him.' Here Wells glanced at me.

'And precisely what,' I enquired, 'is this dangerous mission?'

'According to my friend, Parnell told him that he hoped to move a section of humanity from the past and relocate them in his own time, the twenty-first century, in some kind of reservation in Africa . . .'

Wells strode on, jabbering merrily to himself, for I had stopped and was regarding his strutting figure with astonishment. He realised that I was no longer by his side, and turned. 'You now apprehend the danger!' he declared.

I gestured. 'I no more apprehend the danger than I can see the sense in the removal of humanity from one age to another,' I informed him.

'Aha!' said Wells, striking a pose in the middle of the lane with a finger in the air. 'I must admit that my friend was vague on Parnell's motive for the transportation of the primitives – to him, anyway, it was all a big joke. Similarly, I cannot fathom his reason. However, as for the danger . . . you cannot see this?'

I confessed that I could not. I caught up with him and we began walking again. Wells was enjoying his oration. 'It's quite simple, my dear Wooton. If Parnell has his evil way and moves humanity from the past – then chaos will ensue, temporal pandemonium will break out! It could spell the very end of the human race as we know it!'

The young man flung his arms into the air in an apocalyptic gesture. I calmed him by taking his elbow and indicating a stile in the wall; we climbed this and made our way through the vegetable garden towards the Hall.

'I honestly fail to see . . .' I began.

'Wooton, you are a man of science, are you not? Then apply yourself to the facts: namely, if a large part of humanity is removed from the face of the Earth thousands of years ago, then it obviously follows as a natural consequence that legions of citizens all down the centuries will cease to exist! Thousands, perhaps millions, will go unborn! Why, even you or I might wink out of existence like a snuffed candle!'

'But how can we go unborn when we already exist?' I asked him reasonably.

'We exist now by dint of the very fact that Parnell has *not yet* succeeded in transporting his cargo of humanity from one time to another. That's why it is imperative that he should not be allowed to build his infernal time machine! As soon as he does so, and achieves his objectives, then *whumph!* – mankind will be decimated!'

We came to a halt by the steps of the Hall, and the foursquare architecture of my ancestral seat appeared solid and reassuring after Wells's nightmarish visions. I turned to him. 'Have you thought that this has perhaps occurred to Parnell? Would he go ahead with his plan if it involved the dangers you forecast?'

Wells gripped my arm in conspiratorial earnestness. 'Aha! But how do we know that this is not exactly the end which Parnell desires? How do we know that Parnell is not an anarchist bent on chronic catastrophe?' He pulled his boneshaker upright and pointed it down the drive.

'Well,' I said, humouring him, 'let's just be thankful that so far he has had no luck in enlisting the aid he requires. He appears to be stranded in this age.'

'You say he went to London?' Wells asked, mounting his bicycle. 'To London, then! It rests on me to ensure that Parnell never achieves his evil ends. I thank you for your time, Wooton. Cheerio!' And with this Wells pedalled unsteadily down the drive on his misguided mission to save the world.

Arondel was peeping around the door when I returned. 'Wells?' she asked, dancing from foot to foot with apprehension. I assured her that Wells had gone, and she took my hand as I made my way to the conservatory.

Parnell was attending to his machine when we entered; he stood before the bank of levers, easing them forward one by one. The machine itself was activated; it throbbed, the brass rods rattled, and between the hexagonal frame a grey mist swirled in a hypnotising vortex.

I sat upon the potting table with Arondel beside me.

When Parnell had completed the operation to his satisfaction, he wiped his hands on a large bandana and mopped his forehead. He glanced at me. 'Is something wrong, Wooton?'

'Wells has just been,' I told him.

'And?' he asked, startled. 'Does he know that I'm here?'

'I said that you'd left two weeks ago for London. He told me why he is following you.' And I recounted the strange claims which Wells had just put forward.

By the time I had finished, Parnell was shaking his head. 'As ever, Wells has got it wrong. I sometimes wonder how the young dunderhead will become a famous writer!'

'But there is a grain of truth in what he said?' I asked.

'A grain, yes. But let me explain.' He drew up a reversed chair and straddled it, gripping the back-rest as if it were a ship's wheel.

'To begin with, this 'transportation' of prehistoric citizens was not the reason for my trip back in time. I travelled back to thirty-five thousand years ago on a mission of reconnaissance, a feasibility study, if you like, to lay the groundwork for a team that was due to follow me later to investigate the reason for Neanderthal Man's extinction —'

'Neanderthal Man . . .?' I began.

'The name has probably not yet passed into common usage, but in 1857 in the Neandertal Valley in Germany the remains of a hitherto unknown line of prehistoric man were discovered. By my time, this line was known as Neanderthal

Man, and by the end of the twentieth century it was accepted that these people were a highly intelligent race of hunter-gatherers who inhabited Europe and parts of Asia from two hundred and fifty thousand years ago until thirty-five thousand years ago. It is a fact that they had larger brains than modern man, with the increment located here' – Parnell touched the base of his skull – 'in the cerebellum. This is the part of the brain that governs mankind's spirituality, artistic endeavours, the sixth sense and other "occult" intuitions. It is understood that the Neanderthals were a civilised, compassionate people – and it has been a constant source of mystery and wonder as to why no trace of these people has been discovered after the period of thirty-five thousand years ago. There are three main theories to account for their disappearance. The first is that they did not disappear at all, but interbred with modern man – and no doubt a handful of Neanderthals down the centuries did so, but not in sufficient numbers to bring about the disappearance of the Neanderthals so rapidly. Another theory is that they died out through natural causes, disease, famine, and so forth. The third theory is that they were wiped out in history's first act of genocide by the arrival in Europe of modern man.' Here Parnell paused, shrugged and corrected the slippage of his spectacles.

'Upon my forced arrival in this time,' he said, 'and once I had sufficiently gathered my wits about me to properly take in my companion, I soon realised that Arondel was a Neanderthal girl; her facial bone structure and that of her skull, the shape of her pelvic flange and femur . . . all these are classic examples of Neanderthal anatomy. I realised that it was imperative for me to learn her language, and this I did by painstaking degrees, until I was able to understand her every word. And the story she told me defied my expectations and my wildest dreams.

'Arondel told me that, for as long as she can remember, her people had been the subject of attacks and raids by "foreigners" who years before had come to the island over the frozen waters from the continent of Europe. Before these attacks, her people, the Valley People, as they called themselves, were a peace-loving community, one of dozens that inhabited what is now southern England. They practised arts such as dancing, singing and story-telling, worshipped a sky-god known as Ru and lived in harmony with their fellows. For Arondel, these halcyon days were not even a memory – the tribal elders spoke of them wistfully, and looked forward to a time when perhaps they might be spared the savagery of the invaders . . . These invaders – none other than the ancestors of you and me, Wooton, Modern Man – were uncivilized and unsophisticated, but they were generally stronger than the Neanderthals, and more adept in battle. For years before Arondel's departure from her time, she lived in fear of the barbarian raids that killed her people and destroyed their settlements. One of the reasons that she does not hanker after her own age, and is content in ours, is that she is safe here from the invaders.

'From that day I have been haunted by the visions of slaughter that Arondel's descriptions conjure in my mind. It came to me quite suddenly one day six months ago: there was a way I might be able to save the Neanderthals. I think at first I really did not believe that it could work; it was a grand gesture, a folly bound to fail. What was to stop my unit at Cambridge from going back, taking the Neanderthals and relocating them on the continent of Africa – which in my time is depopulated due to an epidemic which wiped out scores of millions?'

I shook my head. 'But how can you possibly do this? If the Neanderthals are already extinct —'

'You miss the point, Wooton! When we go back to their time, they will not be extinct. They will be there for the rescuing – in fact the very reason that there is no record of the Neanderthals after thirty-five thousand years ago could be that they are moved by us to twenty-first century Africa. Indeed there would be poetic justice in that!'

'At any rate, two months ago, with this fantastic notion uppermost in my mind, I approached an eminent scientist renowned for his philanthropy. Once I had gained his trust and confidence, I told him my story. I made great mention of the plight of the Neanderthals. I even introduced him to Arondel and conducted a conversation in her language for his benefit. I expected at least interest – if not sponsorship. As it was, this eminent man of science, this philanthropist, laughed in my face and threw me into the street. What is more, he made a great joke of the affair to a group of his friends, one of whom was Wells. It is quite ironical that Wells should take my every word as gospel, construe from my intentions that I might bring down chaos on the world, and hound me from pillar to post!'

'I take it that his fears are unfounded?' I interjected.

'Of course! Do you think I would undertake such a scheme without first considering the consequences? Wells thinks that by removing the Neanderthals from their own age, I am endangering the existence of mankind – this is nonsense. Time is immutable, there is nothing we can do to change the events of history. Mankind has *not* been decimated down the aeons as Wells forecasts, and nothing I can do thirty-five thousand years ago will bring this about – *because events then have already transpired* . . . But less of Wells! I am most grateful to you, Wooton, for sending him packing. I have enough on my mind at present.'

'You must almost be ready to leave?' I said, with a degree of sadness in my heart, for despite his occasional irascibility, and periods of infuriating silence, I had come to admire and respect the man.

'The interface is almost ready,' Parnell said. 'I shall depart tomorrow morning.'

I then braced myself for the question I knew I must ask: 'And . . . what of Arondel?' I murmured.

'At first I considered taking her back with me to my own time, before I realised that her presence might take some explaining to the authorities. Our project is top secret, and we wish it to remain that way. It will be far safer if for the time being, Wooton, she remains here with you.'

'And then?' I asked.

'Presently, if and when the Neanderthal tribes are relocated, I will return for Arondel so that she might be reunited with her people.'

'Is that what she wants?' I enquired lightly, emotion stirring in my breast.

Parnell addressed Arondel with a few grunts; she replied, her eyes downcast.

Parnell turned to me. 'She will be sorry to leave you, Wooton. But she misses her people. She is, after all, a Neanderthal girl . . . It is only right that —'

'Of course, Parnell,' I interrupted him. 'I understand. It is only right and proper that she returns to her own people . . .' And yet even as I mouthed these words, contrary sentiments were at work in my head. To cover my true feelings, and in order to change the subject, I suggested that we return to the Hall and celebrate Parnell's last dinner in my time.

24th January, 1884

The day began with Parnell excited at the prospect of returning to his own time, Arondel and myself sad at the thought of his departure, but pleased for him nevertheless.

It is an hour since I wrote that first sentence, and for that long I have been trying to come to terms with the many incidents of the day. However hard I try, I cannot – the magnitude of what happened is too overwhelming to comprehend. All I can do – and, through doing so, perhaps come to some sort of acceptance of the situation – is to set down the events as they happened.

At nine this morning we three proceeded to the conservatory, with the silence and awkwardness that is wont to accompany occasions such as these. I could detect in Parnell's manner a sense of anticipation at what was to come; for more than a year he had cast about hopelessly in this – to him – backward age, dreaming of returning to his own time, yet frequently giving up all hope. At last the future was within his reach, and although he no doubt felt a certain sadness at departing, it was tempered by the knowledge of what awaited him.

He stood before the time machine, his case, stuffed with the many notes he had made pertaining to his experiments, gripped beneath his arm. Behind him, the grey vortex of the interface swirled and tumbled in on itself like a kaleidoscope robbed of colour. The tall levers were arranged precisely, and the date behind the oval glass plate on the plinth read: July, 2001. Although it was two months later than the date to which he should have been returning, it was the closest he could come with the materials available to him.

'When I return to Cambridge the first thing I will do is lobby support among my colleagues to look into my proposal to save the Neanderthals.'

'My thoughts will be with you, Parnell.'

'I will visit you soon. Expect a call at some not too distant date in the future!'

'I'll keep your room ready,' said I.

'Look after the girl, Wooton,' Parnell smiled. He turned to the time machine and placed a foot upon the plinth. He picked up a small black box, with which he would deactivate the time machine when he arrived in the future. He wanted no one from that age unwittingly stepping through the interface and finding themselves in the past.

He shook my hand and kissed Arondel on the forehead. 'Wish me luck, Wooton, and thank you again. Farewell . . .'

He paused on the plinth before stepping through the interface and disappearing into the grey mist, and I held my breath as he did so, and Arondel uttered a little cry.

I stared into the vortex for long minutes before she tugged at my arm and said: 'Bed, Clarry . . . Bed!'

It is difficult to regain the thoughts that were going through my head at noon today; I think I was looking ahead to the short period that I would have with Arondel.

At the same time, some hypocritical and selfish part of me secretly hoped that Parnell's quest to save the Neanderthals would come to nothing – so that I might have Arondel with me for always . . .

Verily, the stuff of desperate fantasy!

I was holding Arondel in my arms when I heard a distant cry and made out the words: 'Mr Wooton . . . Mr Wooton!' Saddler ran along the corridor and hammered on the door like a madman. 'It's Master Parnell, sir! He's at the foot of the stairs in a terrible state!'

We dressed in haste and, hand in hand, ran pell-mell from the bed-chamber and down the stairs. Parnell – or at least a figure who in part resembled Parnell – lay face-down on the floor, one arm outstretched as if he were trying to drag himself up the steps. Saddler's description of his being in a 'terrible state' was something of a euphemism: the man looked as though he had journeyed to Hell and back. His clothes were scorched and in tatters, and the entire left side of his face was blistered and raw. His breath came in pained spasms, and from time to time he cried out in panic.

Between the three of us we managed to carry him up the stairs to his bed-chamber. I instructed Saddler to run into the village and bring the doctor, and then we stripped Parnell of his rags and bathed him where he lay.

As well as the pain that wracked his frame, Parnell was in a state of mental torment. He tossed and turned and attempted to sit up and climb from the bed; it was all Arondel and I could do to hold him down.

'What in God's name happened, man!' I cried at one stage when his rantings had ceased and he regarded me with wide and manic eyes. 'Can you hear me, Parnell?'

He stared at me, through me, and gave vent to a blood-curdling scream, terrifying in its remove from all that was rational and human.

I assumed from the beginning that Parnell had somehow miscalculated the setting of the time machine and had fallen *through* time, slipped between the interstices of reality into some terrible limbo realm. How exactly he had sustained his injuries, and how he had managed to find his way back to the interface, I could not begin to answer.

'Wooton!' Parnell gripped my hand and cried his first rational words. 'All my hopes . . . my dreams . . .' this last he hardly whispered, before lapsing again into a fit of writhing and ranting.

It was almost an hour before the doctor arrived; he examined Parnell with grim thoroughness – after first casting a disapproving glance at Arondel – then stuffed his stethoscope into the pocket of his frock-coat and looked at me. 'What the blazes happened to him, Wooton?'

I had foreseen this enquiry and was ready with a suitable reply: 'He was working on an experiment in the ballroom. I can only assume that he suffered a shock . . .'

'I can give him something to ease his pain, but there's little else I can do for him.' He drew me to one side and told me the worst, and then went on to state that in his opinion electricity was the work of the Devil and should be left well alone. Would that he knew the true cause of Parnell's injuries!

Before he departed, the doctor gave Parnell a sedative and left a vial of pills with me. Arondel and I sat by the bed and regarded the dying Parnell as he slumbered fitfully.

It was perhaps two hours later that he regained consciousness. He was no longer hysterical, though his eyes were wide and staring.

I sat up. 'Parnell! Can you remember what happened?'

Tears appeared in his eyes, gathered and rolled down his cheeks. 'The end, Wooton . . . The end of everything!'

I leaned forward. 'Did you arrive in your own time, Parnell?'

He managed a smile, or rather a terrible travesty of a smile. 'I knew . . . knew there was something wrong. The sky was black, though the sun burned dimly overhead. The occupants of the Hall were in panic. They told me that the first attack had hit Europe the day before, though as yet

England had not been hit. They tried to get me to join them in the cellar, as they said they were expecting the first strike at any time. Reports were that every continent had been bombed, without exception —' Here he began to laugh, and I feared he might lapse into hysteria once more. He controlled himself, however, and terminated his laughter in a bout of convulsive coughing. When this subsided he went on breathlessly: 'Not that there was any hope. Those not killed immediately would succumb to the effects of radiation poisoning sooner or later, and later still the greenhouse effect would ensure the end of everything . . .' During the rambling monologue that followed he used many words and phrases unknown to me; he said that the 'super powers' had finally waged a 'new clear' war, which I envisaged as some terrible conflict between the nations of the future armed, perhaps, with mammoth invisible rays that left nought but death and destruction in their wake.

'I managed,' he went on weakly, 'to get away from the Hall, and then the first missile struck England. The blast turned night into day and destroyed London, and then more missiles fell, and I was caught in the terrible blast and . . . and I crawled through the wreckage of the Hall and located the interface and pulled myself through . . .' He sobbed anew at this and cried: 'Everyone I knew, Wooton, my friends and colleagues and the entire population . . .'

I was silent with shock, unable to find the words to comfort him. Something of the magnitude of the catastrophe began to penetrate my consciousness, and I tried to dismiss the visions of apocalypse with the reassuring solidity of everything about me. I might even have been able to dismiss Parnell's rantings, but for the fact that he lay before me, scarred and burned, the victim of a terrible future war which would bring about the annihilation of the world.

I gripped his hand. 'But is there nothing we can do?' I said. 'Can't we go forward in time to the period immediately before the war and warn the governments of the apocalypse about to befall?' And here I stopped, for Parnell was shaking his head and laughing, as if at a child.

'No, Wooton. You fail to understand. There is nothing we can do to prevent the war – *because it happens*! If we went ahead and warned the governments, it would be to no avail. Don't you see, if there was anything we could do to prevent the war, we would do it, and there would be no war . . . But there is a war – *will* be a war – and we are powerless to do a thing about it. Events are destined, and all the time traveller can do is stand by helplessly and witness the inevitable, immutable incidents of history.'

Presently he lapsed again into the slumber of unconsciousness and I dwelled morosely on the consequence of his report. Then, as now, I was overcome with a pervasive and all-embracing sense of lethargy, or apathy, concerning the fact of my existence. My work, my feelings for Arondel, were made dilute, washed of the very stuff and energy of life by the knowledge that the world as we knew it would cease to exist in little more than one hundred years. It was as if the spectre of Armageddon loomed terrible in the future and cast its retroactive shadow over the preceding century, robbing life of colour, emotions and passions of their vitality. This afternoon it was a mere feeling in my breast, a dull awareness not yet made real by the application of logical analysis. I have had more time to think about it now, and I realise that our lives are only really worthwhile when the future, however nebulous and uncertain, is assured; we might all strive for private gain and personal contentment, but a part of us, however much we might argue otherwise, knows that personal fulfilment is nothing without the hope for a future which we might never even live to witness.

I have been granted a glimpse of the beginning of the end, and I despair . . .

Parnell regained consciousness once more while we were with him, and it seemed if anything that his mental condition had deteriorated; for a full hour he ranted and raved, and then struggled upright and stared ahead with insane eyes.

'We must save the Neanderthals, Wooton! We must . . .' whereupon he fell back to the pillow and fretted like a man with fever. I managed to force a tablet down him with a swallow of water, and presently he took rest.

At eight, with our patient sleeping soundly, we descended to the dining room and contemplated our food. I had no appetite, and Arondel likewise; we picked at the meal without a word, Parnell's vacated seat a cruel reminder of his condition. Later I managed to tell Arondel of the destruction visited on the world that Parnell had witnessed – though I doubt she fully comprehended the import of my words. She did understand, however, when I repeated the doctor's opinion that Parnell was dying. She slipped from the room and I heard her bare feet on the marble as she ran up the staircase.

Seconds later I heard too her cries. 'Clarry!' she screamed. 'Par-nuh! Par-nuh – gone!'

I raced up the stairs and followed her into the bed-chamber, and sure enough there was no sign of Parnell. The bed was empty, his clothes gone. Arondel bit her fist in consternation, tears streaming down her broad brown cheeks.

Seconds later an explosion rocked the foundations of the Hall. 'Parnell!' I cried, taking Arondel's hand and sprinting downstairs.

The blast had brought the kitchen staff up from below, and they milled hither and thither in confusion, while Saddler attempted to calm the situation with talk of my 'experiments'. I assured them that I had everything under control, then dashed through the Hall to the conservatory.

At the far end of the room the grey mist of the interface swirled and eddied. I approached the machine and beheld the small oval plate of the chronometer. The figures therein were a meaningless jumble of digits, but the forward arrangement of the levers suggested to me that Parnell had journeyed once again into the future.

'Par-nuh?' Arondel murmured.

'He has travelled in time once more,' said I. 'Though to

206

what date, and for what reason, I have no idea . . .'

We dragged a *chaise longue* into the conservatory and sat there in a vigil that lasted the rest of the day. Had I been a man of prayer, I might have gone down on my knees and begged for Parnell's swift return; instead I hoped against hope.

The hour was approaching midnight, and Arondel and I were slumbering in each other's arms, when I was half-awoken by something and beheld, as if in a dream, Parnell emerge at a stagger from the interface. He lurched over to the levers and began drawing them towards him. The mist between the hexagonal brass rods accelerated its swirling, and the machine increased its humming crescendo. As he drew the final lever into position, an explosion cracked through the air, for all the world like thunder – and this had the effect of pitching me from a state of semi-sleep and into the reality of Parnell's brief return.

'Par-nuh!' Arondel cried.

I leapt to my feet and attempted to wrestle Parnell to the floor, for it was obvious that he was intent on throwing himself through the interface once again.

'Parnell, are you insane?'

'I have beheld Paradise, Wooton. *Unhand me!*'

Despite his weakness he shrugged me off, evaded my lunge and managed to push me to the ground. 'For the sake of humanity, I must go!'

He ran towards the time machine, paused on the plinth, then dived into the interface, disappearing once again into the unfathomable mists of time. Arondel yelled out and made to follow him – but I restrained her. There was no telling to where the portal opened; I had seen the ravages wrought on Parnell by his journey to the future, and was dissuaded to go after him, or to let Arondel risk her life. In the dim flicker of the vortex I made out the figures displayed on the chronometer, but as before they meant nothing to me. Only the angle of the levers – they were drawn towards me as I stood – hinted that Parnell had travelled to some time in the past . . .

We returned to the *chaise longue* and sat staring at the

malevolent light cast by the portal, our thoughts on Parnell and his insane crusade through the hazards of time to somehow rescue humanity from a terrible fate already sealed.

25th January, 1884
Still Parnell has not returned.

We spent the day in the conservatory. I cannot discount the possibility that Parnell succumbed to his injuries wherever he found himself, and is now lying dead somewhere and will never return.

I recall his claim that he had beheld Paradise, and that for the sake of humanity he had to depart once more, and I can only assume that my friend was driven insane by the sight of the destruction he witnessed in his own age.

26th January, 1884
No sign of Parnell. This morning Saddler reported seeing someone answering to the description of Wells hiding in the shrubbery. Clearly Wells has found out that Parnell did not leave for London, as I told him the other day.

27th January, 1884
If Parnell does not return soon I must seriously think about dismantling the time machine. I have no idea at what age it might open onto, or who might happen through at any time . . .

I have done no work now for a number of days.

Wells sighted in the grounds again.

28th January, 1884
Still nothing.

29th January, 1884
Parnell returned today!

I was dozing this morning when Arondel yelped in delight and pulled me to my feet. I opened my eyes and assumed I was still dreaming; Parnell staggered through the interface between two short, fur-clad prehistoric men, who assisted him over to the *chaise longue* and lowered him to the cushions. One of the men returned through the portal, while the other gazed about him in wonder. Arondel was dancing around and clapping her hands in delight.

I stared at Parnell; he seemed weaker than before his precipitous departure. The right hemisphere of his face was an open, running sore, and his hair, or the little of it that he had possessed, was falling out. He smiled at me, and I was horrified to see that his gums were bleeding. 'I told you, Wooton,' he wheezed. 'I told you I could save them . . .'

I turned at a noise by the machine, and watched in amazement as a never-ending procession of Neanderthals – as by now I had guessed them to be – emerged from the vortex, stepped from the plinth and gathered in the confines of the conservatory: men and women, babes-in-arms and shuffling oldsters – all with the same physical characteristics as Arondel; the same broad skulls, heavy foreheads and prognathous chins, the same squat build of body, thick legs and wide, splayed feet. They could have emanated a sense of threat, so many people I once would have described as 'savages', in so confined a space; yet in fact the very opposite was true. There was a peacefulness about the gathering that I have rarely experienced among my own kind. Arondel was addressing them from the makeshift podium of the potting-table, and I heard my name mentioned more than once, and in the gazes that these strange people turned on me I detected a mixture of gratitude and respect.

I gestured helplessly at Parnell. 'What on Earth . . .?'

'The Valley People are under constant attack from modern man, Wooton. I was destined to save them —'

'But . . .' I stuttered. 'Good God! There's hardly room for all of them in the Hall! What will the villagers say?'

Parnell laughed, though the sound that came from his bent and tortured frame could hardly be described as humorous. 'This is only a temporary measure, Wooton. There are still a few hundred Neanderthals back in the Holocene period, fighting a rear-guard action against the invaders while their people escape through the interface. When they retreat and join us, as I instructed them to do, we will make the final journey. Where do you think I went before I travelled back to fetch the Neanderthals, Wooton?' He was seized then by a fit of wracking coughs, and I watched helplessly as he expectorated blood into his bandana. At last, when he was able to speak again, he told me how he planned to save the Valley People.

It is almost midnight now, and the Neanderthals, some three thousand in total, are billeted safely in the Hall. My staff have departed. At the first sight of the small, brown, semi-naked men and women spilling from the conservatory, the servants dropped what they were doing and ran. I watched them as they evacuated the Hall *en masse* and fled down the drive in panic. At the gate stood the short, pompous figure of Wells, his boneshaker beside him. He questioned my staff as they passed, then smartly mounted his bicycle and tore off in the direction of the village. I can expect a deputation from the local constabulary at first light in the morning.

I am writing this in the conservatory where, with Arondel and Parnell, I await the arrival of the last of the Valley People.

30th January, 1884
The end is in sight . . .

All that remains for me to do is record the events of this final day, and the sad though inevitable fact of Parnell's passing; we can be thankful, at least, that he lived to see the return of the warriors and the exodus of the Neanderthals to their sanctuary.

At dawn this morning I was awoken from my dreams by the sound of my name being called through a speaking trumpet. In a daze I made my way through the Hall to the library and peered through the window, and the sight that

210

presented itself was enough to bring me to my senses. I judged that the entire population of the village was gathered before the Hall. Among them were the familiar faces of my ex-staff, gesticulating and pointing to the upper windows of the Hall, where Neanderthal faces peered out.

'This is your last warning, Wooton. Come out peacefully and give yourself up.' Wells then turned and spoke to the two constables beside him.

I made my way to the main entrance, opened the door and stood on the threshold; a murmur rippled through the crowd. Wells seemed surprised, as if, despite his demand, he had not expected me to show myself.

'You lied to me, Wooton!'

'There is no need to use that thing, Wells. I can hear you well enough without it.'

The young man lowered the speaking trumpet and cleared his throat. 'Do you intend to give yourselves up,' he called, 'or would you rather we forced an entry and arrested you?'

'As far as I'm aware I have committed no crime. Do you have a warrant of search?'

Wells addressed one of the constables, who seconds later pushed through the crowd and hurried off down the drive. Wells faced me. 'We'll give you until noon, Wooton,' he called. 'If by that time you have not surrendered yourself, along with Parnell, the girl and those damned ape-men, then we will have no option but to come in and arrest you all—'

'Are you well armed, my friend?' I asked.

The crowd seemed to take in a collective breath and back off one step. I said: 'I would think twice about entering this place if I were you, Wells. My friends number some three thousand all told—'

'You will bring about the downfall of civilization!' Wells yelled like a lunatic.

'Look about you!' I cried impatiently. 'Do you see any of the catastrophe you forecast?' with which I slammed the door, locked it, and returned to the conservatory.

I reported the encounter to Parnell, and we were discussing what we should do in the eventuality of a raid when the first of the Neanderthal warriors, men and women both, tumbled through the interface. Many had suffered injuries in their last – their *very* last – battle with modern man. I took heart from the fact that soon they would be in a world where war was a thing of the past.

When the last of the warriors had emerged from the interface, Parnell smiled weakly and spoke to Arondel in barely a whisper, and she ran off to summon the rest of her people.

'You know what to do, my friend,' Parnell wheezed from the *chaise longue*.

I stepped up to the bank of levers beside the time machine and, as Parnell had instructed me earlier, eased forward each lever in turn to its fullest extent. As I pushed the last lever into position, there issued from the interface a detonation that well nigh deafened me.

Arondel returned with the Neanderthalers in tow, and we sat with Parnell as the men and women, old folk and children, stepped cautiously through the swirling grey vortex. Many of them paused in front of Parnell and uttered short sounds of gratitude before vanishing into the interface. I could not help but make the inevitable Biblical comparison, as the sea of time parted and the chosen ones made their way to the Promised Land.

Three hours later – with one hour to go before noon and Wells' deadline – the conservatory was empty save for Parnell, Arondel and myself. Parnell closed his eyes, as if in satisfaction, and slept. I stood before the time machine with Arondel, a feeling of sadness in my heart as I contemplated our inevitable parting.

I indicated the portal; Arondel looked from it to me, her expression uncomprehending. She made a small, interrogative sound in her throat: 'Uh?'

'You must join your own people,' I told her. 'You belong with them, not here with me.' I gestured, and then as best I

212

could repeated my words in her own language. She regarded me with those staring brown eyes, and I recalled a time not so long gone when I had assumed her to be a savage, without thoughts or feelings or even passion.

She laughed and took my hand and dragged me towards the time machine. I resisted on the threshold of a future so far in advance of my own time that the machine's chronometer had been unable to calculate the exact age: billennia hence, without doubt.

Arondel tugged at me, and with a gasp I was through the interface and standing on a gentle hillside overlooking what can only be described as paradise, a Garden of Eden recovered from the ravages of war.

The panorama was unlike any I had ever beheld; blue grass extended for miles in a wide, flat plain, and on the distant horizon stood a range of purple, snow-capped mountains. The sun burned huge and molten and bathed the land in a golden glow. The few trees to be seen on the plain were strange and alien, with the delicate beauty of bonsai. The Valley People, the Neanderthals, were minute figures in the landscape as they explored their new world.

Arondel touched my arm and pointed into the sky at a large moon sailing low. It was one phase from the full, and insubstantial in the morning light. Then Arondel indicated her stomach, and with a hand described its waxing in ever larger arcs, until with outstretched arms she mimicked a belly full and heavy with child . . .

She took my hand again and drew me towards the interface, which hung in the air above the grass as if by magic. We stepped from paradise to the conservatory, and suddenly this reality seemed dull and claustrophobic after what I had beheld in the far future.

Parnell had regained consciousness; he looked up feebly when we stepped from the plinth. We crossed to the *chaise longue* and knelt beside him.

'They are safe . . .?' he whispered.

I assured him that the Valley People were indeed safe, and Parnell seemed to weaken perceptibly then, as if he had been willing himself to oversee the salvation of his adopted people, and now could relax his grip on life.

'Parnell,' I said, taking his hand. 'Arondel wants me to go with her, and how can I remain behind? Life will be hard, and I will have to learn many new ways . . . But I will be with the person I love most. How could I remain in this time with the knowledge of what lies in store for modern man? Parnell, can you hear me?' This because his vision had misted, and he seemed deaf to my words.

'Wooton,' he croaked. 'Don't go . . .'

I gripped his hand. 'Don't worry, Parnell. We'll stay with you . . .'

'Don't go,' he said again in entreaty, and it was obvious that he was slipping away from us and feared facing death alone.

'Par-nuh,' Arondel cried, touching his face with her fingers, as his eyes closed and the breath rattled in his throat.

I sit now in the conservatory, with Arondel by my side, and write this final entry. It is ten minutes to midday, and soon Wells and the constables will be here. When I lay down my pen, I will seal this document and leave it in the library, addressed to my solicitor, with the instructions that it should be passed on to you, Charles, upon your twenty-fifth birthday. Then we will step through the interface for the last time, taking with us the body of Parnell for burial in the new land. I have readied an incendiary device in the conservatory, timed to go off following our departure. It is my hope that nothing mechanical will survive the blast.

I trust that this document has gone some way to explaining my motives in leaving this benighted era, and, in so doing, deserting you, my son, to your own life; even if I had it in my power to take you with me, I would hesitate before doing so. I understand that you might despair, Charles, at the knowledge of the catastrophe that is destined to befall mankind, but it is my opinion that to transport you to the future Earth against your will would be a cruel move indeed. I ask you to forgive your father his many mistakes, wish me luck, and rejoice that mankind, albeit of a different type to that which we have known until now, but mankind nonetheless, will survive the ultimate conflict of modern man to become the rightful inheritors of planet Earth.

21st December, 1945
These papers came into my possession one week ago, almost half a century late; for that long I have been in India, and contact between my father's solicitor and myself was lost well before my twenty-fifth birthday. I was twelve years old when I was informed of his disappearance, though I was curiously unaffected by the news. I was never close to my father – as might be clear from the preceding account – and, later, when it came to my knowledge that his wife, my mother, had died in labour, the reason for his disaffection became rather obvious . . . However, the events surrounding his mysterious disappearance did pique my curiosity, and upon my return to England earlier this year I made certain inquiries. Quite by chance, a mutual acquaintance put me in contact with the firm of my father's solicitors, and this document is the result.

I would like to dismiss it out of hand, yet certain facts make this impossible. Strange, hirsute creatures were seen in the Hall by staff and villagers on the day of the 30th January, 1884. The name of Parnell does crop up in the diaries of many Victorian scientists, who describe him as a brilliant crackpot spinning yarns of time travel and ape-men in danger. And, of course, my father did disappear from the face of the Earth in January 1884. It was assumed – and widely reported – that he was killed in the explosion that destroyed the conservatory at Wooton Hall, though no trace of his remains were ever discovered.

But perhaps the clincher is Parnell's account of the future war that destroyed the world – the 'new clear' war as my father so quaintly put it. There could have been no way that Parnell might have described so accurately the effects of nuclear war – nor guessed so precisely the terminology used – other than being the time traveller he claimed and having actually experienced the holocaust himself. We have recently witnessed the horrors of nuclear weapons in Japan, and in fifty-five years from now those horrors will be multiplied a millionfold and life on Earth will cease to exist. I give thanks that I am old man now, and will not be around to see it happen.

There is no doubt in my mind that my father is living – or should that be, will live? – in a paradisaical future Earth with the race of beings known as the Neanderthals. And yet, while I rejoice that mankind has inherited the Earth, as his final entry exhorted me to do, I understand now Parnell's last words. My father himself termed that future world the 'Garden of Eden' – and Parnell, of course, cast my father in the role of the Serpent; for with his dying breath he told him not to go, though my father chose to interpret this as a plea to remain with him while he died.

I rather think that Parnell was being a little pessimistic in his assumption that one man might carry with him into Paradise all the sins of his race. I prefer to see my father integrated into the Neanderthal way of life, and content. His affection for the girl Arondel cannot be denied, and it would be a tragedy to assume that from so strange and poignant a union there might come anything other than love and eventual peace.

Charles Wooton
The Mews, Chelsea
London